PRIMØRDIUM

Primordium is a work of fiction. Any similarities to actual persons or entities of the past, present, or future, is purely coincidental.

TO MY WIFE AND FAMILY

CONTENTS

PART I

PART II

CONTENTS

PART III

PRIMØRDIUM

MARIO LOOMIS

PART I

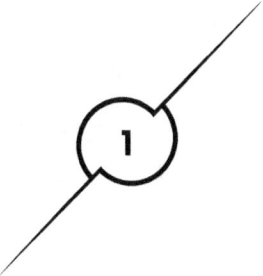

PRIDAPT INCORPORATED

It was a monster. I knew that much. I knew that much. Why else would they be hiding it? So I thought every morning as I walked past the only laboratory door my keycard would not open. Four years I had been working at Pridapt Incorporated, with unfettered access to all the research labs except for the one behind the steel gray doors of the East Wing. Of course, it was not unreasonable of them to keep secrets; research facilities always do—novel ideas, patented techniques and formulas. I was merely a part-time lab assistant after all, hired at thirteen thanks to my mother, one of Pridapt's PhD researchers. But I worked on every other project; why not this one? They could trust me. I wouldn't have told anyone. Besides, whom would I have told? It's not like I went out much. I loved working there, running experiments in the lab, seeing science in action. I would never have jeopardized my employment there. But rules were rules, I supposed. I satisfied my frustration that morning, as I did every morning, by fantasizing about the horrific thing that must be lying there hidden from view.

"Morning, Noah," one of my mother's coworkers called out to me, ending my monstrous fantasy.

"Morning, Dr. Dave," I returned with a smile. I had known Dr. Dave Bernstein for as long as I could remember. When I was a small boy, hanging on to my mother's lab coat, he would crouch down to my level and speak to me. What I recall most vividly, was the way his forehead would crunch up into a stack of little folds every time he smiled at me. It's how I knew he was in a good mood. If he ever looked at me with a smooth forehead, I knew something was wrong. Next to my mother, he was my key mentor, having taught me most of the skills I used in the lab. He was in his fifties, married, with two grown daughters. I was like the son he'd never had and he, the father I'd never known.

Despite having barred me from the East Wing, Pridapt was good to me; everyone accepted me. They were brilliant, some with doctorates in multiple fields, but they always talked to me as if I were a colleague. Sometimes they forgot about the knowledge gap between us, going on and on with their technical jargon until my glazed look reminded them that I was only seventeen. Youth was one of my greatest assets, my mother often told me. Despite their brilliance, Pridapt researchers were clueless about social media and mass marketing. Having always sold their ideas to foundations, other PhDs, lawyers, or CEOs, they'd all but forgotten how regular people think. Walking into the auditorium, I looked up at the banner hanging from the ceiling and smiled.

Destroyed by Man—Restored by Man

That was all me—that catchy slogan—that was my idea. Just a lab tech and a kid, I had come up with the showcase slogan for one of the world's largest biomedical research companies. Across the expanse of seats, I saw my mother beaming at me. She pointed to the banner and gave me a thumbs-up, her steel-blue eyes shining beside her dark-brown hair. Appearing so youthful, people often mistook her for my older sister. She was only thirty-seven, having adopted me when she was twenty. I'd heard bits and pieces of my story over the years: how she had arranged a private adoption from my birth mother, a child herself, abandoned by my father before I was born. I have no memories of it, of course. Never thought much about it either, except when others brought it up. It's good to talk about such things,

I suppose, to put them to rest; but it can work both ways. High school had been difficult for me, socially and academically. My mother had homeschooled me through eighth grade, and while I never had any trouble understanding the schoolwork she taught me, I had a terrible time with the multiple choice tests I was given in school. I still have a hard time with them, and with all standardized tests. Apparently, I read too much into the questions or "over-think" them, as my mother would say. After nearly failing two classes, the school recommended that I receive counseling. During one of those sessions, my guidance counselor asked me a lot of questions about my "father issues." I liked the sound of that phrase, and from that day on, it became my excuse for everything. "I never knew my father," was all I had to say. It worked like a charm until I made the mistake one day of using it on my stand-in father, Dave.

"Don't give me that crap," he snapped back. "You make your own way in this world, good or bad."

I tried to remember that comment whenever I was tempted to fall back on my old excuses, which unfortunately was pretty often. In Dave, I saw my future goals in a nutshell: a scientific researcher, a steady career, family, respect. What else was there? It was getting there that was the problem. My standardized test scores still had a way to go, but with help from my mother and Dave, they were getting better.

All in all, I had good people in my life, and I was lucky to be working at Pridapt.

So this day was a big day for the company. We were announcing the results of ten years of research to reporters who had flocked to the Northern California complex from as far away as New York and Dallas. I wouldn't be making any presentations, but it was my slogan, and I had coached Dave on how to pitch the news to the crowd. He was the lead presenter, and I was as excited as if it were I making the speech. What he would announce that day would shake up the entire scientific community, and I couldn't wait to see it.

"We're a bit early, huh?" a voice from behind me asked. I turned to see a bearded young man with long, curly blond hair, wearing a flannel shirt, jeans, and hiking boots. His eyes darted back and forth behind his round, wire-rimmed glasses.

"It doesn't start for another hour," I explained. "Are you a reporter?"

"Me?" he laughed. "No, National Parks Service. Isaac Dean," he added, extending his hand to me.

"Noah Bolton," I replied, shaking his hand or, I should say, letting my hand be shaken by his. To say he was hyperactive wouldn't do him justice. Energy shot out of him, like static electricity from his flannel shirt. He seemed ready at any instant to pounce on someone or leap onto a zip line to fly across the room.

"Where are you going to sit?" he asked me. "I like to sit right by the podium."

"I like to hang back a bit," I countered, "to, you know, get a feel of the crowd."

"Good thinking, good thinking," Isaac repeated. "How about right here?"

"Okay," I agreed. We sat down and talked while the auditorium filled up over the hour. I tried not to stare at his leg which bounced up and down incessantly. As reporters moved by us, Isaac would blurt out an introductory greeting, trying to bring them into our conversation without success. As the two of us talked, I learned a great deal about Isaac. He was twenty-three years old, and had worked for the National Parks Service since graduating from college with an undergraduate degree in environmental studies. It was the Parks Service that had paid his way to this press conference, but that was not his only reason for coming.

"I also do volunteer work for environmental watchdog groups," he confided. "Word is, there's something..." He stopped cold, peering at me through squinted eyes. "Why are you here, again?" he asked.

"I work here," I answered, and for the first time in an hour his bouncing leg and darting eyes were still. "You are going to love what you hear," I assured him.

"Oh yeah?"

"Yeah, listen to this," I said, pointing to the lectern where Dave was about to begin the first presentation.

"Ladies and gentlemen," he began, "I am Dr. David Bernstein, and I would like to ask you a question." The murmur of voices faded to silence as the crowd settled in to their seats. "If you had the power to save a species on the verge of extinction, wouldn't you do it? Then why not save what we have already lost? Why not restore an extinct species?"

There were sounds of disbelief throughout the auditorium.

"Did he just say what I think he said?" Isaac whispered to me.

"Yes," quipped a reporter, spinning around to glare at Isaac. "You heard right."

"There were rumors that Pridapt wanted to introduce modified species into the wild," Isaac continued. "That's why we were concerned. But this, this is impossible!" I looked at his face, full of confusion and disbelief, and nodded toward the stage.

"I know what you're thinking," Dave continued. "That it's impossible!"

Right on cue.

"Well, here at Pridapt, we've found a way." The stack of little folds appeared on Dave's forehead, and smiling, he explained his point, which was the crux of Pridapt's decade of research. Referring to the image of a stem cell on the screen behind him, he explained how such a cell had the capacity to develop into all the different tissues of the body: bones, muscles, nerves, and organs. Stem cell research had shown that we could now scrape a few skin cells off a person's arm and revert them to their primordial form—stem cells—which we could then turn into something else, like bone, muscles, nerves, and organs. "What if we did that to an animal species?"

His bold suggestion sent a wave of murmuring throughout the audience.

"Similarities between species provide evidence of common ancestry: primordial forms," Dave continued. "An animal's primordium, like a stem cell, would have the capacity to develop into a number of different species. If we revert an adult species to its primordium, like reverting a skin cell to its stem cell, we can then direct it to become something else—a different species."

"You can't revert a whole animal," a voice called out.

"You can," Dave interrupted, "when it is still one cell!" At this point, Dave came out from behind the lectern and walked to the center of the stage, motioning to an aid behind a curtain. "A fertilized egg is, for a short period of time, a one-celled organism. During that time, if we expose it to the proper stimulants, we can revert it to its primordial form, just as we have done with skin cells."

"He's out of his mind," Isaac said out loud, no longer trying to keep his voice below a whisper. The entire audience was voicing similar doubt when Dave broke through the uproar.

"Look at this cell," Dave called out, pointing to the screen behind him. "This is a one-celled chicken embryo. Before it began to divide and differentiate, we treated it with the process I have just mentioned, and it became this." He pointed to a new image of a cell. "While it doesn't look any different, this cell is fantastically different! It is a bird primordial cell—a cell with the potential to become any number of different birds!"

"Come on," Isaac whispered. "That's ridiculous."

"In 1900," Dave continued, "due to overhunting, the passenger pigeon became extinct in the wild. Fourteen years later, the last living member of that species died in captivity, never to be seen alive again. Since mankind destroyed them, mankind ought to restore them. Today, I'm here to tell you we have done just that!" A roar of questions and protests rose from the crowd. Over the cacophony, Dave boomed, "You've heard the riddle, 'Which came first, the chicken or the egg?' Well, the answer is, 'Neither.' The primordium came first!"

An aid brought out a small table with a wooden box on it. Dave moved behind the table and reached into the box. Stepping to the side, he held his arms out before him, raised high above his head. Clasped between his palms was a small feathered creature, whose head was whipping from left to right.

"Ladies and gentlemen," Dave announced, "I give you the passenger pigeon!"

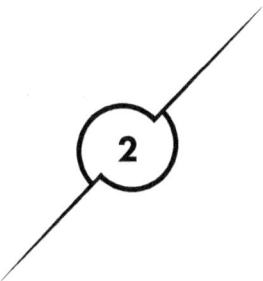

ORIGIN OF THE SPECIES

"I don't believe it," Isaac exclaimed, staring at me. "A pigeon from a chicken egg? How do you know it's really a passenger pigeon? I don't believe it," he repeated, shaking his head.

"It's a passenger pigeon," I affirmed as I stood up and made my way out of the auditorium. *Weren't you listening?* I thought to myself.

"How do you know?" Isaac called out as he trotted behind me. With a sigh, I stopped and turned to him.

"We checked its DNA against the DNA from a stuffed passenger pigeon in a museum. They were close enough to be the same species," I explained. He seemed no less skeptical, so I shrugged and continued on to the locked door outside our labs. I turned again, keycard in hand, ready to explain that he could go no further when a voice rang out behind him.

"Noah!"

I knew that voice. It sounded like... but it couldn't be.

"Noah!" the voice called again, coming from a girl who ran over to us from the auditorium door.

"Zoe!" I blurted out. "You came!"

"Yeah," she chuckled, "no kidding."

Zoe was a girl at my school, wildly popular, and someone I had long admired, albeit from afar. She had dark, wavy hair that was usually pulled back, and large, round, mysterious eyes that turned up like a cat's. She was always the center of attention, holding court within a circle of admirers hanging on her every word. To my knowledge, she had no idea who I was, until one day a week earlier when an announcement was made at a school assembly recognizing student activities in the community. Pridapt had been showcased in the local news as the crown jewel of San Francisco-area businesses, so my working there as a lab technician for the past four years was considered worthy of recognition. After the assembly, I bumped into her outside of school. She not only said hi, which was surprising enough, but then asked how I was doing. I told her I was heading to my job at Pridapt, at the time thinking, *she's not really interested in where I'm going.*

She won't even remember what I say. I could say anything. So I said, "Come see me sometime," immediately feeling like an idiot, yet here she was.

"Cool act with that extinct bird," Zoe beamed. "What was it, the massacre pigeon?"

"Passenger."

"Yeah, right, so..." she continued, peering over my shoulder down the lab hallway. "You gonna give me a tour?"

She could have asked for anything. Whether or not I was capable of complying, and no matter how outlandish her request may have been, my answer would have been the same.

"Sure!"

Zoe flashed a delightful smile as Isaac inched in behind her, his eyes lighting up as if to say, "Me too!" If there had been any concern in my mind about bringing a skeptic like Isaac, who was so openly hostile to Pridapt's work, on a tour of our labs, I was not conscious of it. I was conscious of little else besides Zoe's eyes.

"Well?" she teased, noting my lack of composure.

"Right this way," I finally got out, brandishing my keycard, and with a few fumbling swipes, I unlocked the door.

I led them to my favorite area, the amphibian habitat. Zoe immediately ran to the glass tanks like a child in a candy store. Seeing her enjoy herself so, I felt much more at ease. Looking around the room, I remembered my excitement upon seeing it the first time. I always loved amphibians. I would spend hours flipping through books with photographs of exotic South American tree frogs and poisonous dart frogs, wishing I could see them someday. Then, once I became involved with the primordium research, I saw them and more every day. We even developed amphibians that had never been found in the wild. I lifted a curved rock in the corner of one of the glass aquariums.

"This is my favorite," I said as I exposed a blinking blob of mottled colors, which quickly mimicked the colors and shapes surrounding it. The blob, like the Cheshire cat, became nothing but a set of blinking eyes, which when closed, allowed the creature to disappear entirely. It was some sort of frog, either very rare or perhaps already extinct.

"Are you going to tell us you grew that from a chicken egg?" Isaac scoffed.

"Of course not," I laughed. "It's from an amphibian primordium." I motioned for them to follow me to another habitat. "You've seen these, haven't you?" I asked, pointing to a monarch chrysalis.

"Cool," Zoe chirped as she skipped up to the tank.

"A cocoon," Isaac said nonchalantly.

"Yeah, well that's a metamorphosis," I explained, turning away from Isaac to face Zoe. "It's one life form becoming a different life form. Now, imagine one of these that could grow into a different species."

"That's not possible," Isaac protested. "Every cocoon becomes the same butterfly or moth it's programmed to become. It can't become something else."

"A primordium can," I countered, glimpsing a sparkle in Zoe's eyes.

"A per..." she began.

"A primordium," I repeated quickly, stifling whatever perturbation of the word Zoe was about to articulate.

"What is that?" Zoe asked.

"It's the primordial form of an animal," I explained, "the first one of its kind, containing within itself the potential to become variations of that type—the first mammal, the first fish, the first bird."

I went on to explain a primordium's role the way Dave first explained it to me. He had taken me to a play in which a friend of his was playing several parts. Afterward, we went backstage and met the actor. He looked so plain, his makeup wiped off, the costumes gone. A primordium was like that actor backstage, Dave had explained. Plain, undifferentiated, he had the potential to become a number of different characters. That's what a primordium could do.

"That's where the name of the company comes from," I explained. "Pridapt: it means 'primordial adaptation.' We convert animal embryos back to their primordial forms, and they become like that actor, able to adapt by becoming a different species."

Isaac frowned sternly and was about to ask something when Zoe grabbed me by both arms.

"Will you show us one?" she asked enticingly.

As before, she could have asked for anything.

"Sure!" I exclaimed, and we were on our way to an adjacent primordium habitat.

I remembered suddenly, my reaction when I first saw one. I don't know that I had ever admitted to myself just how unnerving it was. *I should prepare them*, I thought.

"A primordium is sort of larval," I began, "with eyes and a mouth, but also gills." Isaac's eyebrows raised considerably, as Zoe's lips silently mouthed, "cool." I explained that all the primordia are aquatic. They're soft and segmented, making undulating movements in the water; more graceful than typical larvae, as though the external cylindrical shape covered up an underlying complexity, like the sack-like bodies of seals containing fully formed hind limbs.

"They stay dormant in that state, like they're hibernating or something, but once we stimulate them, they start changing within a week or two," I added.

"Stimulate them?" Isaac whispered, staring at me with a mixture of curiosity and fear. I could have, and perhaps should have stopped there, letting his curiosity steep awhile.

The Pridapt press packet he would receive would have answered all his questions. I should have just taken them both back to the auditorium and shown Zoe some other time. But her present fascination was too much for me.

"This is awesome!" Zoe beamed.

It really was. I decided to forget about Isaac's pessimism and focus on Zoe's enthusiasm.

"It's like traveling in a time machine," I suggested. "You get to see the first bird, the first amphibian, the first reptile." I explained how we had gotten a wide range of types to come from our bird primordia: flightless birds, flighted birds, small, and large. Sharing all that information brought to mind something I had always wondered about: was there a primordial form of these primordia? The magnitude of variability that would have to be contained in such a cell was mind-boggling. Could we revert back further, to something before mammals, before reptiles, before birds?

I shared this thought with them—the possibility of crossing primordial lines. "It may be possible, if you take the cell back far enough," I mused, "but, we haven't been able to do that yet. The researchers talk like there's some sort of barrier, like the sound barrier or something. Of course, we've broken that, haven't we?"

"You people are reckless," Isaac snapped. "You know that, don't you?"

"Do you want to see it or not?" I shot back, rather annoyed by his negativity. "You know, there will be loads of medical applications from this," I added defensively, "treatments for diseases that will use our own natural adaptations."

Zoe glared at Isaac with a sniff, then turned to me.

"Go on Noah; I'm listening."

"Well, after we convert the animal embryos back to their primordial form, we stimulate them to adapt to certain stresses, like radiation, different food sources, things like that." I couldn't believe what was happening. Zoe Halpern was now hanging on *my* every word. She, the girl who couldn't have guessed my name two weeks ago, was genuinely interested in what I had to say. It was like a dream come true!

I pushed open the door to the primordial habitat and motioned for Zoe to enter.

"It's in there?" she giggled, peering into the darkness.

"Yeah," I laughed. "Come on." I led Zoe and a hesitant Isaac through the doorway.

"Wait!" Zoe jerked me to a halt by my arm and whispered, "It's not like dangerous or anything, is it?"

"Oh no," I assured her quietly; then, seeing Isaac's profound look of anxiety, repeated, "Of course not! They're perfectly safe."

"Hmm," Zoe sighed, appearing a bit disappointed.

"Let's see it anyway."

The three of us entered the dark room where one wall was the glass side of a water-filled tank. The glass was mirrored on the inside so that observers in the room could see into the tank without being seen. Bluish light from above the water rippled across the floor of the tank, lined with sand and rocks. A foot-long cylindrical shape rested on the sand. Zoe immediately moved to the glass and knelt down to get a closer look.

It expanded and contracted rhythmically, drawing water in through its slightly open mouth, which spanned the width of its front end. The water flowed out gill slits on either side behind what could be called its head. While I had become used to the appearance of a primordium, it was as though I was seeing it anew through Zoe's eyes.

"Hey there," Zoe said, moving her face right next to the glass. "What are you up to?"

"It can't see you," I clarified. "The glass is mirrored on that side to limit external stimuli. That way, we can better control its adaptations." Zoe stood up.

"*Limit external stimuli,*" she mimicked with a robotic voice. So much for hanging on my every word. She had made the move from fascination to mockery in a matter of seconds. The confidence drained out of me, and I began wishing she had not come to Pridapt that day. "You sure it doesn't see me?" she asked, pointing to the primordium which was following her as she moved along the glass.

"That's interesting," I thought out loud. "Maybe it can sense infrared." Isaac, who had been staying about two feet behind us, looked on suspiciously. I explained the various stages the primordia went through: how the initial form underwent a metamorphosis after we stimulated it, turning into a soft cocoon-type structure. That cocoon would then split into two separate cocoons, becoming the male and female forms. All the primordia we had developed went through this same process: the formation of a cocoon which then divided into male and female. The male and female cocoons would then go on to develop into adult forms. Afterwards, they multiplied like modern animals, but with a much wider variety of offspring. Instead of just different hair color or size, their offspring would actually be different species. With selective breeding, we were then able to choose the species we wanted.

"So what's this one going to be?" Zoe asked.

"This is a reptilian primordium," I explained. "We've been trying to develop a new venomous form."

"Why in the world would you do that?" Isaac asked.

"For medical applications," I explained. "Some of the most effective medications are actually dilute forms of toxins. There could be a toxin from an extinct venomous reptile that winds up becoming the next miracle drug."

"You're messing with unknown life forms," Isaac warned, shaking his head. "That's just insane."

I glanced at Zoe and rolled my eyes. She flashed me a charming smile, and I forgot all about her mocking me moments before. Nodding her head toward Isaac, Zoe whispered, "What's with him?"

"Isaac's worried about creating genetically modified organisms. Isn't that right, Isaac?"

Before Isaac could respond, the observation room door opened, flooding the room with light. The three of us squinted toward the shadow of a figure standing in the bright doorway as a voice boomed, "What are you doing in here?"

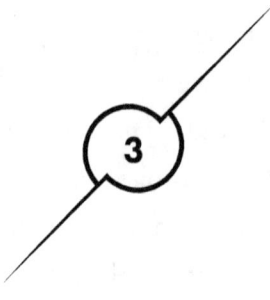

MUTANTS

"It's me, Noah," I called out, still squinting at the light coming in from the hallway, "Noah Bolton."

"Noah?" the shape responded in a less intimidating tone. It was Daniel Smith, a security guard at Pridapt whom I knew fairly well, thank goodness. At six foot five inches and 260 pounds, he was an impressive sight, filling most of the door's frame. "Noah, you know you shouldn't bring people into the observation room, not without guest passes."

"I thought with everyone here for the big presentation it would be okay."

"Not without guest passes, and guest passes have to be approved by the administration. Let's have the three of you wait over here in the conference room." Daniel led us across the hall just as my mother was passing by.

"Noah?" she asked, glancing at Isaac and Zoe.

"I told them they shouldn't be in there, Dr. Bolton," Daniel explained, "not without guest passes."

"In where?" my mother inquired, following Isaac's and Zoe's eyes toward the observation room. "The observation room?" Disbelief was evident in her voice, disappointment in her stare.

"I thought they could wait in the conference room, Dr. Bolton, until they get their visitor passes," Daniel suggested.

"Good idea, Daniel," my mother said, smiling, "though I believe an explanation might be in order first, don't you?"

I felt my mother's steel-blue eyes as they fell upon me, pinning me against the wall with their accusatory gaze. Then, one by one, the eyes of all turned to me. I looked at Isaac and Zoe, thinking they might introduce themselves to take the pressure off of me momentarily, but they simply stared at me, as if to say, "What were you thinking taking us in there?"

"I thought... with the presentation... it would be okay?" I offered.

"I see," my mother replied, her gaze continuing its hold on me. "Why don't we go into the conference room, where you can introduce your friends?"

Daniel held the door for us as we moved around a long

table in the room, then nodded to my mother. "I'll just be over here in the corner, Dr. Bolton."

Did he think she might need security? I wondered what sort of disruption he considered my guests capable of making. Looking at my mother and motioning to Isaac, I said, "This is Isaac Dean. He works with environmental groups and the National Parks Service. Isaac, this is my mother, Dr. Bolton." As they nodded to each other politely, I introduced Zoe.

"Dr. Bolton, I wonder if I might ask you a few questions," Isaac began.

"We can get to that," my mother said without taking her eyes off Zoe. "So you came here from school, Zoe? Are you interested in science?"

"Well, sort of," Zoe said. "Mainly I was curious about this place. They talked a lot about it at school when they gave Noah that award."

"Award?" my mother asked, turning to me.

"Oh yeah," Zoe explained. "Didn't he tell you? It was a big deal—called him up to the stage and everything."

"Is that right?"

"So I came by, and when I saw all the excitement in the auditorium..."

"How did you get in?" my mother interrupted.

"They let me in," Zoe said, glancing at my mother. Zoe,

now the recipient of my mother's steel-blue gaze, displayed some deterioration of her cool demeanor. "Okay," she acquiesced at length. "I told them I was Noah's cousin."

That confession raised all the eyebrows in the room, but most notably my own. After just one high school assembly, I had been transformed in Zoe's world from an unknown entity to someone she would lie about being related to. The day was once again becoming one of the best in my life.

"So you heard the presentation," my mother prompted.

"About primordiums," Zoe added.

"And Noah offered to show you one?"

"Oh, yes." Zoe answered almost immediately. A little qualification would have been nice. It hadn't happened quite like that, after all. I had started by just showing her and Isaac around the lab.

"You know better, Noah," my mother admonished, deflating my ego a bit further. My image had gone from a cutting-edge researcher to that of a child getting a time-out.

"Should they sign nondisclosure agreements?" Daniel suggested from his station in the corner.

"No, Daniel, that's not necessary," my mother replied. "There are photos of the primordia in the scientific report that will be released today anyway."

What? Then it was no big deal! I thought. *If everyone will see it anyway, why make such a scene?* For the first time in my life, I had the sense that my mother was not on my side. She had always been there, in my corner, backing me up, defending me. Now, she seemed to be going out of her way to showcase my poor judgment. Once again, I thought it may have been better had Zoe not come to Pridapt that day.

The door to the conference room opened and Dave backed in, pulling the cart that carried the passenger pigeon's box. Having successfully completed that morning presentation in the auditorium, his mood appeared bright and carefree.

"Oh, sorry," he started once seeing us. "I didn't know there was a meeting in here." His forehead crunched up into its stack of little folds as he smiled broadly at us all.

"No meeting," my mother clarified, "only a gathering of friends." Her eyes darted back toward me for a moment.

"Is that the bird?" Zoe asked, pointing to the brown box on the cart.

"Yes," Dave answered. "Would you like to see it?"

"Of course they would," my mother interjected. "I believe Isaac here has some questions for you as well." She smiled as she moved to the side of room to take a call on her phone.

Dave gently pulled out the passenger pigeon and brought it to Zoe first. "You can touch it," Dave invited. "It won't bite." Zoe stroked the back of the pigeon with her index finger.

"Not a whole lot different from the pigeons I see," Zoe suggested. "I've never touched one of those, though," she laughed.

Isaac approached the pigeon much more carefully than Zoe. When Dave came before him, he didn't touch the bird but eyed it critically from every angle.

"Doctor?" Isaac asked. "How many different species can you get from one of those primordia?"

"It depends on how we stimulate them and the environment we put them in. This bird's primordium gave rise to about thirty different species," Dave explained. "Once the primordium divides into male and female, we breed them and select the offspring with the traits we desire. With each generation, the range of variation decreases, until about the twelfth generation when we only get mature modern species."

"When you say, 'stimulate,' what do you mean exactly?" Isaac asked.

"We direct their adaptation," Dave explained.

"I mean, specifically, what do you do?"

"Specifically? The specifics that we're allowed to disclose will be in the press packet."

"Allowed?" Isaac repeated.

"As employees, we're bound by nondisclosure agreements," Dave explained. "It's the case with all businesses. You must know that."

"I know the devil's in the details," Isaac quipped. "Has this stimulation of immature animals led to any abnormal forms?"

"You mean mutations? Of course, but no more than we see in nature."

"How can you talk so lightly about this?" Isaac exclaimed. "You're completely disrupting the natural ecosystem! People will not stand for this!" Isaac waved his arms. "Look at the amount of resistance with GMO crops. Now you're suggesting we support genetically modified animals as well?"

I could see Zoe's admiration fading with Isaac's growing litany of concerns decrying everything I had earlier been so proud of and admired for. I couldn't let the tide turn so quickly and completely.

"But that's just it," I argued. "They're not genetically modified! Look, we're just like breeders. We revert the cell, and put it in a modified environment. Then, out of the variety of forms that *can* develop, our environment selects the type we want. We don't create them; we just select them."

I watched Zoe turn her attention towards Isaac with a look that seemed to say, "So there, what about that?"

"You've recreated an extinct species," Isaac retorted.

"No, we've selected it from a preexisting variability," I clarified. "There's a big difference. It's not like we are splicing genes or anything. Every animal that develops has already been coded for in the past."

"Except for the occasional mutant," Isaac quipped.

"You have mutants?" Zoe asked, showing a rather disturbing amount of excitement. "Awesome, where are they?"

"Well," I explained, looking at Dave, then Zoe, "the mutants aren't alive. They're mistakes of nature; they die, like a stillborn animal. There aren't very many of them, maybe one in a hundred." I could tell Isaac wasn't really listening to my explanation. He seemed to be fixated on the word "mutant." *A good word to avoid,* I thought.

"Here we go," the security guard, Daniel, muttered as he looked out a window to the front of the Pridapt complex. "Dr. Bernstein, if everything's all right here, I think I'd better go out front. We've got a mob coming up the drive."

"Certainly, Daniel," Dave replied. "You go ahead."

A crowd was making its way up the circular drive in front of the building carrying signs protesting Pridapt's research. *NO MORE GMOs* was a frequent slogan on many of the placards. *KEEP NATURE NATURAL* and *FREED FROM GREED* were on many others. There were about fifty protesters approaching Pridapt's entryway, with another hundred coming up the road.

"What did I tell you?" Isaac gloated.

"They're protesting before they know what they're

protesting," Dave lamented as he moved to the window. His forehead lost its disarming stack of little folds, becoming seriously smooth.

"They know enough," Isaac countered. "Mark my words—this protest will be universal." Isaac looked down on the crowd like a parent at a sporting event, glowing with pride as their child makes the winning play.

"See anyone you know?" I asked him.

"No," he laughed, then reconsidering, he scanned the crowd more closely.

My mother, still in a corner of the room, had been on the phone for several minutes now, and her conversation was becoming more heated.

"I don't care what you think is right; I'm telling you what is right!" My mother's voice shot across the room, leaving a silent hush in its wake. Dave and I quietly moved away from the window toward Zoe.

"A little tension over there," Zoe noted, breaking the awkward silence. I nodded with a grin. "What?" Zoe asked. "You're glad it's taking the heat off you?"

I was. Whoever my mother was upset with at that time, it wasn't me. Anything that would take the attention off of my bringing in people without guest passes was fine with me.

"You have a pretty good gig here, don't you, Noah?" Zoe continued.

"Yeah, I do."

"You like it?"

"Sure."

"They seem to like you, too, except when you bring total strangers into the labs," she chided, elbowing me. Dave smiled, noting our conversation.

"Do you think your mom will tell everyone we were in there?" Zoe asked.

"Probably. She's not very good at keeping secrets," I lamented.

"Are you kidding?" Dave interjected with a smile and a stack of forehead folds. "Your mother's the most private person I know. She'd been working here a full year before any of us even knew you existed."

I looked at Dave, trying to remember when, exactly, I had first met him. My mother had not told him about me for a year? This was a piece of my history I had never heard before.

"Did she keep you in a closet or something?" Zoe laughed.

Adept at finding novel ways to ridicule me, Zoe picked up on Dave's comment. I wondered if anything else could be said that day to make me look like more of an idiot.

"Come on, Noah," Zoe complained. "Don't hold out on me now. Were you a closet child or what?"

"What's a closet child?" I wondered out loud. Before Zoe could answer, my mother's conversation became audible again, louder than before.

"No, don't. No! Under no circumstances are you to go in there!" my mother exclaimed. "I know what that alarm means. I told you, I'm on my way. I'll handle it!"

"What's up?" Dave asked her as she hurried toward the door.

"I have to go," she answered curtly. "I'll be back. Noah," she added, glaring at me, "you know better."

My mother, the consummate multitasker, could maintain her beef with me even in the midst of an ongoing crisis. She whisked out the door and down the hall.

I stood beside Dave and asked quietly, "Where's she going?"

"The East Wing, I suspect," Dave replied.

Zoe, who had slipped up behind Dave and me, inquired, "What's in the East Wing?" I looked at Zoe, then we both turned to Dave.

"That's a good question," I remarked.

"Well, don't look at me," Dave said. "You know as much as I do."

Could that be true? Dave and my mother had worked together for years. I could understand her not letting me in on it, but Dave?

Zoe, who apparently never hesitated to speak her mind, asked Dave, "Don't you work here?"

"Information about the East Wing project is shared on a need-to-know basis," Dave explained. Looking at the two of us, he added, "I don't need to know."

Wow, I thought. There was one area where I did not think I could ever be like Dave. I couldn't just let something like that go—I was way too curious.

"It must be something pretty intense," Zoe remarked with the unsettling sort of excitement she had displayed earlier regarding the mutants.

Intense? Most certainly, and that intensity with its surrounding mystery had always tormented me. I had felt drawn to the East Wing ever since I'd known there was an East Wing. I couldn't stop wondering about it. No, I would never be like Dave in this regard. I could not simply say, "I don't need to know," and coexist with the mystery lurking behind those steel gray doors. Seeing my fervent curiosity reflected in Zoe's round, dark eyes, it was then that I realized: I had to know.

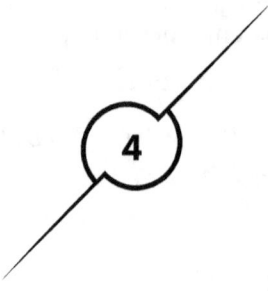

PROTESTS

I loved the way the afternoon sun glittered through the needles of redwoods lining the side and back of the Pridapt property when I came to work. The research building abutted a national park, providing a grand backdrop to the front drive, which, this day, was once again filled with protesters. It had been two weeks since that first demonstration in front of Pridapt, and the size of the daily protests had grown steadily. It was crazy pushing through the crowd just to get to work each day after school. Most of the time, the crowd was quiet, until an employee came up to the front door. Then they would begin their chants, running through a rehearsed sequence of slogans. I now recognized many of the faces, though when I made eye contact with them, they quickly turned away. I suppose my seventeen-year-old face was not the face of corporate villainy that had drawn them from their homes and fueled their daily protests.

Inside, things were crazy as well. There was a big push to complete several experiments before some sort of deadline. By the time I arrived, there was already a long list of procedures for me to run. Most of my duties pertained to DNA sequencing, running tissue samples through electrophoresis machines that separated out the different proteins. There were variations on that theme, such as tagging specific amino acids, identifying DNA damage or changes in the DNA "fingerprint," though the nuts and bolts of what I did was pretty routine. I used to have some downtime while the samples were running, which was when I liked to explore the habitats. Ever since the press conference, though, I simply ran from one machine to the other the whole time I was there.

My mother, too, seemed busy, or perhaps distracted. It was the last few weeks of school, and I had a lot of juggling to do to prepare for finals while continuing with work. I was accustomed to her checking on me, reminding me to keep up with schoolwork and confirming my preparedness for final exams. This year it was as though she had forgotten I had exams. Coming through the front doorway, I saw her hustling across the foyer. I waved and smiled, but she didn't notice me and kept walking down the hallway toward the East Wing.

That figures, I thought, *always the East Wing*, and I wondered if this new deadline had something to do with the mysterious goings-on there. I looked back at the protesters and noticed a familiar face squeezing through the crowd. It was Zoe! We hadn't spoken since she had first come to Pridapt two weeks earlier. I had seen her at school nearly every day but could never quite catch her attention. I rushed out the door to meet her.

"Zoe!" I called out, maneuvering between the tightly packed shoulders and placards. I noticed what seemed like a new crowd of protesters making its way from a bus down on the road. This crowd was much more animated than the sedate demonstrators I was accustomed to. In fact, they moved so quickly toward the building that people began to run out of their way. A wave of panic spread around us, with signs dipping out of sight and people stumbling into each other. Just as I reached Zoe, I heard a crash above my head, and moments later, fragments of glass showered over us. A portion of the "Pridapt" lighted sign had been shattered by a stone thrown from the newly arrived crowd. People were pushing in all directions as a volley of bricks and stones flew over our heads. I grabbed Zoe's arm and pulled her away from the building.

"Come on!" I yelled, and we ran across the grass and into the woods in the adjacent park land. "That's nuts," I gasped between breaths.

"I'll say. Hold on," Zoe added, pulling me around toward her. "You've got glass in your hair." After she briskly picked out several pieces of glass, I noticed the same in hers.

"You've got some, too," I pointed out, and I cleared all I could find in her thick black hair. Catching her eyes, I paused for what must have seemed an awkward length of time.

"Got them all?" she asked.

"I think so," I answered, scanning her hair one more time. We sat on the ground against a broad tree trunk and looked toward the pandemonium from which we had just escaped. Police sirens were getting louder as the recently arrived bus was pulling away. The rock throwers disappeared as quickly as they had appeared.

"Do you think it's safe to go in now?" Zoe asked.

"I don't know," I said dubiously, thinking how I had no desire whatsoever to leave that spot or let go of that moment. "We'd better hang out here a little bit," I advised.

"Nice place to hang out," Zoe agreed, looking around the woods. "So, Noah," she said, shifting her gaze to examine my face, "you must feel pretty good about yourself."

Did she think I was arrogant? I wondered. "Sorry," I apologized.

"For what?" she laughed.

"Sounding arrogant?"

"No, no," she shrugged. "That's not what I mean. I mean, your job and all. You've got it made, right?"

"Well, not like you."

"Not like me?"

"You're only the most popular girl in school," I noted, surprising myself with the boldness of that remark. Zoe mulled over my compliment for a few moments, then turned to me with a smirk.

"That I am," she said, and with a wink jumped to her feet. "Let's walk." She started down a slight hill, thick with ferns.

"We're going to get swallowed in there," I laughed. "Let's go over to that trail." We pressed through the thicket and climbed over a low railing onto a wooden walkway. Leaning against a tree we looked up at the redwoods towering over us.

"There are trees in here that are over a thousand years old," Zoe announced.

"Is that right?"

"Yup. They were cutting them all down, and people decided they wanted to keep some, so they made this park," Zoe explained as she scanned the circle of trees around us. "These are the ones they wanted."

"They're nice," I noted, slapping the trunk of the moderate-sized tree we were leaning against, "especially for a thousand years old."

"Good to be wanted," Zoe added, then turned from the trees to look at me. "So, tell me, your mom's pretty young, huh?"

"I guess so, if thirty-seven is young."

"What are you? Seventeen? Had you when she was twenty?"

"Well, adopted me when she was twenty," I explained.

"No kidding. She was married then?"

"No."

"No? She must have been in college. Single mom in college—that's something. Brothers or sisters?" I shook my head, and it struck me that the information exchange between us was very one-sided.

"What about your family?" I interjected.

"It's just me and my mom."

"Your mom's not married either?" I asked.

"She was," Zoe explained, "and maybe she still is. I don't know. My dad ran off when I was ten."

"Have you heard from him?"

"Not a word," Zoe said bluntly. "Could be dead for all I know or care. Back to your mom," she said, frowning at me like there was some detail that bothered her. "She adopted you as a baby?"

"Yeah, so what?" I asked.

"I have a cousin with a baby, and another cousin in college," she said, shaking her head. "I can't imagine the one in college having a baby. How did your mom get to class? Did she just bring you along everywhere?"

"I never really thought about it," I admitted.

"Well, I'm impressed. You've got quite the mom." Zoe looked down at her watch. "I need to get going. I was just popping in to say hi on my way."

"I should go too," I said. "I'm sure they have a pile of work for me. It's easier to get back to the road this way," I suggested, pointing down the walkway to the park entrance. We didn't say anything the whole way to her car; we just ambled along, feeling the breeze, looking up at the trees, taking in the fragrance of the evergreens. *What a great day!* I thought.

"See you around, Noah." Zoe smiled as she got into her car.

"Yeah, see you around." I watched her pull out of the parking lot and turn onto the highway, feeling eternally grateful for those stone throwing protesters who had set the stage for my time in the woods with her. Maybe they would do it again someday? When I had returned to the front drive of Pridapt, I found that all of the protesters had been dispersed and most of the broken glass cleared off the road. Arriving at my lab, I bumped into my mother outside the door.

"Noah! Were you outside in that?" she asked as she hugged me and checked me for injuries. "Maybe you shouldn't be coming here in the afternoons," she muttered to herself, "not until this blows over. You can just come in on Saturdays with me."

"Mom," I interrupted, "it's okay. I'm fine. I'm sure they'll put some more security out there. It's fine."

My mother reluctantly let go of me and turned to swipe us into my lab. Patting her pockets, she let out an exasperated sigh. "I left my tag in my other coat."

"I've got it," I offered as I brought out my ID card, but my mother quickly typed her passcode onto the keypad instead. I couldn't help but see her do it; it was right in front of me. In an instant, I realized the implications of what I was seeing. The passcode functioned like her ID tag: it gave access to computers, labs, storage cabinets, and—the East Wing! I knew I should not pay attention to the sequence of numbers she was pressing, that she would be appalled to see me watching her enter her code, but I couldn't stop myself. I saw her press the last number and retraced the pattern so I would not forget. I turned my eyes from the keypad, but my focus remained so completely on the passcode that it crowded out any consideration of whether or not I should be doing so. She opened the door, and we entered my lab, the sequence of numbers repeating themselves in my mind over and over, like the melody of a song stuck in your head.

Was it dishonest? I recalled the few comments my mother had made in the past regarding my father. The little she knew, she had learned from my birth mother. My father had abandoned my mother before I was born, and he was a *dishonest* man. That was the word she had used, and that was all I knew of my father: he was dishonest and disloyal. *Was I the same? Was I being dishonest?* The thought genuinely disturbed me, that despite myself and my desire to be good, this dishonest man's blood ran in my veins, making me dishonest. *No, it's not being dishonest,* I reassured myself. *After all, she hadn't asked me about it. I hadn't lied. It was more like a secret.* Everyone has secrets, to be sure. My mother certainly had hers, at least when it came to the East Wing project. This would just be my little secret.

I filled in my lab researchers on what had gone on outside and how we had escaped into the woods that were visible from the lab's window. "Trudging through ferns this high." I motioned to my waist. "It was crazy!"

"We?" my mother asked.

Had I said *we*? Apparently I had. "You remember Zoe," I began awkwardly, with the eyes of my coworkers fixed on my mother, waiting for her response.

"The girl from school," my mother recalled out loud. "You brought her to work?"

"No," I explained over the chuckling of my coworkers. "She just stopped by. I saw her outside in the crowd, so I went out to see her, and then the rocks started flying, so we ran for cover." My fellow lab workers shook their heads and returned to their work. I motioned toward my desk and the line of tissue samples to be run. "I'd better get to work, too," I suggested to my mother, whose eyes softened their stern facade, revealing the love I was more accustomed to.

The rest of the afternoon went by very quickly, partly because of the late start and the heavy workload but mainly because of the happy memory that kept resurfacing in my mind: my retreat to the redwoods with Zoe. It had seemed so easy and natural, like we had been friends for years, so different from the times I had passed her in the halls at school. It was a delightful memory, and it made even the most mundane tasks that day enjoyable.

There was another memory in my mind: the sequence of numbers that played and replayed continuously, becoming embedded in all my other thoughts.

"Your mother had you when she was twenty - 561947?"

"Well, -561947- she adopted me..."

If I were to speak in my sleep, I was sure I would say those numbers out loud. The thought of such a damning nocturnal revelation made me consider duct-taping my mouth shut before going to bed, but I reconsidered. My mother's room was too far away from mine for her to hear what I said in my sleep if, in fact, I actually did talk in my sleep. But when she came to wake me in the morning, the duct tape would undoubtedly be very difficult to explain.

After four hours of such thoughts, it was time to go. I met my mother in the hallway and walked with her to the main lobby. There was a gathering of employees waiting for a brief presentation by the CEO of Pridapt, Mr. Regis Stone. My mother and I sat in a row of folding chairs with Dave, who greeted us with a cheerful stack of forehead folds. I had met Mr. Stone on multiple occasions, and each time it was as though he was meeting me anew. I never took any offense at his not remembering me, being a mere lab assistant, but I did wonder at what point he would decide I was not worth remembering. Was it after I was introduced, after I spoke, or maybe just on sight of me?

Mr. Stone walked briskly around the corner and up to the microphone. He wore a neatly tailored dark suit with shiny black shoes that clipped across the lobby. He had broad shoulders, a broad chin, and broad hands. He tapped the microphone with his massive index finger, then spoke.

"Hello, everyone," he said with a quick scan of the audience. "I'd just like to give you all an update on our dealings with the government and also something about that out there." He waved an immense hand toward the few protesters who had reassembled outside. "There's been talk of a moratorium on our species research, in particular, the reestablishment of extinct species." Whispers of disbelief ran through the audience. "This would not affect other areas of research and could be one of the best things that could happen to us. The same goes for that rabble out there. It's all publicity!"

"Bad publicity," Dave muttered quietly.

"There is no such thing!" Mr. Stone shot back. "There is no negative publicity. What I want to tell you is this: stay the course, continue with your work, and don't worry. Publicity is like a spirited horse. Fear it, and it will strike you down with its hooves and trample you to death, but master it..." He paused and scanned the crowd again as though trying to look each one of us in the eye. "Master it, and you will win the Triple Crown. Make no mistake; I intend to master this spirited horse. Before too long, that riotous crowd out there will be working for us!"

What a command of imagery, I thought as my mother and I left the building. My head was filled with Stone's booming voice and the image of a galloping race horse, jet black, all snorting, neck slick with sweat, clods of dirt scattering behind it like steam billowing out from a launching rocket, and over it, under it, around it, behind it, the incessant melody: *561947... 561947.*

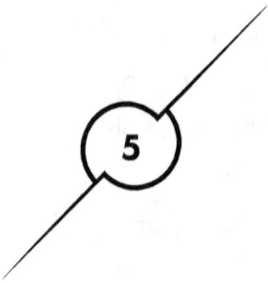

HOPE HAS A NAME

Stone's "riotous crowds" diminished in size over the ensuing weeks, but at the same time governmental scrutiny increased. As Stone had predicted, a nationwide moratorium was passed, halting extinct-species repopulation. That was why there had been such a rush in the labs to finish certain experiments. I hadn't been back to the observation room since being caught there with Isaac and Zoe over a month earlier, and I wondered whether they had managed to develop that extinct venomous reptile in time. Once we had the creature alive in the lab, I assumed we could continue using it for research despite the moratorium. After all, at that point, it was no longer extinct. But the moratorium probably did mean no more development of new primordia. That was too bad. I was going to miss them and the thrill of seeing something totally new arise from them. Hopefully, Stone was right about publicity, and the moratorium wouldn't last too long.

Lying in my bed, I looked out at the morning sky as it became brighter and the fog began to clear. I was reveling in the fact that in only two weeks my junior year in high school would be over. I was imagining what projects I might plan for the summer when my mother burst in to wake me.

"Noah, get up! You've got to come with me this morning," she announced, pulling clothes out of my drawers that she deemed appropriate for me to wear. But it was Saturday. I hadn't had a moment to relax yet, and I was almost a senior. *I think I could at least choose my own clothes.* Before I could voice the objections in my mind, my mother countered with, "I know it's last minute, but I just got the call from Mr. Stone. He wants us to meet him at the hospital. He needs your help with another slogan!"

"My help?" I asked. "He doesn't even know who I am."

"Of course he does. He knows you're my son and that you came up with the pigeon slogan."

"A fat lot of good that did," I quipped as I crawled out of bed. "It just led to a moratorium."

"This is different," my mother reassured me. "Mr. Stone will be announcing the release of our new cancer treatment that has just received FDA approval. It's a miracle drug, Noah," she beamed, standing still for the first time that morning. "I'm going to take you to see the patients in our trials that were cured of leukemia!"

When we arrived at the hospital, we were met in the lobby by a nurse who was involved with the Pridapt clinical trials.

"I'll take you up to the cancer ward," the nurse announced as she darted over to us.

"He's my son," my mother explained, noticing the nurse's inquisitive glance toward me. "He works with us at Pridapt."

"Oh, wonderful," the nurse raved. "Is this the first time he's seen the patients?" My mother nodded. "Fantastic!" Then, whispering to me as though sharing a secret, she added, "Wait until you see them. It's amazing!"

We were joined in the elevator by an aid pushing a patient in a wheelchair, an IV bag hanging beside her. After the elevator doors closed, there was a muffled silence, interrupted only by the regular dinging of the elevator as it passed another floor. I looked at my mother, the nurse, and the aid standing behind the wheelchair. The three of them were glancing at one another momentarily, then looking away before any might speak. The patient looked at no one but simply stared at the space before her. *Are we there yet?*

I found myself thinking each time another ding rang out.

Finally, the door opened, and the nurse looked at my mother and me through narrowed eyes, saying nothing until the aid had eased his patient's wheelchair over the gap between the elevator car and the floor. "This is it!" she breathed, waiting for the patient to be wheeled out of earshot to lead us from the elevator down the hall. "I don't like to speak of the research trial around other patients," she explained once we were alone again. "It's hard enough for them, but to hear about the cures—what they might have been a part of..." The nurse broke off, shaking her head. "Wait for me here," she told us, pointing to a line of chairs. "I'll bring the patients into the consultation room, then come get you."

As we sat down, I noticed a glass wall that enclosed what looked like a children's play area. The similarity to our observation room made me wonder if the glass wasn't mirrored on the other side. All the children were bald, chemotherapy patients I assumed. Several of them were missing arms or legs, and some were lying on stretchers attached to IV bags, the same empty stare on their faces as the patient in the elevator.

"They're kept separate to avoid infections," my mother explained. "That's a special section of the children's cancer ward."

Could there be anything worse? I wondered, looking around the room of children, who should have been outside playing and laughing, but were instead locked within a sterile bubble to keep them alive. *I have no right to complain about anything,* I thought, overcome by the tragic scene before me. Then, from this palette of desolation and despair came a splash of life as one of the smallest children burst into laughter, sitting over a book she was sharing with another child. The other smiled, and the two laughed back and forth, bursting with a joy that refused to be stifled by the weight of their onerous suffering. A light-hearted joy rose in my chest, and I turned to my mother to point out these two children when the nurse reentered the room.

"On we go," the nurse chirped as she returned to the room. "They're waiting for you in here." We entered a wood-paneled room with a long oval table running down its center. A man and three women sat on the side opposite the door. "This is Dr. Bolton and her son... what was your name?"

"Noah," I answered.

The nurse went on to explain the medical history of each of the four patients, all of whom had been treated for leukemia. They were four of the fifty that had been enrolled in the study, the others having been treated at other hospitals across the country.

"All four of us were cured," the man stated, cutting to the chase of the nurse's fairly long-winded review of their stories.

"And the treatment wasn't bad at all," one of the women added. "No pain, no nausea. We didn't lose our hair or anything!"

"We don't use the *cure* word until we're in remission for ten years," the nurse qualified. "But I can say that these patients' remissions were so rapid and so complete..." The nurse smiled. "It's like nothing I've ever seen, and I've been an oncology nurse for fifteen years!"

It was a study in contrasts, the rosy-cheeked, vibrant individuals talking to us in that conference room and the pallid faces of those just beyond the walls undergoing traditional cancer treatments. *This should be a pretty easy sell,* I thought.

After thanking the patients and the nurse, we returned to the first floor to meet with Mr. Stone.

"This is quite an honor, Noah," my mother reminded me as we stood in the hospital lobby waiting for Mr. Stone. "For the CEO to want your input is huge. It means he trusts your insight." I barely had time to digest that thought when Mr. Stone strode up to us.

"Is this the kid?" he asked my mother.

"You mean my son?" my mother clarified, politely but

pointedly. Mr. Stone paused, as if at a loss to understand the difference between those two titles. "Yes, this is my son. His name is Noah."

"Okay, kid," Mr. Stone fired at me, "let's hear it."

I stared blankly at him, taken aback by the immediacy of his question. *Weren't we going to sit down in a conference room again?* I wondered.

"Let's go. I'm giving a press conference here," Mr. Stone snapped as he breathed a heavy sigh toward a man at his side.

"Well, Mr. Stone," I began, "we just got done meeting with some of the patients who were in the study, and I was really..." I could see Mr. Stone's impatience growing with my every word. "I mean, well," I stammered. "What about, 'We're doing the most good for the most people?' or something like that?" Stone looked at the man at his side and shrugged.

"Rather cliché, don't you think? What else have you got?"

I stumbled through a few ideas about the children with bald heads from chemotherapy.

"I'm on in five, kid; give me the bullet," Stone shot out then kept his gaze fixed on me.

"Okay," I stuttered, "hope... hope on the horizon... there's hope on the horizon..." I watched as Stone's eyes began to wander again. "And that hope has a name: Pridapt."

Stone's eyes stopped moving for a moment. "Hope has a name, hope has a name; I like that, kid. Frank, you got that?" he asked the man at his side. "Work it into the speech. You've got three minutes. Make it shine."

While my mother smiled broadly at me, Stone thrust his massive index finger towards me and bobbed it up and down repeatedly.

"I like it, kid!" he boomed, grinning at my mother. "Annette, you came through again. Strong work."

Stone moved to the corner of the lobby where the press was already gathering to cover his speech. My mother looked at me and shook her head.

"What?" I asked.

"You, thinking on your feet like that." My mother beamed. "That was a lot of pressure. I'm sure Mr. Stone will remember you now."

"Yeah, he'll remember all right; I'm *the kid*." I laughed, and we took seats on one of the benches against the lobby wall to listen to Stone's presentation. Behind the crowd of reporters and cameras, I spotted a familiar frame jogging back and forth. It was Isaac. Right when I saw him, he noticed me and moved briskly over to join us. *What on earth could he find to protest about a successful cancer treatment drug*, I wondered? I reintroduced Isaac to my mother quickly, not wanting to sully my moment of glory by dredging up memories of the day I had brought him and Zoe into the observation room. Fortunately, Mr. Stone began to speak promptly so there was little time for reminiscing.

"Ladies and gentlemen," Stone began, "I'd like to share a dream with you, a dream I've had ever since I was given the reins at Pridapt Incorporated ten years ago. It's a dream of doing the most good for the most people. Now, I know you've heard that before, and it may simply seem like another empty political promise, but not today. No, today that phrase actually means something.

"Upstairs in this very building there are patients, children, under attack, their lives threatened, their childhoods robbed by a villain that all too often gets away with murder. I'm speaking of cancer. Who among us doesn't know someone—a relative, friend, or coworker—who has been assaulted by this horrendous killer? In my mind, it's public enemy number one.

"Now, this hospital is filled with some of the finest doctors and nurses in the country, and they're doing their best to combat this heinous assault, but I'm afraid it's just not enough. We are losing lives. Every day, we lose more lives to this killer. Our success is limited, and our treatment options are fraught with side effects and complications. Someday, we will look back on these times aghast that we used to cut off arms and legs to treat bone cancer or used toxic chemotherapy and radiation to stop the growth of blood cancer cells. Someday, we will no longer even consider such painful approaches to cancer treatment and instead will treat patients with effective, natural, and holistic treatments that heal them promptly and painlessly.

"That day, my friends, is now on the horizon. It is very near, and for some it has already arrived. The FDA has just approved our revolutionary treatment for leukemia. Yes, hope is on the horizon, and that hope has a name—Pridapt Incorporated." A spontaneous applause rose from the listeners, and my mother and I quickly joined in.

"Quite the introduction," I commented.

"I'll say," Isaac cheered. "It sounds fantastic!"

Stone looked at each of the front-row reporters one by one, as if sealing the memory of their faces in his mind.

"There are press packets for all of you, and our doctors will be available for questions in a room down the hall behind me," he added before turning and breezing out of the lobby.

"I'm glad to see your company is focusing on more appropriate research like curing cancer rather than modifying animal species," Isaac said.

"We've been working on this cancer treatment for ten years," my mother pointed out. "It's always been a part of what we do."

"Really?" Isaac asked. "Well, with this FDA approval, maybe you'll keep on this line of work and forget about recreating extinct animals."

"The moratorium has taken care of that," I grumbled.

"Hate to say 'I told you so,' but..." Isaac shrugged. "Anyway, holistic cancer treatments, that's something I can get behind wholeheartedly," Isaac pronounced with a smile.

"So glad we have your approval," my mother muttered, her lack of respect for Isaac's opinion evident in her tone. His ignorance of what real research work entailed was obvious, but I don't know that I would have risked offending him and losing a fan. As it turned out, Isaac hadn't noticed my mother's tone as he raced to join the reporters gathering to receive their press packets.

Isaac's ignorance of our research reminded me of how little I knew of this revolutionary leukemia drug.

"Ten years working on this?" I asked my mother. "Which lab?"

"The treatments were derived in one of the cell culture labs, but there are other arms of Pridapt that deal with clinical trials," my mother explained.

"Cell cultures," I thought out loud. "What kind of cells? Cancer cells?"

"You can't treat cancer with cancer cells," my mother chuckled. "We tested the serum on mice initially. When we found that it cured them of tumors, we moved on to human clinical trials."

"What serum?"

"It really has been ten years," my mother continued. "The first few years were all bench-work research, then it took years to get approval for human trials, then finally, approval for treating all patients with leukemia. It's the end of a very long story, Noah," she said with a placid look of profound relief, "a truly happy ending."

I realized that she hadn't actually answered my question about the serum, but it was all right. It was still a good day. Once again, I was the kid who came up with a slogan, a slogan that had been very well received, regarding a new drug that had been well received. It was a good day indeed.

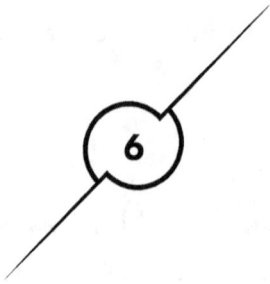

A NEED TO KNOW

I stared through the blackness at the ceiling of my room, barely perceptible in the darkness. Only a glimmer of light slipped under my door from the kitchen where my mother was preparing to go to work. My eyes were fully accommodated to the darkness, and yet, I couldn't make out any of the details in front of me. I knew what was there. I had stared at my ceiling enough to know that there were cracks in the plaster and all sorts of little bumps and irregularities whose shapes and positions I knew by heart. By sheer will, I decided I would see them in the darkness, like an owl seeing a mouse in the dead of night. I imagined random shapes and lines, my mind desperately trying to deliver on my will's unreasonable demands. *Does everyone stare at their ceilings?* I wondered.

Out of the blackness, the image of the true ceiling appeared in a flash as my mother opened the door to my room allowing in a flood of light. It startled me, and I swung up to sit on the edge of my bed.

My mother gasped and leaped back into the doorway. "Noah?" she asked anxiously, as though I might be someone else.

"Yeah," I replied matter-of-factly. *Who else could it be?*

"Honey, why are you awake so early?" my mother inquired as she eased back into my room.

"Just thinking."

"Don't you have a final exam this morning?"

"Yeah."

"Noah, you need your sleep," she advised, coming alongside my bed. "Why don't you sleep some more?"

"I'm not tired." I wasn't. I had too many things on my mind to sleep. Staring into the darkness often helped me straighten out the clutter of thoughts in my head. Two days earlier, I had been riding high, having come through for the CEO with a PR phrase already posted on the company's website and run in the local papers. But what did that amount to, really? It was just a gimmick. I wondered if I would ever make it to the type of position my mother and Dave had. I was no longer failing any classes, but my grades were not the type that would win me any scholarships to big-name science programs. I wanted to be more than the slogan guy. I wanted to work on the science end of things, to help plan the next research project, or at least to be in on the ones we were already doing. *Tell me!* I thought. *Just tell me!*

"Well, come have some breakfast," my mother suggested.

561947—there it was again. I had never written the sequence down, but I had not forgotten it either. Even if I had wanted to, I don't know that I could have. "Sure," I agreed with a smile.

I sat at the kitchen table while my mother prepared some eggs and toast for me. I felt it was a safe time to bring up the reptile primordium. Enough time had passed from that fateful day, when I had brought Isaac and Zoe in without permission, to talk about it without repercussions.

"Say, whatever happened to that reptile primordium?" I asked nonchalantly. My mother looked at me from the corner of her eye and frowned. "Did we get the venomous form in time, you know, before the moratorium?"

"I'll tell you about the reptile work," my mother acquiesced, "but it is confidential. You cannot be telling your friends about it. Okay?"

"Sure," I agreed.

"No, really, Noah," my mother stressed, turning and staring at me.

"I promise, I won't tell anyone," I pledged, immediately

feeling a pang of guilt about watching her type in her passcode the other day.

"Well," my mother began as she served me my breakfast, "we did indeed manage to develop an extinct venomous reptile before the onset of the moratorium. The exciting thing is, it's led to our developing two new medical applications."

"What does it look like?" I asked, unable to contain my excitement.

"It's interesting, brightly colored…" my mother halted. "You are not to see this thing ever. Don't go looking for it, you understand, Noah?"

"Of course."

"It's very dangerous," she continued. "It sprays its venom into an attacker's face, causing debilitating muscle spasm, like instant tetanus."

I did my best to suppress the smile breaking through my staid exterior.

"So the venom has two significant traits," my mother continued, shifting the description away from the brightly colored, venom-spraying, muscle-paralyzing demon-lizard back to medical science. "It is absorbed very quickly through the skin, and it works immediately on the muscles."

"So, that's good for drugs, right?" I asked.

"Absolutely. It's a perfect vehicle for administering drugs because it can get them rapidly absorbed through the skin. It will also be a great model for studying muscle spasm, so it may help us discover new ways to treat back and joint pain."

"What does the venom look like?" I asked. "Is it brightly colored, too?"

"The venom? No, it's clear, not very remarkable," my mother noted, "but it's funny. It has a very strong smell of nutmeg. When we first isolated it, I smelled that and thought someone had brought eggnog into the lab or something."

She laughed, and it struck me that it was the first time she had smiled that morning.

So she had been working on the reptile toxin project. That must have been what was in the East Wing, and that was why she wanted no one else going in there, why alarms had been going off that day when she was called in there so urgently. That would make sense.

"So, where is this reptile?" I asked. "The East Wing?"

"No, it's not in the East Wing. Never mind where it is. I don't even know. After we discovered how useful the venom would be, Mr. Stone had the reptile and all the venom we had collected moved to a high security room in the administrative wing."

"There are places more secure than the East Wing?" I asked, incredulously.

"Oh yes. Only two people have access to those rooms—Mr. Stone and the Chairman of the Board.

She had been sharing so much information, I felt the time was right to ask again about the cancer drug.

"What about that serum?"

"What serum?"

"The one you used to develop the leukemia drug."

"What about it?"

"Where did we get it?"

My mother picked up a folder of papers lying on the table, looked through them briefly, then dropped them on the table.

"It's a secret," she sniffed, "and we all know how good you are at keeping secrets, how you like to share them with total strangers and casual acquaintances."

561947—the sequence flashed across my mind with rebellious indignation. "So *that's* what's in the East Wing," I teased.

"Will you stop?" My mother sighed with a half smile. "Honestly! Enough about the East Wing." She mussed up my hair and went to fill her cup with more coffee. "I have to leave soon. I need to finish up my work early today in order to get to an afternoon conference."

"Oh yeah," I remembered, "that genetic conference. What's that about, or is that a secret, too?"

She shook her head at my jab but seemed to appreciate the change of subject. "It's a presentation on the theory of genetic memory."

"Memory in the genes? If that's true then I should remember the inside of a jail cell," I declared.

"Why on earth would you say that?" my mother asked, not looking up from the folder she was leafing through.

"Well," I answered, "because of my father, of course."

"Your father?" she scoffed, looking at me with a blank stare. "Why would... oh yes, yes, right." One of the few details my mother had told me about my birth father was that he had been in jail. "Well, it's not really that sort of memory they're talking about, you know."

My mother had a curious look on her face as she turned, looking down the hall toward my room. "Why *were* you up so early?" she asked with an unsettling degree of concern.

"What does it matter?" I asked.

My mother slowly turned her gaze from my room as if breaking free of some magnetic force. "It doesn't," she said with a seemingly forced smile on her face. "It doesn't matter at all." She kissed me on the head, grabbed her briefcase, and ran out the door, calling over her shoulder, "Do well on your test!"

As the door closed and I was left in the silent, empty house, I began to wonder which was the greater enigma: what lay behind the steel doors of the East Wing or what lay behind my mother's steel blue eyes.

Later that morning, after finishing my exams, I drove to

Pridapt and had lunch in the cafeteria. My fellow lab technicians, my mother, and Dave had all finished their lunches
before I had arrived, so I ate mine alone by an outside window. I often had my lunch alone like this, in that very spot:
the same chair, the same table, the same scratches on the
glass that looked out onto the front walkway of Pridapt.
The predictability of it all comforted me, especially when
the burden of loneliness weighed me down. If not friends, I
could at least have the company of my routine.

I finished the last of my sandwich, and through the
window scratches, saw Zoe coming up the front walkway.
I hadn't spoken with her since the day we escaped into the
woods alongside Pridapt, though I almost caught her eye a
couple times in the halls between classes. I ran to meet her in
the lobby, getting her an official visitor's pass. I didn't want
another embarrassing scene with a security guard or my
mother.

My heart was lifted as I walked side by side with Zoe
down the hall to my lab. As we turned a corner, we saw my
mother talking with Dr. Joseph Strauss, a retired physician
and part-time ethics adviser at Pridapt. He was short, wore
round glasses, and had a wave of white hair that fell onto his
forehead like the part of a horse's mane that hangs between
their eyes. When he spoke, he motioned with his head and
his white mane would swish back and forth. I could see it

swishing a lot right then.

"There's *Supermom*," Zoe announced as soon as she saw my mother, fortunately outside of earshot.

"Supermom?" I asked.

"Single mom in college, remember, you told me? Pretty cool, though I still think she should let you into that secret lab. What is it called?"

"The East Wing."

"Yeah, that's it," Zoe affirmed. "I think it's a trust thing. You know, if she trusted you, she would let you in. If she doesn't let you in, then she doesn't trust you." Zoe stopped walking suddenly.

"Come on," I urged, turning back toward her.

Nodding down the hall, she countered, "Think we might want to hang back a minute or two. Something tense going on."

I turned to see my mother getting quite agitated by her conversation with Dr. Strauss. We could hear them now.

"Annette," Dr. Strauss spoke, gesturing with both his hands and head, "we need to talk about this."

"I know it's your job to play the devil's advocate," my mother shot back, "but this is not a good time right now. You need to..." She saw Zoe and me standing down the hall and stopped. "Later, Joe," she ordered, ending the discussion. Walking down the hall toward us, she greeted me with a stern look. "Visitors' day again?"

"I got her a pass this time," I offered with a smile. "I don't start work for a bit, so I thought I could show her around, the different labs, you know... just show her like, I don't know, the East Wing?"

The words surprised me as they came out of my mouth. I should have known that it was no time to be putting her on the spot. I guess Zoe's comments about trust were still ringing in my ears, and I felt the need to prove myself.

"You and the East Wing!" my mother snapped. "This is what it's about, isn't it: you impressing your friends? Well, the world doesn't revolve around you and your friends!" She glared at me then turned and marched away. I was mortified. Unable to speak or move, I stood, humiliated, in front of Zoe. I knew I was no one to her at school, but at Pridapt I was somebody in her eyes, and in an instant, that respect had all been stripped away. I had never been so embarrassed.

"Sorry about that," I managed to get out finally, still not looking at her.

"That?" Zoe laughed. "Heck, that's nothing. You should hear my mom. That's like a 'good morning howdy-do' for her. At least your mom wants you around. She lets you work here with her. Not my mom—nothing I do ever pleases her."

"Really?" I asked, appreciating the change of subject.

Zoe elaborated on her mother's resentment of her at

some length. Apparently, her father left them when Zoe was about ten years old. It seemed he did not want the responsibility of raising a child, and in a strange shifting of guilt, her mother blamed Zoe for her father's abandonment. Since then, her mother had developed diabetes and was in poor health. I was surprised that Zoe was sharing all this information with me, but didn't mind.

Zoe ended her exposé with a longing: "I wish I could do something big for her so that she'd see it, plain as day, couldn't deny it, and be pleased with me at least one time." Zoe had been looking up at the ceiling as she spoke of her wish. She returned to the present reality and asked, "So, what are you going to show me today?"

561947, the sequence resurfaced with greater intensity and clarity than ever before. The surge of embarrassment had now been replaced by a smoldering resentment. "Hang out in the lobby coffee shop for a bit," I suggested. I knew my mother would be going to her conference shortly. "I'll come get you at around two o'clock."

"Then what?"

"Then I'll show you the East Wing."

"Are you serious?" Zoe gasped, wide-eyed and grinning.

"Of course I'm serious," I whispered, "but not a word. If my mother ever found out, she'd kill me! I mean it; she'd really kill me!"

Then don't do it, Zoe might well have said, and I half hoped that she would. *Stop me; tell me it's not worth it. Tell me to wait until I'm allowed in properly. Why press the issue now, when emotions are running high?*

But then again, I knew she would say no such thing. If anything, she would bolster my resolve to do it. She was the one who had brought up the East Wing that day. That's why I put it on her. I looked to her to stop me instead of my own conscience which had been trying to stop me all along.

When two o'clock arrived, I brought Zoe from the lobby to the steel-gray doors of the East Wing. Without hesitation I began to type in the code. *56-* I stopped and turned to Zoe.

"You have to look away," I told her. "It's secret."

It was my secret, and I was not one to let secrets slip through me like a sieve despite how my mother had chided me that morning. I *could* keep a secret. I was my mother's son, after all.

I finished typing in the code, and with a click of the lock, the mystery that had eluded me for years, teasing and taunting me daily with its obscure, hidden treasures, was before me. The East Wing's steel doors opened effortlessly at the touch of my hand.

SECRETS

As we entered the room, the lights came on, illuminating a square white space with black lab benches running along each side. The wall opposite the door had a central glass window about three feet high by three feet wide, looking into an adjacent room. Next to the window was a second steel door. There was no lab equipment in this first room, only a computer terminal and some file cabinets. One of the file cabinet drawers was ajar, and there was a chart open on the nearby lab bench.

Zoe was the first to approach the window, pressing her face up against it to see past the reflection from the light above.

"It's dark in there," she mumbled, her cheeks still pressed against the glass. "Take a look." She rubbed off the fog from her breath and stepped back to allow me to see. It was dark in the next room, but there was enough light filtering in for me to see that there was yet another room beyond that one. They weren't labs; the most distant one was more like the habitats we had for the primordia, but those were surrounded by observation rooms. I couldn't understand why there would be a habitat off by itself.

I moved closer to the window again and craned my neck to see into the corners of the back room. Shifting my head back and forth, I tried to see past some distortion along the edge of the glass.

"It's blurry in the corners," I commented. "Maybe the glass is double-paned."

"What's this?" Zoe asked, pointing to the open file on the lab bench.

"Hopefully something good," I sighed, disappointed at the anticlimax of our break-in. I picked up the file, and we both scanned the pages as I leafed through it. "Vitrology Beginnings," I read. "What do you suppose that is?"

"That's an invitro lab," Zoe replied. "I have an aunt who used them. Cost her a bundle."

"Used them for what?"

"To have a baby, of course," Zoe laughed, shaking her head.

A Human cell lab, I thought. *They must have provided the cell line for the serum.*

As I looked back down at the file, I noticed something in my peripheral vision, a familiar pattern of shapes I took note of but had not yet recognized. Then it struck me—eyes, eyes were in the window! I jerked my head back toward the glass pane and could not say if I had simply imagined it, or if there had indeed been a pair of eyes in the window looking back at me. In any case, there was nothing there now.

"What?" Zoe asked. "Did you see something?"

"Did you?" I asked cautiously. Zoe shook her head. "My mind's playing tricks on me, I guess." I stared into the room again, now more intently, the way I would stare at my ceiling in the darkness. I saw a few more details: a glass wall and another door leading into the habitat.

There was a blurriness in my peripheral vision that disappeared whenever I tried to focus on it. It gave the scene in the next room a mottled, swirly appearance. The hair on my arms rose, and I felt a tingling run up and down my back. *Maybe it's a migraine coming on from the stress of lying,* I thought. I had had a migraine once. It had given me blurry vision and strange sensations then, too.

"Why don't we just go in there?" Zoe asked as she went to open the door next to the window.

"Wait!" I said, louder than I had intended to. She looked back at me, uninterested, and pushed down on the door handle.

"Locked," she explained. "Have a key?"

I shook my head, put the chart back on the counter, and pulled out drawers in search of a key. After trying all the drawers, I tried the door handle myself.

"Still locked?" Zoe asked. I nodded, then remembering that my mother's code also allowed access to computer files, I raced to the keyboard and logged in with my mother's name. Scrolling down a list of files, I found a set of video log entries that looked promising. "Click on the last one," Zoe suggested. "Cut to the chase. It's like reading the end of a book first—you don't waste your time."

I considered her suggestion but thought we might understand more if we saw the entries in order. I compromised by opening the next to last video in the folder. It was my mother looking through an observation window and narrating what she was seeing.

"Well, there it is. It's changing, splitting." Moving away from the window and facing the camera she added, "It's dividing."

"I think we need more than that," I said and clicked the next entry.

"There's something happening." My mother was again narrating. "It's something big, a sort of change. Oh my, what is that? Hold on..." and the clip ended abruptly.

Just as the video stopped, I heard the sound of a keycard

swiping. My hand fumbled around the edges of the computer monitor, finally finding the *off* button, then Zoe and I scrambled to hide alongside two file cabinets in the corner of the room. The door swung open, and my mother stepped inside, whisked to the second door, unlocked it, and disappeared into the back room. The steel lock clicked shut behind her.

I slipped up to the window to look around the corner where my mother had gone.

"Are you insane?" Zoe whispered. "Let's get out of here!"

"In a minute," I whispered back. With light now filling the back room, I couldn't resist the opportunity for a quick look. The room was similar to the one we were in, except that most of the back wall was a very large glass window, with a door alongside of it. Beyond the glass window was the habitat. My mother stood at that glass wall, apparently searching for something within it. Without warning, she turned and looked straight at me. I rushed back to Zoe, who was heading to the door, and shook my head.

"She saw me," I moaned, my mind racing to think of some explanation to give my mother.

"What did you see?" my mother fired out at me as she burst into the room. "Hmm? What?"

"Nothing."

"Noah," she commanded, "what did you see?" The intensity of her question startled me.

"I saw you rushing down the hall," I stuttered, "and I thought something must be wrong, because you were supposed to be going to the conference, so we just followed you in here to make sure you were okay." The excuse had come to me as I was offering it. I knew it was a shot in the dark, but surprisingly, it seemed to strike a chord.

"Well, thank you for your concern," my mother said, extending her arms as if to sweep us out of there.

"Why did you come running in here?" I asked.

"I noticed an unauthorized entry."

"You did?" I asked, sharing a distraught look with Zoe.

"It wasn't us," Zoe piped up, with a defiant and guilty look.

"I know it wasn't," my mother replied, to our surprise. "The computer log recorded it at eleven o'clock this morning. You two were taking exams then, I trust."

Zoe nodded.

There's a log? I thought in horror. I wondered if she would notice that there were two entries around this time, demolishing my lie. Just as we were about to leave, my mother looked toward the open file on the counter and stopped.

"You've been in my files," she accused.

"It was out like that," I offered. "We just glanced at it."

My mother picked up the file and, replacing it into a drawer, slid the drawer shut. She did not appear to be angry with us, though the silence in the room begged for something to be said.

"So you used an in vitro lab?" I asked her, more to make conversation than to seek an answer.

"Why do you say that?" She whisked her head around to me with renewed vexation.

"The name, Vitrolo—I don't know. What was it? Zoe recognized it as an invitro lab," I struggled to explain. Zoe glared at me for bringing her into the fray, but my explanation seemed to calm my mother. "Is that where you got the cell line for the cancer serum?" I asked, regretting the question as soon as it left my mouth. This, apparently was my mother's *last straw*.

"Come with me," she snapped, grabbing us both by the arm and leading us out into the hallway. "You just couldn't let it go, could you?" my mother barked out as she marched ahead of us down the hallway. "Just because you couldn't see, you had to see."

It was all my fault, Mrs. Bolton. I was the one who egged Noah on, I imagined Zoe admitting in my mind. But there would be no such self-immolation on my behalf. Zoe walked two paces behind me, stone-faced and silent. I was hung out to dry with no one coming to my aid.

"I have another idea for Mr. Stone," I offered in an attempt to defuse the tension. "I was thinking of the John F. Kennedy speech, about the space program." My mother did not reply, but her pace seemed to slow a bit. "He could start with that, with a video of Kennedy's commitment *before this decade is out to land a man on the moon and return him safely*. Then he could say that we had a commitment like that, and then he could use Neil Armstrong's line, how our latest achievement is *one small step for Man...*"

"That's good, Noah." My mother sighed, shaking her head at me, then Zoe. "Zoe, we'll see you to the door now." After walking Zoe through the lobby to the front door, we bid her a brief farewell, and she left. As we made our way back to the labs, I felt pretty good. All in all, things had not gone that badly, given the circumstances. I was even considering bringing up the cancer serum again with my mother, when Dr. Strauss turned the corner in front of us, his white mane-like hair bouncing with every step.

"Joe, a word?" my mother fired out at him. "Stay here, Noah." She marched directly up to Dr. Strauss and seemed to confront him about something. Her voice suddenly rose, "So you were looking through my files?"

It was Dr. Strauss who had gone into the East Wing that morning, I realized. *Looks like someone else was in the hot seat now.*

"You haven't seen them, have you, Annette?" Dr. Strauss asked. I moved closer to hear her response.

"I was told the issue was resolved," my mother replied.

"Resolved?" Dr. Strauss retorted with a swish of his mane. "How could such a thing ever be resolved? Annette, I'm beginning to think we need to halt the whole project. In fact, I'll be recommending that to Stone tomorrow. "

"Maybe you need to make a visit to the cancer ward to be reminded of why we're doing what we're doing."

"I've been to the cancer ward."

"And you've been in my lab, where you have no business."

Did she say, "My lab?" The East Wing was her lab?

My mother broke off their conversation and looked back at me. "Come on, Noah." She started out at her usual brisk pace but then slowed, allowing me to come alongside her. "You want to know about the leukemia drug, don't you?"

I hesitated, then nodded.

"You want to understand how it works, how we made it, where we got the serum, right?"

I wasn't sure where her line of questioning was headed, so I said nothing, afraid even to nod.

"It's okay, Noah." She smiled. "Really. I'm ready to tell you. You deserve to know. If Strauss has been snooping around in there, why not let you see too? You'll understand;

you'll listen to me, right?"

"Sure," I answered, still wondering if it was a trick question.

As we walked, my mother explained the mechanism of action of our new drug. "It's derived from the serum produced by a human cell line we have in culture. Almost by chance, we happened to test this serum on mice and found that it dissolved cancer tumors. The tumors literally disappeared overnight! It turned out that the serum contained a factor, a sort of retrovirus, that inserted a gene into the animal's DNA. This gene coded for the destruction of the cancer cells. After the mice, we moved on to human trials. We started with leukemia patients too sick to undergo any other therapy, and, well, you know how successful that was. Now, we're set for many other trials, like bone and muscle tumors. Can you imagine, Noah, being able to cure a child's cancer without amputating an arm or leg?"

She paused for a reply. I hadn't really followed all that she was saying. My mind stopped at the bit about inserting genes. *Did that mean the patients got someone else's genes?* I wondered. The idea troubled me.

"Noah?" she prompted.

"Oh yes, sorry." I looked up and realized we were standing in front of the East Wing doors. With a swipe of my mother's card, we were back in the room where Zoe and I had just been hiding. My mother pulled out a key from her lab coat pocket and slid it into the lock of the second door.

"All right, Noah," my mother began with a sigh, "I'm going to show you now, but..." She hesitated as if at a loss for words. "Prepare yourself."

"Prepare myself?" I asked. *For what?*

"Just keep an open mind," she said, nodding her head for me to follow. As she unlocked the door and pushed it open, I stepped back. Her words confused me. Her tone frightened me. Suddenly, I was very nervous about going into the next room. Even as a child I had always been fascinated with secrets, always longing to know them, to discover them and expose them to the light. Now for the first time since I had learned there were such things as secrets, I did not want to know what they were.

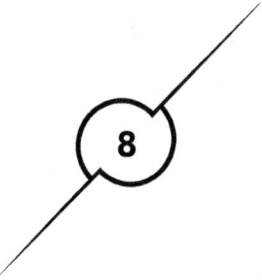

8

THE FACE OF THE MONSTER

We entered the second room, and fluorescent lights blinked on, giving me a good look at the space I had only glanced at earlier. Next to the large glass window on the back wall, there was a video camera on a tripod, another metal door, and a set of file cabinets. My mother pulled out one of the file drawers, and slipped in a sheet of paper. As she pushed the drawer shut, I caught a glimpse of a folder titled, "Birth Certificate."

A table with chairs stood just in front of the glass window, and my mother motioned for us to sit down. She flicked a switch, and light flooded the habitat behind the glass. In the back corner, there was a large tank of water with a platform alongside it. Steps led up to the platform from a carpeted area below outfitted with several chairs and tables.

On the table before us, I noticed a framed photograph of my mother in a graduation gown.

"College graduation?" I asked, nodding toward the photograph.

"Yes," my mother answered, only momentarily taking her eyes off of the habitat.

"Where was I?" I asked, remembering Zoe's question of how my mother had managed being a single mom and a full-time student. "Was I in day care or something?"

"Where were you? Oh, you were somewhere." She sighed, turning from the habitat window. "Then, as now, you must have been sneaking around places you weren't supposed to be."

"Very funny," I scoffed.

"So..." My mother swiveled her chair to face me directly. "I'll tell you about the serum. I told you it was produced by a cell line we had in culture, but I didn't tell you where those cells came from. You were right—we got the original human cell from that in vitro lab you read about. We stimulated that cell to revert to its primordial form..."

What? Its primordial form? I had thought they were just normal human cells.

"It was like the experiments you have been involved with, only this was human," she continued. "We introduced stressors to bring about adaptation, and as soon as it became apparent that it was, in fact, a human primordium, we harvested the initial sample of cells which we then grew in culture."

"You made a *human* primordium?" I gazed at her, stunned.

My mother halted her almost manic account and looked at me with a combination of sadness and defiance. "Yes, Noah, but just for the cells. You see, there was an opportunity. The cell we got from the in vitro lab was actually a single-celled embryo. They said it wasn't suitable for implantation, so if we hadn't accepted it for experimentation, it was going to be destroyed. This way, some good would come from it."

"So you developed a line of cells from it?"

"Yes," my mother answered after a short pause.

"Where are they? I don't see any incubators in here," I noted, looking around the room.

"The cell cultures aren't here. They're in another facility now, where we have been purifying the serum and preparing it for patient injections." Swiveling back toward the habitat, she continued. "After we had obtained the cells... I found... It all happened so quickly."

I had never known my mother to stammer so.

"We weren't prepared for how quickly it would transition," she continued. "You see, this was the first primordial reversion of any type that we had tried."

"The first? You mean, before any animals?"

"That was not our plan, of course," my mother explained, "but the opportunity presented itself..."

"What do you mean, it transitioned quickly? Into an adult? You grew an adult human primordium?" Before my mother could answer, the implications of that conclusion became instantly apparent to me. *That's what's in here!* It wasn't just a monster being hidden in the East Wing, it was a *human* monster!

My mother looked at me, then turning to the habitat, answered, "Yes."

"And it's in there?" I gasped, pointing to the habitat behind the glass wall.

"*She* is in there," my mother corrected. "She's not an *it,* though she is different in some ways. You see, as it was the first reversion we had ever done, we didn't know how far to go. We meant to do what we do now, what you have been doing with the animal experiments, to revert to an animal's original type: the first bird, the first amphibian, the first reptile. Instead, it seems we pushed it a little too far, past the human primordium to something more primal, to a prior commonality. It was like playing God though we had no intention of doing so. It led to some unusual adaptations."

"Like what?"

"Well, the first stressor was radiation. Since radiation causes cancerous cell formation, the primordium adapted to the stress with production of the anticancer serum we are now using on leukemia patients. Unfortunately, the radiation also caused some permanent damage to her."

I scanned the beige walls of the habitat from top to bottom and still saw no sign of the thing. Behind the carpeted area with chairs and tables, there was a small, cave-like alcove and an entrance to another side room. I assumed it was hiding in one of those areas. "How old is it?" I asked.

"*She*," my mother stressed, "is nine."

"So you must have started the project right after we came here."

"More or less," my mother replied as she opened the door to the habitat. "Come on in."

We entered the habitat, and I continued to look for it, though now a bit more nervously. My mother stood still and signaled for me to do the same. Looking over at the water tank, I noticed some blurriness in my peripheral vision, similar to what I had seen through the front window earlier that day. Jerking my head quickly toward the periphery, I saw what looked like eyes suspended in midair! As quickly as I saw them, they disappeared.

"What was that?" I gasped, pointing in the direction of the apparition.

"Be quiet," my mother whispered. "You'll frighten her. And don't look at her eyes."

"Why not?"

"Just don't. If she turns toward you, look away. She has a sort of hypnotic ability." My mother must have seen the doubt in my eyes because she added, "Trust me, just don't look at her too long." Putting a hand on my shoulder, she whispered, "Never be alone with her either. Promise me."

"Never be alone? Is it dangerous?"

Where the eyes had been, there was a mass of wavy shapes, like heat waves rising from a road on a summer day. Out of the distortion, I saw a shape emerge, a figure crouched on all fours, moving slowly along the platform by the water tank. It had no hair, or very short hair on its head, points of its spine protruding along the length of its back, and dark lines running down the sides of its neck. It seemed to have come out of a sort of camouflage, like my favorite toad in the amphibian habitat. It was moving away from us hunched over. Then it stopped, and its head turned around and looked squarely at us, as if it had twisted a full 180 degrees on its neck. Its eyes were wide and round, the whites visible around the whole circumference of its pupils. It was like the face of a startled animal, but the startled look didn't go away, no matter how casually it seemed to be moving or looking around. It was a horrible face.

Suddenly, it spun and dove into the tank. It swam down to the bottom, turned upright, and pressed itself against the glass, looking out at us. The dark lines on its neck were open wide and gaping as it began drawing water in through its mouth.

It has gills?

The sight unnerved me: its mouth opening and closing sequentially with the slits in its neck. Although I was used to this in the early forms of other primordia, before the cocoons and the metamorphosis, seeing it in an adult human was different. This thing was monstrous, truly monstrous.

"Why does it look like that?" I asked.

"You mean her eyes?"

"Its eyes, gills, camouflage, everything!"

"We think it was from the radiation. It caused atrophy of the muscles around her eyes. They became fixed in their sockets. She adapted by developing several additional vertebrae in her neck, which is why she can turn her head so far."

"And the gills and camouflage?" I asked.

"Like I said, because we pushed her reversion too far, she developed some more primal adaptations. I think her gills would close and atrophy if we took the water away."

"Why don't you?"

"We tried once, and she got extremely agitated. It's sort of like taking a security blanket away from a child. I'll have to do it sometime, but there's just so much else going on now."

"A security blanket?" I scoffed. "Right. So, we're using cells from that thing?"

"We harvested the cells before she developed into her adult form."

"But still, this is what they became." I felt uneasiness at the thought of this thing's cells being injected into people. My eyes examined it the way they would take in some bizarre deep-sea creature at an aquarium. It looked back at me, unblinking.

"Don't look at her eyes!" my mother reminded me.

"It looks pretty big for nine years old."

"As with the other primordia, she grew very quickly after the metamorphosis."

My revulsion was becoming fascination. It was our own little monster, kept safe here in our habitat. "Does it bite?" I asked playfully. "Does it have any venom or anything?"

"She's never bitten me, though if you keep talking about her that way she just might bite you."

"How can you call it 'she,' and how did you ever get a swimsuit on it? How can it disappear anyway? That suit doesn't have camouflage."

"She keeps the skin of her arms over the material if she wants to stay hidden."

"Clever. Does it let you touch it?"

"She is not an 'it'! Why do you keep saying that?"

"Are you kidding? Look at it! It's a monster! There's no other word for it," I retorted. Shaking my head, I peered into the tank again. "Now where is it?"

A plastic chair flew at us from the corner, barely missing my mother's head and whizzing by my ear. The primordium became visible at the origin of the chair's trajectory.

"That thing is quick!" I gasped crouching down, expecting another object to come hurtling toward us. "Where is it?" Then, out of the corner of my eye, I saw motion. The thing was scrambling up the corner of the room toward the ceiling, pushing off the two adjacent walls. At about twenty feet above the floor, it scurried onto the top of an arched metal beam that spanned the length of the habitat. Crouching there, like a rat on a rafter, it peered around the edge of the beam and stared at me with its owl eyes.

"Don't look at her eyes!" my mother admonished once again.

"How can you help it? It's like a bat flying around the room; you can't take your eyes off it."

"Well, take your eyes off it—her," my mother corrected. "She's agitated, probably jealous."

"Jealous?"

"Yes, and you're making it worse."

Just as I turned to my mother to share an indignant look

of dismay, I once again saw rapid motion in my peripheral vision; this time, it was like a squirrel running along a telephone line. The thing was scampering along the narrow ceiling beam directly over our heads! I instinctively jumped back toward the door.

"Let's get out of here!" I yelled.

"Calm down, Noah," my mother chided me. Before I could open the door, the creature leaped from the ceiling beam onto the edge of the water tank, then dove back into the water, turning to stand again, against the inside of the glass.

"I told you, she can…" my mother began, but seeing the look of revulsion on my face, she halted. "I should never have brought you in here."

The primordium moved to the back to the water tank and curled up in the corner, disappearing with its camouflage. My mother said something more, but I was no longer listening. I was thinking about Zoe and what she would make of our little monster.

She would love it! I thought.

"She's acting out," my mother was explaining to my deaf ears. "I shouldn't have brought you in here. I'm sorry, Noah. It would be better if you just forgot about ever coming in here."

Forgot? If there was one thing I knew, it was that I would never forget this experience, and I definitely had to see this thing again. I knew I would have to bring Zoe in to see it too.

"Come on, Noah," my mother sighed, leading me out the door. After the habitat door clicked shut, I quietly grabbed a roll of tape that was on the table. When she led me through the next door to the outer room, I slipped a strip of tape over the door's locking mechanism.

"So, what was that alarm the other day? Did that thing go berserk or something?" I asked her once we were back in the outer room.

"No, she didn't go *berserk*. There are motion detectors around the inner habitat." She flipped a switch over the lab bench, turning on the motion detectors. "See? If she ever gets out of the habitat, it sets them off."

"She got out?"

"She did that day. I must have left the inner door ajar or something."

A sudden jolt of fear flashed through me as I thought of the tape I had just placed on the outer door lock. "You closed it well today, though, right?" I asked.

"Yes, I double-checked it. Why? Are you afraid of her?"

My mother's mocking tone made me feel indignant. Was it unreasonable to be afraid of a monster? Who wouldn't be? My mother couldn't consider the situation rationally; she was biased, too invested in her research to see clearly. But

I had seen it clearly, clearly enough to have second thoughts about the tape I'd just put on the outer door. There was no taking it off now, not without my mother finding out what I had done. I would be back later that afternoon, and I would take if off then. In any case, the habitat was locked. Like my mother had said, she probably left that inner door open that day. The thing was contained. My fears allayed, I mused again about the wonder of it all, our own little monster—how excited Zoe would be when I told her!

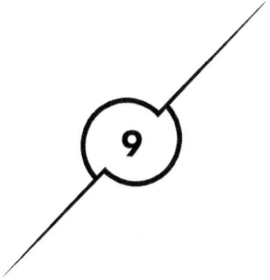

NEVER BE ALONE

My mother was finally leaving for the conference she had planned to attend that day, hoping to catch the last two presentations. On her way out, she stopped in to see Mr. Stone, and I set up one last electrophoresis run in my lab. While the specimens were running, I went outside to clear my head. Standing along the edge of the woods, I could see my mother's car in the parking lot. As I waited for her to leave, I watched the shuttered sunlight coming through the trees.

It was good to be away from that habitat. Seeing that monster was like hearing music being played horribly out of tune with wrong notes and screeching instruments. Now, in the fresh air, there was peace. The beauty of nature was well aligned and ordered with everything in its proper place.

There were no monsters here.

This was where I came to start over, to reboot. It offered me a chance to get things straight. I would lose myself in those trees, that air, and in those columns of light and shadow. I thought if I looked hard enough, I could find the answer to any question.

My mother's car left the parking lot, and left the woods. Walking along the grass that led to the driveway, I felt the peace of that moment gradually fade as the discordant reality of the monster made its way back into my mind. My fascination with the thing resurfaced, and before long, I could think of nothing else.

I started up the driveway back to Pridapt, thinking how I wished Zoe was still there to take advantage of my mother's absence, when, as luck would have it, she stepped out of her car not twenty feet from me.

"Hey, Noah," she called out.

"Zoe! Have I got something to show you!" Seeing the coincidence of her having stayed as some sort of providential sign, I eagerly brought her into Pridapt with me. She still had her visitor's pass from the morning, so we walked by the security guard, Daniel Smith, with a cheerful nod, and returned to the East Wing. I again made sure Zoe looked away as I typed in my mother's code. *What about the log?* I thought, panicking for a moment. It was so close to the time that my mother had been in there, I felt it would be okay.

"So?" Zoe prodded me as the steel door shut behind us. "Tell me, what is it?"

"It's a human primordium."

"No way! That's insane. Is it a freak?"

"Totally."

"Whoa. That's got to be tough."

"For who?" I asked.

"For it."

Wait, was she empathizing with the thing? She hadn't even seen it yet, and she was feeling sorry for it?

"What do you mean?" I asked her.

"Well, if it's a freak, I'm sure nobody wants to be around it. It probably grosses everyone out, right? It's worse than being nothing. Nobody pays any attention to 'nothing,' but everyone stares at a freak."

"Well, don't stare at this one."

"Why not?"

"It's got some sort of hypnotizing ability."

"Cool!" Zoe exclaimed, her eyes filled with wonder and excitement. "So, where is it?"

"Back there," I said, pointing through the small window as I turned on the lights. "In that back habitat." Zoe craned her neck to see the full extent of the room behind the window. "Do you want to go in and see?"

"But that door's locked," she complained, pointing to the door I had taped the lock of.

"Not today," I boasted, and Zoe ran over to pull it open. "Wait! Hold on, I have to turn off the motion detectors. Otherwise, my mother will be back here in a flash." I felt like I had pushed my mother just about as far as she would go. I did not want to see how she would respond to my breaking in here again.

After switching off the motion detectors, I led Zoe into the next room and the metal door closed behind us with a thud, gently tapping against the door jamb. We went to the large glass wall, and I turned on the lights in the habitat.

"What does it look like?" Zoe asked, looking around the space behind the glass.

"Oh, you'll know it when you see it," I assured her.

Passing the file cabinet my mother had opened earlier, I pulled out the drawer and grabbed the file labeled, 'Birth Certificate.'

"Whatcha got there?" Zoe asked as she continued her visual exploration of the habitat.

"Just checking something."

I read the documents quickly. They turned out to be my naturalization papers instead of a birth certificate. They said my mother was an illegal alien and, oddly, that I was adopted at age seven.

"I don't see anything in there, Noah. Though I can't see into those little nooks in the back."

"Just wait; it will appear," I suggested, but Zoe had already stepped over to the habitat door and pulled it open.

"The door's open! Let's go in and look around."

"No! Wait!" I yelled. "I don't have keys for that door."

"It's open."

"On this side, but it's locked on the inside." I was not eager to go back in there.

"So just tape it, like you did the other one." Zoe winked as she picked up a roll of tape on the table and tossed it to me. I reluctantly complied, taping the habitat's door latch open, then repeatedly opened and closed the door to be sure it was safe.

"I think that will do it," Zoe quipped.

"I'm not taking any chances. And listen, we don't go any farther than about two feet from this door. I mean it. This thing is freaky." I pulled the door open, and we slowly moved in, just beyond the threshold.

What happened next I still think of as the most frightening moment of my life. It was just a sound, a sound that in other circumstances would have been unnoticeable it was so ordinary. Such sounds can be the most terrifying of things when they occur in the wrong context. The sound of a chair scraping on the floor when you push back from a table is unremarkable unless you happen to be home alone and you hear that sound coming from a room upstairs. The metal door to the monster's habitat swung shut behind us, and instead of the soft thud of the taped lock thumping against the frame, I heard the metallic click of the door's latch. Spinning around, I dove onto the door handle and pushed down on it, to no avail. The door was locked! Jumping aside to the window, I saw the monster standing just outside the door, staring at me with its owl eyes, dangling a strip of tape in its hand.

"What happened?" Zoe asked, trying the door for herself several times. "What is it?"

"It's the primordium. It locked us in!"

"What? You said it was in here!" Zoe rushed to my side to look through the glass, but by then the primordium had vanished into its camouflage. I reached for my phone, finding there was no service.

"There's got to be a phone or intercom somewhere in here," Zoe rattled off, her calm demeanor deteriorating.

"There are no phones in here. It's the primordium's habitat! There's no service in here either; the walls are too thick." *The motion detectors!* I thought with sudden relief. They'll alert my mother—but I had turned them off!

Just as that momentary hope had passed, I detected motion beside us in the habitat!

It can't be! Are there two of them? My thoughts raced as I moved from side to side trying to see a shape through the blurry motion near the ceiling beam.

"You see something in here?" Zoe gasped.

"There it is!" I shouted.

I saw it again on the ceiling beam, peering down at us! This time, Zoe saw it too.

"That's it?" she groaned, the playful fascination gone from her voice.

An eerie sound emanated from the thing—a low growl the likes of which I had heard only once before. My mother and I had come upon some park rangers who were putting down a rabid animal. It was a mountain lion, glassy-eyed, frothing at the mouth, with a low gurgling growl coming from deep in its throat, pulsing in waves through the foam over its teeth. It was an unnerving, unforgettable sound, now nearly duplicated by this monster perched above our heads. It seemed to be gulping air into its mouth then forcing it out its gills.

Zoe shrieked. "We have to call someone. Get the guard, now! We need to get out of here!"

"Don't look at its eyes!" I told her.

It growled again and leaped down, first to the water tank, then to the carpeted area about ten feet from us, its head and eyes following our every move.

Zoe grabbed the door to the habitat, shaking the handle up and down and throwing herself against the door. The thing blurred out of view.

"Look for anything that's out of focus," I shouted to Zoe. "If it seems blurry, it's probably it." Zoe's breaths became louder and more rapid. "And slow your breathing: stay calm," I added.

"Calm? How am I supposed to stay calm? When is your mother coming back?"

"Not until tomorrow."

"Tomorrow? I'm not spending the night in here with that thing. We have got to find a way out! It must have gotten out somehow. We can get out that way."

I scanned the habitat nervously looking for any means of escape.

"It must have gotten out by that ceiling beam," I suggested, looking up at the corner of the room where there was a small gap between the ceiling and the beam that the thing had been crawling on.

"How could we ever get up there? That's impossible!"

The primordium jumped between us and the corner, then turned and scampered up the corner almost effortlessly pushing off the adjacent walls, returning to its post on the ceiling beam.

"Show-off," I quipped.

"This isn't funny," Zoe snapped.

"You're the one who had to come in here."

"Fair enough," she acquiesced, "but you're gonna get me out of here, right?"

"Right," I agreed reluctantly.

"Is it poisonous or anything?"

"No, it doesn't have venom. It's just a freak."

"Sort of like a giant possum." Zoe laughed, a little too loudly to sound like genuine laughter. The primordium moved its head from side to side, then bobbed it up and down, like a lizard. It stared at us from the ceiling beam as though sizing us up. Then, its eyes disappeared.

"It's on the move," I warned. I could no longer see its body extending out from the sides of the beam.

"Where is it?" Zoe whispered again.

"Come on, we'll grab a couple of those chairs to hold out in front of us." Step by step, we made our way onto the carpeted area and snatched up two chairs. Looking to our left and right, we tip-toed back to the window beside the door.

The minutes seemed like hours as we stood with our backs up against the glass wall, chairs held in front of us as defensive shields. Both of our chairs had gradually drooped down to wind up resting on the floor, and I was about to suggest that we sit on them, when I saw eyes appear on the opposite wall. I tapped Zoe's shoulder, motioning toward the eyes, which then moved as the shape of a body emerged, running straight for us. Instead of the low, grunting growl it had made before, it now let out a high-pitched scream, its arms flailing at its sides. Zoe screamed in return, hurling her chair toward the monster, then cast herself full force against the door. This time, however, the door offered no resistance, flying open and landing Zoe flat onto the floor in the next room. I dropped my chair and scrambled after her, slapping the door shut behind me. It closed with a quiet thud.

At the same time, the outer door opened, and my mother walked into the room, stopping to pull the masking tape off of the door latch.

"Forget about the motion detectors?" my mother barked as she marched toward us. We must have been visibly shaken because her demeanor softened as she approached us.

"I turned them off." My voice cracked. "Before we came in. At least I thought I did. Thank God they kept working! Mom, that thing is rabid. It charged us." I panted. "You've got to get rid of it!"

My mother opened the door to the habitat and casually pulled off a strip of tape from the latch. Zoe and I stared, open-mouthed at the tape hanging from my mother's hand. The habitat door swung shut with a metallic click. My mother rolled up the tape and threw the ball into a trash can by the window.

"Well, you weren't planning on leaving that on, were you?"

"That tape wasn't there a minute ago," I insisted.

"Oh really?"

"That thing took it off. It locked us in there!" I explained.

"And she put it back on? Why?" my mother asked.

"Yeah, why did it do that?" Zoe asked.

"*She*," my mother corrected. "Don't you start that too."

"Okay, why did *she* do that?" Zoe asked.

"You tell me," my mother demanded.

"How should we know?" I rushed to explain, still out of breath, my voice wavering. "It's up to something. It must have taken that tape off the second we went in, then put it back on before scaring us out of there. To make us look... foolish, I don't know. But, I'm telling you, it knew exactly what it was doing. It played us."

"How did you get in the outer doors?" my mother inquired, unmoved by my accusations regarding the primordium.

"They weren't closed all the way," I lied.

"Really? Well, like I told you," my mother sighed, "she's probably just jealous."

"It moved in and out of that habitat like it was nothing," I stressed. My mother seemed disinterested.

Then it dawned on me. That's what triggered the

motion detectors! The primordium came into this middle room before I had turned them off. It must have seen me tape that door earlier and knew that I would be coming back. It actually understood that and had come out to trap me! I would never underestimate that thing again.

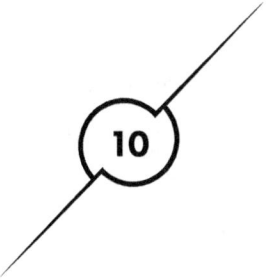

ONE SMALL STEP FOR MAN

I wonder, can you can stare too long into darkness? When you do, it seems, you begin to see things. The morning after our terrifying encounter with the primordium, I woke up early. Once again, I found myself staring at the ceiling, wondering.

What would people think if they saw that monster? I figured the last thing anyone would want would be to have some of its genes shot into them. Then again, people had been drinking cows' milk for centuries, and women had been taking a hormone replacement derived from horses for decades. Did anyone really care about the source of their therapy as long as it helped them? If you could be cured of cancer, what would you care if the cure came from a monster? Still... my thoughts were curtailed by something blurry in my peripheral vision. It was to my right, against the wall: a narrow, oval shape hovering midway between my bed and the door.

Was that thing in here? My heart pounded as I swung around, sitting on the edge of my bed. The oval shape did not move. I shifted my position left to right to gauge some sense of depth or motion. There was neither. I closed my eyes, and the shape remained, like the ghost of a bright flash that persists even when your eyes are closed. *Not another migraine,* I thought, though I had never had an aura like this.

I was certain there would be a pair of owl eyes appearing at any moment, and the more I anticipated that materialization, the more my heart pounded. I felt its pulsations radiating up into my throat. *What should I do?* The room was totally dark, with no moonlight nor trace of dawn in the window. The harder I tried to see in the darkness, the more I saw nothing but that oval shape.

Then it moved. Like the oval pattern of light from a spotlight, it floated across my wall to the door. I turned my head side to side still trying to make out something more definite about its shape, when the door opened, allowing a flood of light to enter the room.

"Noah?" My mother's voice came through the light.

"Mom," I gasped between breaths, "it's you."

"Of course. Are you all right?"

"Yeah, yeah, I'm fine. You?" I asked, still looking beside and behind her for any sign of the primordium.

"Bad dream?" she asked.

"Yeah." I considered the idea. "That must have been it." *What else could it have been?* The light from the hall now illuminated all the dark recesses of my room. There were no more shadows where monsters could hide. It had to have been my imagination.

"Come have some breakfast," my mother suggested.

I sat with my mother at the kitchen table for over an hour. I had the time since my next exam wasn't until later that morning, but I knew that my mother rarely had time to spare. She always had somewhere she needed to be, so I realized that she was missing something important for my sake.

Surprisingly, she didn't seem angry with me for sneaking back into the East Wing. It wasn't that she thought it was all right. She still told me I would have to pay for that mistake in one way or another. It seemed she was more concerned with what Dr. Strauss would say to the CEO, Mr. Stone, that morning.

"There's nothing the two of you could do to hurt us more than what Dr. Strauss will probably do."

"What's that?"

"I suspect he'll recommend that the clinical trials be stopped."

"Stopped?" That seemed extreme. Modified, I could understand, but stopped? I imagined Dr. Strauss's white mane swishing across his forehead as he insisted the research come to an end.

"I spoke to Mr. Stone about it in advance, hoping to soften the effect of anything Strauss says. I also gave him your idea about the race to the moon, by the way," my mother added. "He liked it." She brought her coffee mug up to her lips and held it there as if she hoped to drink up the answers to all of life's problems. "It all depends on how he reacts to Strauss today."

"Well, the cancer patients have already been treated, haven't they?"

"The leukemia patients, yes, and that drug has already received FDA approval. But it's not just cancer, Noah. We have so many projects in the works, degenerative disorders, diabetes..."

"Diabetes?" I interrupted.

"Yes, diabetes, and many others. There are literally millions of people who can benefit from the therapies we're looking to develop. Many of the clinical trials are ready to start accepting patients."

"Even the diabetes trial?" I asked, remembering what

Zoe had told me about her mother's diabetes.

"Yes, that one is about to start. Why, do you know someone with diabetes?"

"I do—well, a relative of someone I know."

"They would have to be a good candidate for the study, fit the criteria, consent to everything, but if they are interested, I can give you the paperwork they'll need to fill out."

"That would be great, thanks." I felt so comfortable talking with my mother right then that I felt it was time to ask about those naturalization papers I had seen the previous day.

"I saw my adoption papers yesterday."

My mother shook her head. "You just happened to open that file cabinet?"

"Sorry, but I was a little confused. The paper said I was seven when you adopted me." My mother sighed, then turned her chair to face me directly.

"Noah, I have to tell you something. I was married when I adopted you."

So she wasn't a single mom in college. Zoe was right to have doubts about that scenario.

"My husband was not a good man; he did not want... it turned out he never really planned on staying and he didn't want to have to pay child support, so he was opposed to my adopting you, and he insisted I hold off on the papers." She stood up and began to pace slowly back and forth in the kitchen. "He first left when you were very little, so you wouldn't remember him. After that, he would just pop in, out of the blue. I would get up in the morning and just see him there in the kitchen. It would scare me half to death. I finalized the divorce when I was twenty-six and filed your naturalization papers right afterward. I didn't want to burden you with any of this. He's not worth my remembering nor your knowing. It's over; that's all that matters. It's all over now."

"Sorry I made you think about that," I apologized, regretting my insatiable curiosity.

She continued to pace for a few more minutes, stopping occasionally to hold her mug to her lips again. "In a lot of ways, those were the worst four years of my life."

"Six."

"What?"

"You said you were twenty-six when you were divorced. You were twenty when I was born, right? So, twenty to twenty-six—that would be at least six years you were married."

"Right, six," she agreed, seemingly uninterested in the details. She sat back down and looked at me. "But that wasn't the most disturbing thing you saw yesterday, was it?"

"Not even close."

"I know it's shocking to see her at first. But after a

while... I've been with her every day, every day of her life."

"What did Dr. Strauss think when he saw that thing?"

"He hasn't seen her. No one else has, except Mr. Stone." My mother shook her head at my referring to the primordium as "that thing."

"I guess you get used to it, huh?"

"Once you stop calling her 'it,' yes." We sat for a few more minutes together, not speaking but simply resting in each other's company. It had been a long time since we had sat together like that. Soon, my mother regained her usual sense of urgency and rushed out to her next appointment, and I went off to my final exam, the next to last of the year.

When I arrived at Pridapt that afternoon, I paused for a few minutes in the parking lot, leaned against my car, and looked out at the trees. It may have been their old age, their magnificent height, the colors of green, reddish-brown, and black, or the way their tops swayed with the breeze, but they always calmed me. I loved the way the light moved between them. Lines of sunshine seemed to dance among the darkness, sweeping it away so effortlessly.

I wished I could dispel the darkness that easily. I had no answers to the questions I pondered in the dark, no explanation for the shapes I saw or imagined, but in those woods I could find peace. With that peace, I made my way in to another afternoon of work.

As soon as I crossed the lobby, I saw Mr. Stone's massive frame moving alongside my mother. Judging by the smile on my mother's face, the CEO had not been swayed by Dr. Strauss's words, and the clinical trials had not been shut down.

"We moved on your idea, kid, another winner," Mr. Stone said to me, thrusting a huge thumbs-up in my direction. "We'll keep him around, Annette."

"Very glad to hear that, sir," my mother replied.

"Say, Annette, don't we have a program to support higher education of Pridapt's employees?"

"Yes."

"Well, I'd say this young man would be a prime candidate, wouldn't you?"

"I believe it's geared for postgraduate studies, masters and PhDs, isn't it?" my mother asked. "Noah's still in high school."

"Well, you can't very well do postgraduate studies before you've done undergraduate studies, now can you? We have an excellent state school system here in California, kid. How would you like a full-ride scholarship to one of them?"

"That would be amazing! But..." faltering, I added, "I have some trouble with standardized tests."

"Standardized what?" Mr. Stone shot back with a bellowing laugh. "Son, I'm the standard around here." He bobbed his colossal index finger at me. "I say you're in—you're in."

"Sounds good to me," I replied, beaming.

"We'll get you the finest education, then you can come back here and continue doing great work for us. What do you say to that?"

"I don't know what to say."

"Just say yes."

"Yes, absolutely," I answered, glancing at my mother, who was watching me with such pride that I was certain all my indiscretions regarding the East Wing had been forgiven.

"Son, this time you're really going to see your idea come to life. The press conference is at three thirty. I'll see you both there." My mother and I stood together in the lobby for a few moments while Mr. Stone returned to his office.

"Wow." I had meant to say something more profound, but that was all that came out.

"Yeah," was my mother's equivalent response. "See you at the press conference."

I performed my lab work effortlessly, the time racing by. Everyone in the lab was finishing early to be down in the lobby for Mr. Stone's presentation. In fact, all of Pridapt's employees were instructed to be present for this one. When I returned to the lobby, I found that nearly every square inch was filled with chairs, except for the semicircle of reporters with cameras and microphones standing in front of the lectern. I saw Dave, smiling with a full compliment of little forehead folds, sitting beside my mother, and took a seat beside them.

There were no protesters this time, coming on the heels of a very good response to his "Hope has a Name" speech.

At precisely three thirty, Mr. Stone walked up to the podium and received applause from the audience. The screen behind him lit up, with a still shot of President Kennedy.

"In 1961," Mr. Stone began, "John F. Kennedy delivered a speech to Congress calling for an expansion of the space exploration program. I'd like us to listen to a portion of that speech right now."

A video began playing on the screen behind Mr. Stone:

"First, I believe that this nation should commit itself to achieving the goal, before this decade is out, of landing a man on the moon and returning him safely to the earth," President Kennedy stated.

It then jumped to another portion of his speech: "In a very real sense, it will not be one man going to the moon— if we make this judgment affirmatively, it will be an entire nation. For all of us must work to put him there."

"In 1969," Stone continued, "just eight years after Kennedy's call to action, we did indeed send a manned spacecraft to the moon. It had not been easy, inexpensive, or without risk. As the lunar module was descending to the moon's surface, Neil Armstrong was in command. He had to improvise, manually steering his craft, the *Eagle*, through an area filled with boulders. When it finally set down, it had only seconds of fuel remaining. The *Eagle* had landed on the moon! We all know what happened next."

Another video played on the back screen, showing the film of Neil Armstrong stepping off the ladder onto the moon and speaking the infamous statement: "That's one small step for man, one giant leap for mankind."

"Here at Pridapt," Stone spoke, a still shot of Neil Armstrong remaining on the screen behind him, "we are facing a new frontier, a frontier not in the outer reaches of the skies but one within the inner recesses of our very being. It is the human body, the essence of health, and the curing of disease. I declare our commitment, before *this* decade is out, to the goal of discovering, refining, and making available the cure for ten diseases, one disease per year!"

There was silence as we all took in the ramifications of that last statement. Some whispering began among the reporters and a hand was raised, but before anyone could speak, Stone continued.

"This is a challenge, to be sure, but as President Kennedy said, it is a challenge 'that we are willing to accept, one we are unwilling to postpone, and one which we intend to win.'

Last week we announced our cure for leukemia. That was the first in a decade of cures to come. It was one small step for man, but a giant leap for mankind, because it set us on the path to a new era in health and longevity. Join me in this challenge, this commitment, this bold, far-reaching goal of mastering the new frontier of the human body."

This time, when he stopped, there was not silence but prompt applause. We were all impressed, forgetting, for the moment, the daunting implications of the goal of yearly cures. We were doing good for people. We were healing them, and it actually was "we." I was on the team. I was in line for a scholarship, a free ride to college, teed up to become a full-fledged researcher. Stone wanted *me,* and like Zoe had said about the redwoods in the national forest, it was good to be wanted.

As for the owl-eyed growling monster scampering around the rafters of the East Wing, that would just have to be our little secret.

PART II

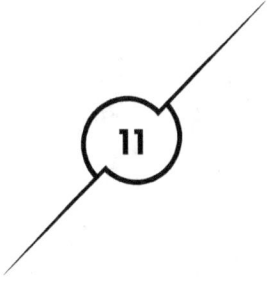

CANCER VACCINES

I watched a little girl's head rock back and forth as she tottered across the Pridapt lobby to her mother, one of our researchers at Pridapt. Her grandmother had brought her to say hello to her mom during the lunch break. I was sitting in one of the large chairs by the front window, having just set up some specimens to run. It was a quiet afternoon, with only an occasional person passing by—very different from the week before, when the lobby was filled with folding chairs for Mr. Stone's press conference. I turned from the little girl padding her way across the marble floor and looked out at the pines.

As I focused on my wooded sanctuary, I saw a familiar face cross the foreground. It was Isaac, our hyperactive skeptic turned ardent fan. I had not seen him since Mr. Stone's "Hope has a Name" speech, where he had expressed his full-fledged support for our "holistic medical treatments," as he called them. I jumped up to meet him at the door.

"Hey, Noah," Isaac called out. "I was hoping to catch you here." It turned out that Isaac had been assigned to a project in the redwoods. "I'll be working here all summer into the fall," Isaac explained. "When I learned of my new assignment, I thought of you right away. Maybe we could catch up a bit?"

"Sure, I just have to finish up a few things, then we can talk."

"Fantastic! Listen, I don't know if I told you before, but I have a blog. It's got more to do with my environmental watchdog work, but I talk about all sorts of things on it. It's got over a million followers right now."

"No way!"

"Yeah, it's actually large enough that I have a few sponsors, mostly tax-exempt organizations, but I'm starting to get some commercial ads for outdoor hiking and camping gear. I was thinking of doing a story about your natural cure for cancer."

"It's not my cure," I clarified. "You'd have to work with the PR department on that one. They're very particular about what is said to the press."

"It could be anonymous."

"Anonymous? How? I'm the only person you know here. It would be pretty obvious who leaked the information. Listen, things here are looking really good for me right now, and I don't want to jeopardize anything."

"Oh, I understand. No worries. How about this: I do a story about you working at this high-tech company but also enjoying a lunchtime walk through the redwoods?"

"Now that I could do. Let me finish up my work in the lab, then I'll be done for the afternoon, and we can go out to the woods."

Isaac went back outside and sat on a boulder by the circular drive. I logged the data from the last set of specimens, cleaned up, and was hurrying out to meet up with him when I bumped into Dave who smiled at me, his forehead full of folds.

"Noah, where are you in a rush to?"

"Oh, I just finished up, and I'm going for a walk in the woods with a friend."

"Wonderful. Well, I won't keep you. I just wanted to congratulate you on that scholarship I heard you received."

"Oh, yeah, that's something, isn't it?"

"It certainly is. You must have really impressed Mr. Stone. He doesn't hand out that sort of thing lightly." His forehead suddenly became smooth, and he kept looking at me.

"Well, my friend's out there waiting," I said, breaking the silence.

"Oh yes, go ahead." As I turned to leave, his little forehead folds returned and with a smile he added, "I'm proud of you, Noah. I'm really proud of you."

"Thanks. Thanks a lot," I answered. This time it was I who held on to the moment. *What a nice guy,* I thought. He always knew just what to say to me.

"Oh no," I heard Dave mutter as he looked over my shoulder, "here we go."

I turned and saw the swishing mane of Dr. Strauss approaching.

"Dave, you need to say something," Dr. Strauss argued. "Stone needs to hear from more people than just me."

"What do you want me to say?" Dave asked.

"Just point out the obvious. This isn't science. It's commercialism! One cure per year—that's absurd!"

"He's a CEO. He thinks in terms of marketing; that's what he does."

"That's why he needs restraint."

"We don't want to see the kind of restraint that was laid on our species repopulation work, do we?" Dave asked, his forehead as smooth as marble.

"That came from outside the corporation," Dr. Strauss protested.

"Yes, but it was the same sort of knee-jerk reaction that is born of fear. Now, that whole line of research is dead in its tracks."

"I'm sure we'll be allowed to continue again, once there is some level of oversight."

"But in the meantime," Dave countered. "We lose ground. Granted, there's no urgency with the species work, but with the medical applications, there is. We are helping people, people who need help now."

"Absolutely, but what I wonder is when does the noble cause of helping others end and ambitious commercialism begin, or are they one and the same?"

"What's wrong with making money by helping people?" I interjected, feeling compelled to stand up for the team that I was now an official member of.

"Nothing," Dr. Strauss answered, swinging his lock of white hair in my direction. "Noah, is it?" I nodded. "Son, money is neither good nor evil, but it exerts a powerful influence, and the amount of money we're talking about here is staggering. Are you aware of the next wave of research?"

I shook my head.

"The vaccines?" Dave suggested.

"Yes, vaccines!" Dr. Strauss stressed, as though the word itself articulated all his concerns.

"Vaccines for what?" I asked, casting a quick look toward

Isaac, who seemed perfectly content sitting on his boulder.

"Cancer vaccines," Dave explained. "The idea grew from the success of the leukemia treatment."

"Vaccines aren't just for the few with a disease," Dr. Strauss warned, speaking now directly to me. "They're for everyone. Most people do not get cancer, so most people would be getting the vaccines unnecessarily and therefore taking on risks unnecessarily. But with over three hundred million people in the United States, at a minimum five-dollar profit per vaccine, that's at least one and a half billion dollars profit!"

"So?" I asked, honestly not knowing whether or not that amount of money was exorbitant for a large biomedical company. "If it cures cancer, doesn't that save money that would have been spent treating it?"

Dave gestured toward me with raised eyebrows and a cocked head, as if to say, "How about that?"

"That's not the point," Dr. Strauss countered. "With that enormous carrot dangling in front of us each year, what corners will be cut? What data will be buried? That is the powerful influence of money. Believe me, I know. It affects me, too. I've been with Pridapt since before we were Pridapt, and I've received multiple stock options. With this leukemia treatment alone, my options are worth a small fortune. Every one of these vaccines would mean millions for me. You don't suppose that affects how I think?"

"Who do you think is cutting corners or burying data?" Dave asked him.

"No one, I hope. But the temptation will certainly be there."

"That's why you're here, Joe," Dave said with a smile, "to keep us all honest."

"It can't be just me." Strauss shook his head. "It can't be just me."

"I've got to get back to my friend," I mentioned, nodding to the front window. With a subtle wave, I gladly took my leave of the discussion and made my way out to Isaac. From his boulder, we went down to the park entrance and walked up the wooden boardwalk where Zoe and I had strolled that day of the protests.

"What I like most about this blogging business," Isaac explained, "is how quickly I can share something. After our walk here today, I'll post some photos and a few notes, and within an hour, over a million people will have seen it. Isn't that amazing?"

That was amazing. "Better make sure you get everything right."

"How so?" Isaac asked.

"Well, if you make a mistake, it's out there for a million people to see."

"That's true, but I triple-check my posts, so don't worry."

When we arrived at the spot where Zoe and I had sat, I stopped walking and leaned against one of the trees. "Can I ask you something, Isaac, off the record?"

"Sure."

"I mean it, no blog or anything, right?"

"On my honor."

"If you do something good, but make a lot of money doing it, is that unethical?"

"Why would it be, if you're doing something good?"

"Well, maybe too much money would tempt you to do the wrong thing."

"Hmm." Isaac pondered the scenario briefly, then concluded, "Then I'd just give a lot of the money away. Problem solved."

"That would do it," I concluded, laughing. "What about your concerns of messing with nature? Cancer is a natural process, so if we cure it, we're changing nature."

"That's different," Isaac explained, looking around at the towering trees over us. "That's working with nature. Take this park. This is a perfect example of how to work with nature, by respecting it, not 'messing with it,' as you say."

The image of the primordium kept surfacing in my mind. *Talk about messing with nature,* I thought.

"There are people," Isaac continued, "who want to clear-cut old wood forests like these, harvesting everything they can in one shot. But then it's gone, and all the future harvests are gone, too. And not only that, but there are mudslides and erosion as a result. Forests like these have taken thousands of years to grow naturally, and they should not be swept away rashly. The biological design of living things, likewise, should not be toyed with lightly. But it is possible to make a path, like this one. Enter the forest, respecting it even as you benefit from it, and even as you profit from it."

"Right," I agreed quietly.

"Ooh, that would make a good blog, a pharmaceutical company doing the right thing. Remember what I just said, okay?"

Even in the midst of my doubts, Isaac's optimistic creativity rubbed off on me, and I found the next slogan popping into my mind: "We cure cancer naturally, before it begins!" It was a very appealing concept. I would be sure to share that one with my mother tomorrow, who would pass it on to Mr. Stone.

"Another way to look at it, Noah, is like something I've written about conservation. We're not looking to put a big fence around nature and never go in. If we'd never gone into the old wood forests, not only would we not know their beauty, but there are tons of medicines we would never have had: glaucoma drugs, hypertension drugs, muscle relaxants, cortisone, and even a drug to treat childhood leukemia all come from plants and animals in the forests! It's the same sort of thing with your company, isn't it? You've cut down some trees, made a path into the forest, and found some amazing cures. As long as you don't start clear-cutting the forests, you should be fine. Your cure works within the body's natural mechanisms. That's what I read in the press packet. If it's working within the confines of nature, how is that messing with nature?"

"Right," I agreed again, a little more quietly. I knew that if he saw the primordium, he would not consider our treatments as working within the confines of nature. That thing was completely unnatural, and I still wondered if people shouldn't know that it was the source of the treatment they were receiving, especially if they were healthy and receiving vaccines. These would not be people on the verge of death. They might well choose *not* to receive cells from that thing if they knew what it was.

"So," Isaac began again, still fashioning his next blog post, "you explore the old wood of the human body for cures with respect, staying on the trails, not trampling the undergrowth, not exploiting and destroying. Just like us here, coexisting with these old trees."

I nodded, then froze. My heart pounded, pulsing up into my neck.

"What's wrong?" Isaac asked.

I could see, off to my left in my peripheral vision, a pair of eyes! I fought the reflex to turn my head to them, trying to convince myself that it had to be my imagination; it was simply something that looked like eyes. *That thing could not be out here!* Finally, I jerked my head to the left and rapidly scanned the tree trunks looking for a contour, a blurry shape, and eyes. My thoughts were racing as quickly as my pulse, and then I saw it: two eyes against the tree trunk, immobile. I didn't answer or take my eyes off of it.

"What are you looking at?" Isaac asked. "Oh! An owl," he remarked after following my line of sight. "You looked like you'd seen a monster," he chuckled.

Just an owl, just a freaking owl! I couldn't even see a bird in the woods without picturing that monster!

"Fantastic creatures, aren't they?" Isaac continued. "Now where did it go?"

"Yeah, they're great," I agreed, trying to find the pair of eyes again. "It must have flown."

"Or maybe just closed its eyes," Isaac suggested. "Their camouflage is amazing."

"Amazing, yes. It just startled me a bit," I explained. We sat quietly for a few minutes, after which Isaac told me he had to get going.

"Nice job, spotting that owl! Here's my blog address," he said, passing me a small sheet of paper. "No quotes, I promise."

"I'll head out with you," I suggested. My heart rate simmered down as I tried to erase the thoughts of the primordium brought to mind by this little owl. Walking back to Pridapt's parking lot, I saw Isaac off, then stopped inside to say goodbye to my mother.

When I went by her office, I saw her at the end of the hall, going into the East Wing. I started to call out, but stopped myself. I had no desire to see another pair of owl eyes that day. Instead, I walked to my car and started out on the drive home. I did not want to dwell on the monster, nor did I want to ponder the dangers of high profits. These were not my problems. I wanted to think about good things, how Dave was proud of me, how I'd earned a scholarship, how I had a path to future success.

Will I ever get that monster out of my head? I wondered. I wished I had never seen it. My mother was right. It would have been better had I never been inside the East Wing.

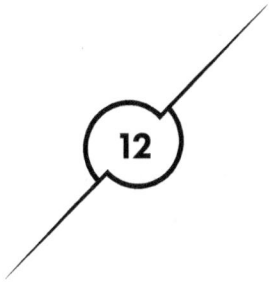

ONE GIANT LEAP

Several days later, I was preparing for the last school activity of the year—my nemesis—a standardized test. That morning, I finished my lab work at Pridapt and stopped by to say goodbye to my mother, who was speaking with Mr. Stone.

"There he is," Mr. Stone announced, bobbing his monumental index finger toward me.

"Hello, sir," I replied.

"I was just telling your mother that you scored another winning slogan. It's in today's paper." He grinned, handing me a copy. "You're on a roll, son, and so are we. We're set to make some big moves in the coming weeks."

"Cancer vaccines," my mother explained, replying to my confused look.

"I heard something about that," I offered, then said no more, afraid that Mr. Stone might ask who told me, and I didn't want to make trouble for Dr. Strauss. Fortunately, Mr. Stone paid no attention to my comment and continued his conversation with my mother.

"Political connections are powerful but fickle. We can't take any chances with reelections. We have some very influential people on board with us right now, so now is when we move. Strike while the iron's hot, eh?"

"What about our research looking into the serum's mechanism of action?" my mother asked. "It looks like it may not be necessary to use gene insertion."

"Annette, we know what works now. Do you know how many labs there are out there trying to beat us to the punch on this? If we don't run with this, someone else will. Later on, if you find a better way, a second-generation therapy, great, but for now, this is our window of opportunity."

"There could be a backlash if there are any problems," my mother warned.

"Problems?" Mr. Stone laughed. "Damn the torpedoes, full speed ahead!" Then thrusting his hand and finger in my direction asked, "Who said that, kid?"

"Besides you?" I blurted out, compelled by his enormous digit which began to move up and down like a conductor's baton. My eyes followed it, as though it were his finger that interrogated me. Without hesitation, I readily handed over all I knew. "Captain, or... Admiral David Farragut. It was during the Civil War—the Battle of Mobile Bay—he was leading the Union fleet through a bay full of mines to attack the Confederate ships. That's when he said, 'Damn the torpedoes,' and gave the order to move ahead. They won the battle, and it became a PR thing for the North. That's why his order became so famous. It helped Lincoln get reelected and..."

"By golly, they are teaching you something in school!" Mr. Stone exclaimed. "My taxes are doing some good after all."

"Actually, my Mom taught me that in seventh grade, but I'm sure the kids at school know it, too."

"She did? That's right; she homeschooled you. Well, you had quite a teacher there son. She's a smart one, and so are you," he added, with another finger-thrust. "Keep up the good work, kid." Turning toward my mother before he left, he added, "Now's the time, Annette. Everything's in place. Make it happen." Mr. Stone marched down the hall to his office, leaving my mother and me looking silently at each other.

"He's on a roll," I noted.

"That he is," my mother remarked quietly. "Don't you have a test soon?"

"Not for a couple of hours, but I was about to head

over." My mother wished me luck, and I went off to school for the last time as a junior.

After arriving, I sat on a stoop in the front of school, looking at Mr. Stone's copy of the morning paper. There, on the front page, was the slogan I had thought of while in the woods with Isaac: "Curing Cancer Before It Begins." Mr. Stone must have really liked that to use it so quickly. The article went on about the moonshot speech and had a picture of Mr. Stone with Dave and my mother beside him. It introduced the whole concept of a vaccine for cancer, all cancers. The article explained the number of lives affected by cancer, the degree of suffering it caused, and the cost of treating cancer patients. Those numbers dwarfed the costs of the vaccines that Dr. Strauss had worried about. The vaccines might have meant billions in profit for Pridapt, but they would save tens of billions in medical costs.

The vaccine, I read, would be delivered with a liquid medication, taken by mouth. There was no mention of a retrovirus being in that liquid, though I knew that's what it had to be. Once ingested, a retrovirus actually infects a person's cells, inserting its genes into that person's DNA. I wondered what people would think of that. But then, there was no mention of genes, either. Even the reporter, whose job it was to ask questions, did not think of asking about the mechanism of action of the vaccine. They were told that the vaccine worked, and that was all they needed to know. Maybe *how* it worked was not that important.

The article quoted Mr. Stone explaining that children and teachers at public schools and government employees would be receiving the vaccines *automatically*. I wondered if automatically meant it would be mandatory. These early vaccine recipients were privileged to be the first in line, according to the story. Maybe they were. Who wouldn't want a vaccine against cancer? In any case, things were certainly moving very quickly. It was the beginning of the "giant leap for mankind."

I put down the paper and looked out across the lawn in front of the school. Students were making their way in now, streaming along the walkways that radiated out from the front doors, like ants filing into an ant hill.

It was a pleasant morning during a very nice time of year. The air was fresh, with a gentle breeze blowing through the overhanging tree branches. The leaves swayed back and forth, and birds darted from the grass, up to the trees, then back down to the grass.

Zoe would surely be coming by this way soon, or so I expected. Despite the multiple times I'd been with her, including some very memorable, albeit terrifying, times, I still felt like I was nobody to her outside of Pridapt. She never acknowledged me in the school hallways, never sought me out, and never offered to trade phone numbers. This would be my last chance this year to secure her contact information.

An occasional passing face gave me a brief nod, but I was looking for one in particular. Before long, I noted Zoe coming toward me, stopping every ten feet or so to talk with another group of fans. From a distance, she acknowledged me briefly with a slight gesture but then continued working the crowd around her. The stoop I was positioned on was directly in her path so she could not avoid walking by me. When she reached me, I had my opportunity.

"Zoe, how are you?"

"Good, you?"

"No nightmares from the other day?"

She began to smile, then was distracted by a boy passing by. "First place tonight!" she called out to him. He smiled and gave her a thumbs-up in return.

"Why do you do that?" I asked her once I had her attention again.

"Do what?"

"Look away in the middle of a conversation."

"What? I'm just saying hi."

It's rude, I wanted to say but said nothing.

"What?" Zoe repeated, then looked at me curiously. "It's not like you're the only boy I know. What, am I the only girl you know?"

"Of course not," I lied, "but..." I stammered. I could see the interest drain from Zoe's face as her eyes darted across the walkways again, scanning for more interesting interactions. "Can I, uh, have your number?"

"What for?"

"To stay in touch, you know, over the summer?"

"I know where to find you," she replied, then turned to a passing group of boys as though she were catching a passing train. And that was that. It was time to go in to take my exam, so I resigned myself to social failure and focused instead on doing as well as I could on my test.

Afterward, I sat in front of the school again and considered the fact that another year was over. I saw a group of students throwing rolls of toilet paper over tree branches. Others, seniors I supposed, were driving onto the grass, spraying the neatly maintained sod up into the air. I wouldn't admit it to myself, but I was waiting for Zoe again.

It struck me that of all the people around me at that moment, I was the only one who was alone. Prior to high school, I was rarely alone. I was always with my mother, my substitute father, Dave, other researchers at Pridapt, or their children. Those other kids and I always got along well. I guess it was because we had Pridapt in common. It seemed strange to me that while homeschooled, I never felt isolated and got on easily with my peers; but here, in the crowd of a large public school, I felt alone. Watching the students walking away from the school, joking and laughing with each other, it was clear that I didn't belong there.

A large flock of birds, moving like a cloud of smoke from a tree, flew down to the field beside the school, then quickly back up to a tree. I watched them with fascination. There were so many you could actually hear the sound of them turning in the air. A few stragglers brought up the end of the flock. They rushed to catch up, late with the next turn, always being left behind.

That's me, I thought—on the fringe, scrambling to catch up. *Why don't those birds just give up and go their own way? Why don't I?* I watched the birds for several minutes, focusing on the stragglers. It was difficult, like following the pea in a shell game. But the whole time, not once did a straggler go off on its own. It was as though breaking away was not an option. They had to stay with the flock. But I didn't have to, and I didn't really want to anymore. I was ready to break away, grateful that I was not a straggler bird, not cursed to scramble after the crowd endlessly. I would accept being an outsider, and let the flock fly off without me.

Embracing my new title, I hopped off my perch and headed to my car just as Zoe emerged from the school. She was telling a story to some friends. She was always telling a story. On sight of her, my misanthropic resolve evaporated, and I was once again irresistibly drawn toward the prospect of approaching her.

I walked in her direction and panicked, realizing I had no new material to use on her. If she were at Pridapt, it would have been easy; but here at school, she was in her element, and I was not. She glanced up at me briefly, just enough to recognize who was approaching her, and continued on her way. I was tempted to call it quits when I remembered the diabetes trial, which would be a perfect excuse to flag Zoe down again and ask for her phone number.

"Say, Zoe, about your mom," I called out, trotting over to intercept her. Zoe frowned and excused herself from her bewildered friends.

"My mom?" Zoe hissed as she drew closer. "Uncool, Noah, why are you yelling about my mom?"

"I wasn't yelling. I just... Your mom has diabetes, right?"

"Yeah, what about it?" she asked, already looking over my shoulder at others passing by.

"I forgot to tell you before about a new trial we're starting at Pridapt. It's for diabetes, and, well, maybe your mom could... "

"Diabetes? You have a cure?"

"Well, it's a trial, you know, testing a possible cure, but maybe I can get your mom in, if she qualifies."

"That would be awesome!" Zoe exclaimed, throwing

her hands up into the air. She grabbed me by both shoulders and, beaming a huge smile, said, "Noah, you don't know what this means to me. She'll be thrilled! I hook her up with a cure, and she'll be off my back; she might even appreciate me! That's fantastic! What does she need to do?"

"Well, I can just call you when I get the application form."

"You do that, Noah!" she said, pointing at me as she turned to go back to her friends. "Fantastic! Girls, get this!"

"I do need your number, though."

"That you do," Zoe agreed, spinning back toward me and jotting it down on a scrap of paper. Pressing it into my palm she cooed, "I'll be waiting." She smiled broadly then ran off to join her friends.

I looked at the numbers on the paper, then tucked it into my pocket. I did feel a little used, but that felt better than being the straggler left behind. The diabetes trial was my ace in the hole, and I'd played it well. It worked better than I could have hoped. I looked up at the swaying leaves and blue sky, took in a deep breath, and savored the warm comfort of being securely within the flock.

THE GOOD OF SOCIETY

"We've created a monster!" The words echoed down the hallway from the staff lunchroom at Pridapt. I literally stopped in my tracks when I heard them. Was the word out? Did someone leak the information about the primordium? I knew my mother would blame me. Who else knew? Besides my mother and me, there was only Mr. Stone, and he surely would not have told anyone. Turning the corner into the lunch room, I saw Dr. Strauss's white forelock swishing at the table, and realized that he had made that proclamation to a group of Pridapt employees.

"It's monstrous, this frenzy to crank out cures like cars on an assembly line!" Dr. Strauss continued. "It needs to be kept in check."

I breathed a sigh of relief when I realized that he was not speaking of the physical monster locked behind the East Wing doors but merely the metaphorical monster of corporate greed.

"In war," Dr. Strauss continued, "innocent civilians are always caught in the crossfire, but we should hope that none of those casualties are deliberate. Even though there is always 'collateral damage,' the goal is to have the least amount possible. If there is an alternative tactic that will lead to fewer civilian casualties, we choose that. It's the same in medicine. We know that there will always be unexpected side effects and complications. We accept that, but our goal must be to have the fewest possible, so we, too, must seek the alternative with the least collateral damage. That takes diligence as researchers, but it also takes time, time to consider all the possibilities and test the alternatives. Beware of these time constraints and deadlines; don't compromise your priorities."

The circle of researchers, whose attention had waned shortly after Dr. Strauss had begun his address, nodded politely and stood up to leave. I noticed two men leaning against the wall of the cafeteria whose attention had not wavered in the least as Dr. Strauss spoke. They wore dark suits and spoke quietly to each other while never taking their eyes off of Dr. Strauss. I thought I recognized one of them as part of Mr. Stone's security team.

Dr. Strauss noticed me and called me over. "Hello, Noah, can I buy you lunch?"

"Already had some, actually. Just came for a doughnut."

"Well, then, can I buy you a doughnut?"

"Sure, thanks."

As we moved along the line past the coffee machines, I grabbed a cup to fill for Dr. Strauss. I didn't drink coffee myself, but whenever I was there with my mother, I always filled a cup for her.

"Coffee, Dr. Strauss?"

"Yes, please." He smiled. "Oh, not that one. I hate flavored coffee. I don't know why. It's just one of those things."

"Sorry," I said, tossing the hazelnut-scented cup and filling a new one with plain black coffee. I had the feeling he wanted to tell me something, so I asked him about his concerns. "Dr. Strauss, is it just the money you're worried about with the vaccines?"

"No, it's not just the money, Noah." He sighed, directing my attention toward the tray of doughnuts we were passing. "These vaccines will snowball. Soon, all of this will be too big to fail, too big to be stopped. It will be seen as a service to society too essential to be questioned: reducing the cost of treating cancer. The name, Pridapt, will be synonymous with 'The good of society.' Why, the way Mr. Stone talks, we're the saviors of humanity."

"But we are saving lives, aren't we?" I asked as we sat back down at a table. "Those cancer patients in the trial were cured."

"That doesn't mean what we did was right."

"But they would have died."

"Everyone dies," Dr. Strauss countered dryly. I studied his face as he sipped his coffee.

What an odd thing to say, I thought. He hadn't struck me as a cynic before. Seeing this pessimism, I was losing interest in what he had to say. If you couldn't agree that it was good to save a sick person's life, what could you agree on?

"We never save lives. We only postpone death," Dr. Strauss elaborated, apparently noting my frown.

"So we live longer with less disease. Isn't that good for society?" I asked.

"Good for society," Dr. Strauss repeated, "and when the good of society is not in line with your good—what then? When the good of the many conflicts with the good of the few, who wins? Noah, what good will it do to cure ten diseases if in the process, we lose our humanity?"

"I don't understand."

"It's in our nature as human beings to care for the least among us—the weak, the fragile, the individual—not merely 'the good of society.' That's why we should move slowly, to find the way with the least injury, the least collateral damage, as I was saying to your fellow researchers just now."

"What about the people who will die in the meantime?" I asked, remembering Dave's defense the other day.

"In the meantime, we should resist the temptation to sacrifice some in order to save others."

"Who is being sacrificed?" I asked. When he didn't answer, I got up to leave. He grabbed my forearm, then gently pulled me back into my seat.

Looking at me steadily in the eyes he asked, "When are you free?"

"I'm finishing a set of specimens in ten minutes."

"Come with me this afternoon. It won't take long."

"Come with you where?"

"To a hospital outside the city, up in the hills."

"What for?"

"To see the ones we've sacrificed."

"You mean patients?"

"I mean our collateral damage," Dr. Strauss said as he stood up and pushed his chair back from the table. "Think about it," he added, his eyes casting a look of benevolent concern. "I'll be in the lobby at two o'clock. Meet me there if you decide to come."

As Dr. Strauss left, I noticed the two men in suits leave the cafeteria behind him. I went to finish up my work in the lab then visited my mother.

My mother was always happy to see me stop by, and this day was no exception, until I explained that I was thinking of going with Dr. Strauss to see the patients from the trial who had suffered complications.

"What on earth for?" she asked. "What good will it do? Those things happened early on, and we changed the protocol since then. The later patients did fine; you saw them."

"Yes, so shouldn't I see these, too?"

"Why? I haven't."

"Maybe you should."

"Are you going to lecture me now like Strauss?" My mother's indignation was palpable. She stood up from her desk and paced back and forth.

"Knowledge is always preferable to ignorance. You taught me that. I don't agree with him, Mom. I think he sees the worst side of every situation and can wreck the best of moods."

"You're right about that," my mother agreed with a chuckle, sitting back down next to me.

"But to disagree with someone, you have to first see things from their perspective. You taught me that, too."

My mother sighed, and her look softened. I knew I had her with that one. She really had taught me those concepts, with those very phrases. I had a keen memory for such things. I not only remembered what I had learned but how I had learned it: the situation I was in, who was teaching me, and what I was seeing or experiencing at the time.

"You always have to see things for yourself, don't you?" my mother asked.

"I'll see for both of us," I suggested. "Once I've seen what he's seen, then we can put his gloom-and-doom attitude to rest."

"Fair enough," my mother conceded.

As I looked at her, it struck me as very odd that she had not seen those patients. Even odder was the fact that Dr. Strauss, with his unlimited access to the trial patients, had never seen the inhabitant of the East Wing.

"How is it Dr. Strauss has never seen the primordium?" I asked her.

"You could only imagine what he would have to say about her," she said, rolling her eyes. "It's safe to say he wouldn't understand."

She had already told me how the primordium had developed more quickly than she had expected. She had just obtained the cells that they would later grow in culture when it rapidly grew into adult form.

"Since the project had begun as a typical laboratory experiment, as opposed to a human clinical trial," she explained, "approval from the ethics committee was not needed. Dr.

Strauss was not involved. Then, when the primordium developed beyond the cocoon stage, her appearance was so shocking that Mr. Stone restricted access to the project to himself and me. He was ready to abandon the whole line of research until we discovered the anticancer effect of the serum. Since then, I've remained the only researcher with access to the East Wing, until Dr. Strauss managed to get into the front room the other day."

"After getting those initial cells, what did you do with the primordium for the next nine years?" I asked.

"For nine years I've been her caregiver."

You mean zookeeper, I thought. "No other experiments on it?"

"I've been recording her adaptations to our original stimulations, but no, since she developed into adult form, we no longer exposed her to anything that was potentially harmful. If I had known... I would never... My hope has always been to mainstream her."

"Yeah, right." I laughed, then realized that she wasn't joking. "You're serious?"

"Of course."

"How could it ever...? I can't imagine that thing on the outside."

"Stop calling her that! Just stop it!" she cried. "You don't know anything about her. You're such a great inquisitor, always asking questions, always needing to see for yourself. Stop coming to conclusions before you know everything."

"What don't I know?" I asked.

"Sometimes we just have to make the best of a difficult situation." She sighed, putting her arm around me. "I feel responsible for her. She didn't ask to be in that habitat; I put her there. I'm sorry if my obligations here have ever taken my attention away from you. You're everything to me; you know that, don't you?"

The sincerity in my mother's voice was so real, I almost thought she was about to cry. I had never seen her cry. She often spoke to me tenderly, but her voice never wavered and her eyes never welled with tears. But I did know how she felt about me. That, I never doubted.

"I do," I replied and never felt more at home than at that moment. Despite the cold, stainless-steel lab benches, glass beakers, and fluorescent lights, I was surrounded by love. It was there in the lab that I belonged. More than at my school, it was the lab where I was wanted, appreciated, and loved.

With my mother's blessing, I went to meet Dr. Strauss in the lobby, to vanquish ignorance with knowledge. I was a little unnerved when I thought of what this collateral damage might be, but I was comforted by the fact that I'd already seen the patients who had been successfully treated. I knew how the story ended.

I arrived in the lobby at two o'clock and found Dr. Strauss by the front door waiting. He held out his arm toward me with a smile.

"I knew you'd come," he boasted. "You're someone who needs to know the truth for yourself. I could tell that about you. The first time I saw you, I could tell that about you."

I joined Dr. Strauss in his car, and the two of us drove up into the hill country, to the edge of a rocky hillside where a long stretch of iron fence led to a gated entrance. A bronze plaque beside the gate read, "Whispering Acres." Dr. Strauss typed in his passcode to open the gate, and we drove up a winding driveway to a sprawling one-story brick structure that looked more like a prison than a hospital. The closer we came to the pentagonal building, the more a string of words kept surfacing in my mind. It was Mr. Stone's booming command in the hallway the previous day: "Damn the torpedoes! Full speed ahead!"

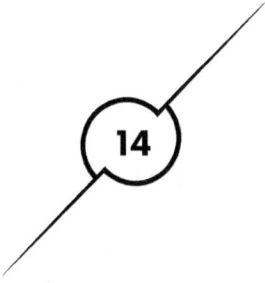

SIDE EFFECTS

Whispering Acres was a medical facility specially designed for Alzheimer's patients, Dr. Strauss explained. A ten-foot-high fence surrounded the grounds of the facility. Except for a parking lot and a circular access road, there were no lawns or open areas between the building and the fence. A center courtyard made up all of its outdoor space. There were five faces of the building, each with its own doorway leading to a specific wing. The wings were not open to one another, to keep patients from getting lost.

"What if there's a fire?" I asked. "If you can't get to the only door out..."

"In the event of an emergency," Dr. Strauss explained,

"the doorways between units open automatically to allow for safe exiting and access for emergency medical personnel." Then, studying me for a few moments, he added, "Clever of you to think of that so quickly."

I don't know if *clever* was the right word. It was just that little discrepancies always presented themselves to me. I couldn't help but notice things, things that other people seemed to overlook. The constant flow of information such attentiveness generated could make it hard to focus at times.

We entered one side of the pentagon, and Dr. Strauss signed in at the front desk. An electric door opened, and we entered a small foyer, standing before another set of doors. I looked for a button on the wall to open the doors as there were no handles.

"We'll have to wait until the first set of doors closes," Dr. Strauss explained.

"It's like a jail," I whispered as I looked through the door at a man on the other side staring back at me.

"Here we go," Dr. Strauss prompted, taking my arm and leading me into the unit. The gentleman who had been staring at me began to walk into the foyer but was immediately stopped by an aid stationed at the door. "To avoid getting lost," Dr. Strauss nodded to me, "it is sometimes necessary to impose limits on freedom."

"I guess they don't really know what's going on," I

concluded, looking back at the man being redirected away from the door.

"Why do you say that?" Dr. Strauss asked, stopping and turning to face me.

"Well, you said they have Alzheimer's. They don't remember anything, right? So they must not know they're sick or even that they're trapped here. Blissful ignorance." I chuckled.

"Oh, they know all right." Dr. Strauss looked intently at me. "Haven't you ever struggled to remember something, something you knew was important? It's on the tip of your tongue, you know you should be able to remember it, but you just can't. Frustrating, isn't it? Now multiply that frustration by about one thousand and imagine feeling that way every waking moment of your life, knowing you should remember your family members' names, but you can't. You can't even remember what they look like, how many of them there are, where your own home is. These patients look at people passing by them every day and they can't recognize a single face, even though they know they should. Surrounded by people, they are totally alone. There's nothing blissful about that. Some would call it a 'living hell.' So never joke about it."

"I'm sorry. I didn't mean..."

Dr. Strauss held up his hand.

"It's not your fault. You didn't know." He started down the hall again, then looking sideways at me, added, "But now you do."

We walked down the circular hallway past a central courtyard and sitting area.

"So, why are trial patients here?" I asked. "Did they lose their memory?"

"They're kept here for privacy, though they do share the wing with several Alzheimer's patients. Those are trial patients there, at that table in the courtyard," he said, pointing through the glass wall. "Let's go visit them."

The way to the courtyard was through a pair of locked steel doors controlled by a keypad. Their similarity to the East Wing doors gave me a momentary chill. It was to keep the patients with Alzheimer's from wandering into the courtyard during inclement weather. The other patients, our trial patients, were given the keypad code for free access whenever they liked. Dr. Strauss typed in his code, and we entered the courtyard to join the patients sitting under the shade of a tree.

Four men sat around a table. They had been talking among themselves but stopped the moment they saw us enter the courtyard. They all looked away, except for one, who watched our approach closely.

"Good afternoon, Dr. Strauss," he called out to us.

"Noah," Dr. Strauss said, leading me by the shoulder toward the man, "this is Mr. Carter. He likes to be called just 'Carter.' Carter, Noah."

The man looked as though he were going to extend his hand to me but then suddenly turned away from us, jerking around in his seat to face the opposite direction.

Seeing my confusion, Dr. Strauss whispered to me, "Give him a moment."

"Don't get angry," another patient beside Carter said. "It only makes it worse."

"Thanks for the words of wisdom!" Mr. Carter shot back at the man, shifting in his chair to face him. I heard myself gasp quietly when I saw his face and arm. Unfortunately, Carter heard it too, and whipped his head around toward me. "Well, take a good look, kid. Isn't it just fine?" His arm was an array of mottled colors from jet black to parchment white. His face had patches of the same extremes, along with other completely inhuman skin tones, changing from green to orange, then white.

"Take it easy, Carter," Dr. Strauss rebuked him and asked that he move over a seat to allow us space to sit. "I hadn't told Noah about your condition yet because I believe a person should be introduced as a person *before* introducing their ailment."

"Point taken," Carter replied. "Sorry, Doc, it just caught

me off guard this time. Pleased to meet you, Noah."

"Likewise," I said, trying not to stare. As I looked around the table, each time I caught one of the men's eyes, he would immediately look down, his face flushing with a bizarre skin color.

"Side effect of the cancer treatment," Carter explained. "A little tidbit they failed to mention."

"They didn't know," a tall elderly man across the table from me added, his face flashing a tone of forest green.

Carter looked at me, then nodded at the elderly man. "He's 'Mr. Green Jeans.' He only turns green."

"I'm George Bloomfield," the old man asserted. "Don't listen to him." Then, turning to Carter, he added, "You ornery old coot!"

Another at the table spoke. "At least we're alive. We would have been dead." He looked directly at me. "Every one of us, we would have been dead."

"And they take care of us," another added.

"Keep us locked in, you mean," Carter quipped. "And why put us in here with Alzheimer patients? They can't possibly get used to us. They see us fresh every day!"

"Would you rather be on the street?" the man Carter called Mr. Green Jeans asked. "That's where we'd be if they turned us out. Where else could we go? We signed up for this. We knew there could be problems."

Damn the torpedoes, I thought, only it hadn't been we who had taken on the risk of maneuvering through a mine-field; it had been these patients.

"It would have been better had we just died," Carter grumbled as he stood up and left the courtyard.

After a few awkward moments, Dr. Strauss and I likewise got up and left. Back in the unit hallway, he shared some additional history with me. When it was found that the serum cured mice of cancer, Dr. Strauss had recommended that more work be done. He said my mother had recommended the same. But Stone wanted to move more quickly.

"There's always the push to be the first," Dr.Strauss explained, "to capitalize on the finding before someone else does." The argument was, these were lost-cause patients—they were going to die. They had nothing to lose. It was a persuasive argument, a "conundrum," as Dr. Strauss called it. How could letting people die have been the better route to take? So they took the quicker, less careful route of using the serum directly. "But once on that route, the train kept moving faster and faster, and now it's nearly impossible to change direction," Dr. Strauss argued. "There are more lives to save. Now we need to stop cancer before it begins." He paused and looked at me as though ensuring that I caught the allusion to my latest slogan.

"People think when there isn't a clear, definitive answer

to a question, that all possible answers are equal—one is as good as another. It's not true; some *are* better than others," Dr. Strauss continued. "We know there are always risks, but there can be an inordinate amount of risk."

"Didn't we tell the patients about the risks?"

"Oh, we got informed consent, if that's what you mean, but you can't ask a drowning man to differentiate between a line of rope and a live electrical cord thrown to him. He will grab anything tossed his way. It's up to the person throwing the line to be sure that what they are throwing is safe. That was our responsibility."

"But while we try to find the safest line to throw, people die."

"That's the conundrum, yes. But it's different now, isn't it? Now, we're talking about vaccines, and these vaccines are not intended for people who have nothing to lose."

Our conversation was interrupted by the scream from a patient down the hall from us who was pointing at Carter.

"It's a monster!" she screamed. Dr. Strauss came to Carter's aid by leading him away from the patient and into a small conference room.

"I see what you mean about them not getting used to you," I noted.

"Same thing every time," Carter nodded and sat down. "They give us everything we need here: food, entertainment, fresh air, everything but our freedom," he lamented.

They were pretty isolated. While some family members had initially come to visit them, before long, like the family members of the Alzheimer's patients, they made their visits less and less frequently. Why bring the grandchildren if they will only be scared?

"So, we play chess and talk about things you young kids wouldn't remember," Carter explained.

"Try me," I said. "I have a good memory."

"Oh, yeah? Tell me, who was Charles Lindbergh?"

"That's easy. He was a pilot who won the Congressional Medal of Honor for making the longest trans-Atlantic flight," I answered promptly. "He also butted heads with FDR by opposing our entering World War II, which led to him being called a Nazi sympathizer. Then, there was the horrible story of his baby being kidnapped."

"How do you know all that, kid?"

"Like I said, I have a good memory, and I had a good teacher."

"You must have," Carter said, smiling without a hint of odd coloration in his face. We talked some more about Charles Lindbergh, FDR, and World War II. Then he quizzed me about the Federalist Papers and the Constitution. An hour slipped by and I think we could have talked for an hour more had Dr. Strauss not indicated that he needed to get back to Pridapt.

"It can seem like prison on the outside, too, sometimes," I offered as I was getting up to leave. As soon as I'd said it, I was afraid it trivialized his situation, but he only nodded.

As we headed out, I turned back and said, "It wouldn't have been better, sir."

"What wouldn't?"

"If you'd died... I would never have met you, and I'm glad I met you."

Carter looked up at me and grinned. "I'm glad I met you, too, Noah."

We went through the foyer and the double-locked doors without speaking. Sitting in Dr. Strauss's car, I broke the silence, blurting out, "You're wrong."

"About what?"

"About these patients, about how we shouldn't have treated them. I meant what I said to him back there, how it wouldn't have been better had he died. It's worth it. His life is worth it, to me anyway."

"To me, too, Noah," Dr. Strauss answered with a warm smile. "That's why I come see him every week."

I had underestimated him. He did care.

After a brief pause, he added, "Every life has meaning and purpose. Do you believe that?"

I nodded automatically as I considered what he had said.

"A single person in the right place at the right time can change the world," he continued. "Remember that. Maybe you'll join me again next week?"

I thanked him for bringing me to Whispering Acres and enthusiastically accepted his offer to take me along with him the following week.

Back at Pridapt, I felt a strong need to see the primordium again, the wellspring of the conundrum and the source of those patients' deformities. It was already a quarter to five, and everything would be closing down in fifteen minutes, but I convinced the security guard to let me in briefly just to "check something." My mother had already left for the day.

Typing her code into the keypad, I reentered the East Wing for the first time since that day with Zoe. Looking through the small window in the outer room, I saw the primordium sitting in its habitat. *It's too far away,* I thought. I needed to be closer, to look at it again with my new perspective. Like those patients with the horrible flashes of inhuman skin colorations, wasn't this monster also collateral damage? Hadn't it, too, been sacrificed?

I felt irresistibly drawn to it. I stood up and paced the floor of the outer room, still having no key to the next door. Out of frustration, I pulled on the door's handle, and to my surprise, it offered no resistance—the door lock was still taped open! I thought my mother had removed that tape when she had found Zoe and me in there the other day, but I must have been mistaken. I turned off the motion detectors and went inside.

The lights blinked on as I walked over to the glass wall and took a seat directly facing the primordium, which had remained seated on the other side. I looked at the thing, and the thing looked at me. Remembering our last interaction, I was sure it wanted me to be afraid of it. It was still revolting to look at, but if I could get past the appearance of those patients at Whispering Acres, why not this thing? At the very least, I could get past my fear of it. I had been glancing intermittently at its head, its legs, the floor, the walls, then finally, I looked at its face. I fought the revulsion, the impulse to turn away like the elderly woman who cried, "It's a monster!" and I let my gaze rest completely and steadily on its eyes, repeating to myself, over and over, "I am not afraid of you!"

MONSTROUS CONUNDRUM

Was death ever preferable to life? After talking to Carter at the hospital for over an hour, I was certain it was not. All life was precious. How often had I heard my mother say that to me? Then what of the life of this primordial monster? The cell from which it had arisen had been slated for destruction. Its life, such as it was, would have ended then and there had it not been for Pridapt's research. Would it have been better that way, for it to have been destroyed at the earliest stage of life? What of the good that had since come from the thing—the cures?

I was calm, keeping my gaze on the center of its eyes. They seemed less hideous that way. I was no longer afraid of it; that was certain. But I still had a subtle uneasiness, something keeping my mind on low alert, a distant ringing in my ears—a reminder to stay on guard.

A knocking at the door startled me, and I turned around to see Zoe's face in the window. Jumping up, I opened the door for her to join me.

"What are you doing here, Zoe?" I laughed, surprised and delighted to see her.

"I just wanted to see you."

"Really? I mean, great! I have a lot to tell you."

I led her to the table I had been sitting at in front of the habitat. The primordium had moved from the chair and was now crouching in the corner, its back to us.

"You won't believe what I saw today," I started, ready to tell her about the patients at Whispering Acres. Then I worried that I should not be talking about those patients to anyone outside of Pridapt.

"What?" Zoe asked.

"Some of the cancer patients, the ones cured of cancer," I diverted.

"I thought you saw them already," she noted.

"Yeah, but these were very interesting, all cured of cancer."

"That's nice," she replied monotonously.

I thought it strange that she didn't ask about the diabetes trial.

"I'm still working on getting those application forms for

the diabetes trial, you know, for your mother."

"That's nice."

"I hope to have them soon," I added, still waiting for the excitement I had noted the day before.

"Tell me, Noah, would you still be happy to see me if I was in there?"

"What do you mean?" I asked, frowning at Zoe, who was staring into the habitat.

"Would you come to see me? Come visit me? Or would you just leave me here?"

"Why would you be in there?"

Zoe got up and strolled along the window toward the door.

"Why won't it look at us? Is it afraid of us?" She continued as she ran her finger along the glass. "Why don't we let it out for a bit?"

"No!" I shouted. *Was she insane?*

"Are you afraid?" Zoe laughed. "You are, aren't you? I knew it. You're all the same." She shook her head at me, turned, and opened the door. "Well, I'm going in."

"Stop!" I cried, but it was too late. She disappeared into the habitat, the door clicking shut behind her. I pressed my face up against the glass wall to see where she was, and I saw the primordium whip its head around, looking back over its shoulder at her. It was gulping air again and forcing it through its gills. The low growling sound resonated through the glass. Zoe's cavalier attitude disappeared as she grabbed the door handle and jerked it up and down repeatedly.

"Let me out!" she shrieked. "Noah, get me out of here!"

I ran over to the door and opened it, letting her back into the room.

"What were you thinking, Zoe?" I chastised her. For the first time, she was genuinely annoying me. I had come in here to clarify my thoughts regarding this monster, and she showed up, ready to rekindle the terrors of the other day! *How did she get past security?* I wondered.

"Just sit down, please, and stay put." I told her. Surprisingly, she complied.

"I don't know why I did that," she said. "It was like it made me do it somehow. It's not my fault, Noah."

"It's okay," I said, "but, let's just stay put for now, okay?"

"No problem, Noah. Say, just wondering, would you save me if I was in there, like if it attacked me and was biting my arm or something?"

"Don't go in there and that won't happen."

"I won't, of course, but if I did?"

I happened to glance back into the habitat and noticed that the primordium had moved again. It was not near the water tank, nor in the area with the chairs.

"Noah?"

I held my hand up to Zoe and pointed into the habitat. "It's moved," I alerted her. "Help me look for it."

While the two of us scanned the habitat from one end to the other, I became aware of a shadow behind me, moving along the wall. Turning around, I saw it, right where I had imagined it, passing along the wall by the back door, but there was no one there to cast the shadow. It was then that I noticed that the lights were off in the entry room.

Security must be shutting everything down!

I shoved back my chair and ran to the door. Pulling on the handle, my heart sank when it clanked against the door jamb, locked closed. *But it was taped open!* I thought. I bolted to the window and looked into the front room. In the dark, I saw light from the window shining onto the table, and in the center of the patch of light was a strip of crumpled-up tape!

Who would have... Zoe? My patience was at an end. I spun around and started toward the table, but she was not there. I ran to the glass wall and, looking into the habitat, saw Zoe crawling along the ceiling beam! *How could she have gotten up there?* I wondered. I knew she was not capable of climbing to that height. Zoe lay down on the beam and grinned at me.

"Come on in, Noah!" she called out. "It's so cool!"

This can't be real, I thought. It was like a hallucination.

Back on the beam, Zoe was gone! I scanned the habitat, and she was nowhere in sight, nor was the primordium. I now realized that there was nothing in the habitat.

If not Zoe, what had I let out when I opened the habitat door?

Fear gripped me as I considered the likely answer. Was that thing on the loose? Had it escaped and then pulled off the tape from the door, locking me in? Was it in the room with me now?

I felt a sudden jerk of my shoulder, yanking me sideways, then another. Convinced that the monster had sunk its teeth into my shoulder joint and was beginning to tear me apart, I lunged away from it. It drew me back upright, tearing again into my shoulder. I tried to call out, but no sound came from my throat. I could barely breathe, and my chest felt crushed. There was a slap and a flash of light. I heard my mother's voice calling as though from a great distance. The glass wall before me came into clearer focus, and behind it sat the primordium where it had been before, motionless, its owl eyes fixated on me.

I turned to my side and there was my mother, grasping my shoulder and leaning over me.

"Noah, it's me," she said anxiously. "Can you see me?"

"Yes." I gasped. "Is that really you?"

I looked behind her for the shadow that had been

moving along the wall, but there was none.

It was my mother who had been shaking my shoulder and who eventually slapped my face to bring me out of a hypnotic trance.

"Is Zoe here?" I asked.

"Zoe? There's no one else here, Noah. How did you get in here?"

"The door was open," I lied again. "What time is it?"

"It's six-fifteen. The security guard called me when you didn't come back to the front desk after an hour. What do you remember?"

"Nothing that was real, apparently," I muttered as I looked into the habitat. The primordium sat there, still in the same position it had been in when I had arrived. It had put all that into my head, just playing with me, ensuring I remained afraid so it could have the upper hand.

"It did this to me," I muttered. "I know you told me to never be alone with it. You told me and I did it anyway. I know it was stupid. I let it get into my head."

"Get into your head?" she asked me.

"I saw Zoe in here. It was so real, as real as I'm seeing you right now... Wait—how do I know this is real? How do I know anything is real? It got control of my mind. How can I be sure of anything?" I was panicking.

"I know I told you to never be alone with her," my

mother said calmly, "but that was only because I thought she might have a mild hypnotic ability, like we see in some reptiles. She can't control your mind or make you see things that aren't there."

"But you just told me, Zoe's not here, and I saw her, plain as day!"

"You thought you saw her. You must have been asleep. If she had any effect on you, it would only have been to make you fall asleep."

"No, you warned me to never be alone with it. You must have seen it do something like this before."

"Nothing like what you're describing. I was always careful to keep her hidden whenever anyone came in with me. Once, an aid caught a glimpse of her before she could disguise herself. He kept staring at her, even after she was in full camouflage. I think he could still see her open eyes. Afterward, he was perfectly calm and convinced that he had just *thought* he'd seen something. I always figured that she had put him into a dream state so that it seemed unreal to him."

"That's the opposite of what it just did to me," I protested. "It was completely real to me!"

"Noah, why did you come in here?" my mother asked. I wasn't satisfied with my mother's complacent evaluation of the primordium's attack on my mind, but I appreciated the change of topic.

"I needed to see it again, where it all started."

"Where what started?"

"The cures. They came from its cells, its genes, right?"

"I've already told you that, Noah. What's wrong?"

"I saw them, Mom—your first patients."

"The ones Dr. Strauss took you to see?"

"Yes—the ones that were all going to die and were cured, except they have some pretty bad skin mottling. It changes with their mood."

"He told me they were horribly deformed," my mother grumbled. "All that fuss over some skin mottling."

"It's pretty bad," I explained. "The colors are very unnatural, so they can't really be out in public."

"I'm told we take care of them though—free room and board for the rest of their lives. Free medical care, too."

"That's great," I agreed. "Still, it's pretty lonely there. I'm going to go visit them again next week."

"Good for you, Noah," my mother said, nodding approvingly and sitting beside me. "You've got a good heart." Then, frowning a bit and examining my face more closely, she added, "You feel all right?"

"Yeah, I'm good. About that serum..." Now it was my turn to change the subject. "Couldn't we find a way to treat people without putting genes into them?"

"I was just speaking to Mr. Stone about that the other

day. We've come a long way with that work, and I think we'll have the answers soon. That was our original plan, you know, but it was taking too long."

"Too long for what?"

"People were dying."

"You mean Mr. Stone was putting pressure on you to begin the trials?"

My mother gave a brief nod. "He told us to use the serum we had used on the mice. I said there were some unknowns but... well, you heard him the other day, 'Damn the torpedoes!' That was his attitude. Once it worked, it was impossible to deny it to others in similar situations. You saw them, Noah, those healthy patients at the hospital. They're cured and now lead totally normal lives, and they would have been dead. How could we not keep moving forward?"

"Dr. Strauss said you started with last-resort patients, but now you'll be treating everyone."

"The cures were so spectacular we felt we should offer it to everyone, yes."

"Offer," I repeated.

"What's that?"

Offer, I thought. That was a key word. That was different from giving the vaccines automatically.

"And there haven't been any more complications like that skin mottling?" I asked.

"Oh, no, that problem was resolved."

"But what if there are other problems we don't know about yet?"

"We'll be keeping a close eye on the patients, Noah. Don't you worry."

As we made our way to the front room, I fought the impulse to look back at the primordium. All that I had just seen, or thought I'd seen, was rapidly becoming like a dream to me. But despite what my mother had said, I knew it was no dream. It was a deliberate illusion.

We walked into the front room, and my mother pulled the tape off of the lock of the door. "When did you tape this door again?"

"I didn't. I thought you must have left it on from the last time," I explained.

"Why in the world would I do that?" she asked, laughing. "You really didn't put it on there, honestly?"

"No, I tell you. I found it that way."

My mother looked at me and frowned, then glanced toward the primordium habitat and sighed.

That thing did it! I realized. It must have snuck out again and slipped that tape onto the door. It had set another trap for me, leading me in there so that it could have a good close look at me and cast its spell. And to think I was feeling sorry for it. I hated it. I hated that monstrous thing!

HER NAME IS EVE

The following day was sunny. Without the usual filter of clouds, the sun sparkled through the glass in Pridapt's front lobby, making everything appear bright and new. I needed something new, a fresh outlook, a clear mind. It was late morning, and I appreciated the silence of the quiet lobby, despite a dull ringing in my ears that had been present ever since my experience with the primordium the night before.

Now that it was summer, I worked at Pridapt every weekday, often driving in with my mother. There was always enough work for me to do, given the constant push for our annual cures. I had just dropped some specimens off at another lab and was taking a moment to appreciate the sunlight pouring in the windows when my mother passed by.

"Forget something?" she asked.

"More like trying to forget something," I grumbled. I was trying. Gazing at the sunlight drew me away from the darkness of the previous night's illusion, the fear of losing control, and of being controlled. Noting the direction my mother was headed, I asked, "Off to the rat cage?"

"She'll never be civil toward you if you keep saying things like that," my mother chided. "Come in with me again," she suggested, "but come with an open mind."

I'll never open my mind to that thing again, I thought, but agreed to walk with her. It would be prudent to gather more information on the thing to better protect myself should I ever need to be near it again, though I didn't see that happening any time soon. "I'll come, and I'll be quiet," I agreed.

While I did hate the thing for what it had done, luring me in with the taped door and manipulating my mind, I had to admit I was intrigued. It had demonstrated an impressive degree of sophistication with its conniving plan. Avoidance would be my primary approach always, but should it ever get its tentacles on me again, I wanted to have the upper hand. To have that, I needed to understand it better.

My mother stopped about thirty feet before the East Wing doors. "Wait," she said, holding her arm out in front of me. "She'll see us there." I looked down the empty hallway. "You have to be more careful about what you say,

Noah, and how you act around her, okay?"

"How could it see us?" I asked, still scanning the hallway, wondering from what vantage point we could possibly be seen.

"She can sense infrared."

"I saw the reptile primordium doing that," I recalled, "that day I brought Zoe into the observation room. I could have sworn it saw Zoe through the mirrored glass wall!" I got over my initial excitement and considered the implications of my mother's warning. "But that was very close, just the other side of the glass. You're not saying it can sense infrared through multiple walls, are you?"

"Her range is about sixty feet, and yes, through walls."

"Sixty feet! That's insane!" I exclaimed. "But it's only vague shapes, right? I mean, it can't tell the difference between you and me."

"She does recognize me. I don't know if she can identify you through the walls, but since you're with me, I'm sure she'll know it's you, so..."

"How can it sense so far?"

"It was a capability I'd been evaluating in her. Apparently, by testing the limits of her ability, I was helping her develop it further. She had greater acuity each time I tested it, her ability increasing in response to increased need. It would be like a person getting better vision each time they read an eye chart. It's really quite fascinating."

"And disturbing," I added.

"Her hearing is also very acute."

"Don't tell me it can hear us from here."

"Not from here, but from the habitat she can hear us in the front room, so do watch what you say, or better yet, just say nothing."

"It understands English?" I chuckled.

"Of course," my mother snapped. "She's understood everything you've said. That's why she doesn't trust you, Noah. You need to rebuild her confidence in you."

Doesn't trust me? What about me trusting it? How could I, after what had just happened? And now I knew that it could hear through walls!

"I'm the only person she's seen for most of her life," my mother explained. "I'm imprinted on her."

"Oh, so you're like its mother?"

"Yes."

I agreed to keep my mouth shut, which satisfied my mother sufficiently for us to proceed to the East Wing doors. In the outer room, my mother shared more information with me, some of which was clearly meant for the primordium to hear.

"Noah, I'm going to show you the outdoor habitat now. Keep in mind that you are a guest in another person's home. Do you understand?"

I nodded, but my mother motioned for me to verbalize my agreement out loud. "Yes, absolutely," I said and followed my mother through the central room, then into the habitat. I could feel its eyes on me, following me. I kept my eyes focused on my mother's shoulder as she walked in front of me. The desire to turn and look at it was overpowering, but I resisted. It was trying to draw me in again, I thought, but not this time. I suspected that it was crawling along the rafters, peering down at me, waiting for me to cast a glance its way, but I was prepared. I would not be fooled again. I followed my mother across the habitat floor and into a side alcove, the ringing in my ears growing louder.

We passed what appeared to be sleeping quarters and a bathroom, continued down a short hallway, then went through a door leading outside. My mother held the door for me as she stepped onto a stone path. I hesitated to follow her, looking at the door.

"That door doesn't lock," she assured me, with a tone that I thought downplayed the known risk of that thing toying with locked doors.

After we had walked along the path for several minutes, and well beyond the sixty-foot range, I began to speak. My mother held up her hand to stop me.

"Even here?" I whispered. My mother nodded and continued walking.

Who's master of whom? I wondered, evaluating this bizarre relationship between that thing and my mother. Maybe it had influenced her mind, too, but not in as obvious a way as it had mine: no frightening hallucinations, just subliminal influences. *Maybe she only thinks she's never been hypnotized because she has been. How would she know? It could be influencing both of us right now!*

The trail wound through a densely wooded area, much like my forest retreat. I assumed there was a fence enclosing the space, but I couldn't see it. We were easily two football fields away from the habitat door by then, so I felt certain we could speak freely.

"So there are no consequences for last night?" I asked. "No time out in its room?"

"I've spoken to her about it," my mother replied, then glancing at me added, "and what happened to your promise to remain quiet?"

Motioning to the distance between us and the habitat I began, "We're... it's..." Pointing to my ear I asked, "From here?"

My mother nodded and continued walking. After we had gone another fifty feet or so, she stopped.

"As I told you before," she said to me, "in hindsight, it would have been better had you never come in here, nor gone to see those patients. Now that you know..."

"Ignorance is better than knowledge?"

"Some questions have no clear-cut answers. Some things just are. As difficult as it may seem, they just are. In those circumstances, yes, ignorance can be preferable."

Now I knew she was not in her right mind. This was not the mother who had raised me.

"Who *are* you? I mean, really, why teach me these things if you don't believe them yourself?"

"Well, what good has come from all your curiosity?" my mother asked.

I thought about that question for a bit, then replied, "Carter."

"Who's Carter?"

"Just some old guy trapped in a hospital because of a nasty side effect, but he appreciated my talking to him. We had a long conversation about history, and, like I said, I'll be going back to see him next week. Did you know Dr. Strauss goes out to visit those patients every week?"

"Does he?"

"Yeah, so there's that, anyway. Even though it's just one person, that made it worthwhile. So it's true, knowledge is better than ignorance."

"Okay then." My mother chuckled. "I suppose it is." I watched her walk alongside me, a serene smile on her face. "Noah," she began.

"Yeah?"

"You're a compassionate young man. It's good that you can empathize with those patients." She paused. "You know, Eve is your age."

"What are you talking about? She's nine."

My mother smiled and I realized that I had actually referred to the primordium as "she."

"Like all the primordia," my mother continued, "she developed very rapidly, growing to the apparent age of eight within one month of life. So she, like you, is basically seventeen."

"Hmm," I mumbled, looking around the woods. "Do you come here often?"

"When not at that desk outside the habitat, I'm back here with Eve. I basically homeschooled her, like I homeschooled you."

"And you dress it and everything?"

"Of course not! I taught her to dress herself, just as I taught you," she answered, frowning at my return to the use of the pronoun, "it."

I saw a blur in my peripheral vision. "Is it out here?"

"She's not an *it*!" my mother railed. "Her name is Eve. Refer to her by her name, or don't refer to her at all!"

I looked at my mother in astonishment. Given that choice, I knew I would have to stop referring to the primordium altogether.

"Let's go back to the habitat," I suggested as I nervously scanned our surroundings.

"Eve," my mother called out. "It's okay; you can come over."

My mother was looking at a tree trunk to our left. As I stared at it, its base moved, and I saw that the primordium had been sitting cross-legged at the tree's base, its arms wrapped in front of itself with its skin camouflage matching the tree bark nearly perfectly. It quickly swung up to a branch of an adjacent tree, wrapped its arms around the trunk, and promptly disappeared.

That's pretty cool, I admitted to myself, then turned away to avoid eye contact.

My mother led me along the path again when a blur passed by us and landed with a thump. Out of a waviness in the air before us, a shape emerged. The primordium materialized and held its hand out in front of my mother. It then picked up a rock and threw it into a thicket, flushing out a bobcat which ran off through the trees.

"Thank you, Eve," my mother said calmly.

"You're welcome," the primordium replied.

You're welcome? It talks? Hearing the spoken word come from that thing was as startling to me as a chipmunk politely asking for directions. It didn't just talk; it talked like a person, with a person's voice—a girl's voice!

I began to fear it even more, though at the same time, I considered the advantages of such a thing as a sort of pet or guard animal. *If it could be trained,* I was thinking, *it might be a pretty handy thing to have around, but could I ever turn my back on it?*

It stood a few feet ahead of us, looking throughout the woods like a safari guide, then turned back and stood quietly before us.

"All clear?" my mother asked. The primordium nodded, then promptly camouflaged itself and disappeared into the woods. As we continued on to the far end of the habitat, it struck me that the primordium was being quite civil. Like a cat dropping a dead mouse at its owner's feet, it had seemed to be trying to impress and perhaps even get along with me. The sound of its voice—a girl's voice—kept coming back to my mind, leading me to wonder if it wasn't that bad after all. Remembering how real Zoe's presence was in the East Wing the previous night, I reminded myself that I couldn't trust my own inclinations as long as I was in the presence of that thing.

At the end of the path, we reached the corner of the outdoor habitat. The fence was topped with barbed wire and had security cameras directed along all of its sides. I wondered how the bobcat could have gotten in, then I saw it climbing along a fallen tree that was leaning against the fence. It struck me that it would be fairly easy for the primordium to get out that way too.

"It could climb right over that fence. What keeps it from escaping?" I asked.

"Escape? The fence is there to keep people and things out, not her in."

"What will happen, you know, when the research is over?" I asked. "It's not like it..."

"*She* will be mainstreamed at some point. I've been assured of that. She was supposed to be mainstreamed already, but things kept coming up. There may be a need for more serum, for the diabetes project. They kept..."

"They?"

"Mr. Stone," my mother clarified. "He kept telling me, 'Not yet.' I wasn't ready yet, either. Whenever and wherever we do it, I know it will be difficult. Look at you—still calling her *it*."

"And soon we'll be vaccinating all our teachers and government workers with its genes."

"The newspapers always play things up, Noah. There won't be any vaccines ready for six months at the earliest. We still have time to develop a version without the retrovirus. Like I said, we're getting very close. I'm sure we will have a formula by the time Stone wants to start the next wave of human trials."

"I heard there are laws being passed."

"Well, of course. It takes a long time for such things to get through Congress. If you don't start early, it will never happen. You have to get the ball rolling."

"You sound like Mr. Stone."

"Be careful what you say, Noah," my mother admonished me. "We're doing good work here; remember that. Mr. Stone has given you tremendous opportunities, opportunities few seventeen-year-olds could ever hope for. Never forget that."

She was right. I just couldn't get that word, *automatically*, out of my head. I was anxious about what I had read in the paper two days previously, the big announcement of our curing cancer before it begins. The vaccines would be given "automatically." But my mother was right. I needed to keep my mouth shut about a lot of things. Thinking out loud could get you into trouble.

I followed my mother back indoors, looking overhead occasionally for any signs of the primordium, but I didn't see it again that day. As we exited the East Wing doors, the dull, persistent ringing in my ears became more distinct and intense. It quickly grew to dominate my thoughts and memory to where I could think of nothing else, leaving me with a vague but potent sense of uneasiness and dread.

HER BOYFRIEND?

It was the scratching that disturbed me most, waking me in the morning. The ringing, while ever present, was more of a dull background noise, almost unnoticeable until I focused on it, but the scratching was unavoidable. The sequence of scratches, much too rapid to be the sound of a hand tool or other human activity, were like the sounds of a rodent. I found myself counting the number of scratches or scrapes between pauses: five scrapes, then a pause. The sound conjured an image of chiseled teeth methodically gnawing on some object, then stopping to process the matter and begin again. Five scrapes, then another. The sound was perfectly clear and loud as though it came from a microphone inches from some vermin's mouth. It wrenched me out of peaceful sleep, and I bolted upright, spun my legs down to the floor, clasping my hands to the sides of my head to silence the noise. So I had awoken the past two mornings. There was no doubt in my mind that this was a residual effect of the primordium's hypnosis.

Hours later, I was sitting in the woods by Pridapt, still trying to rid myself of the memory of that sound. It had been two days since my mother had given me a tour of the primordium's habitat. Although I had almost come to admire its abilities, I couldn't help wondering if it had put that thought of admiration into my head just to gain my confidence and get me to lower my guard.

So I came to the woods to clear my head and rid myself of that thing's effect on me. There was always peace in those woods, my woods, as I thought of them. Here, there would be no monster swinging from the trees, peering down at me. Here, I could understand myself.

Free of the gnawing sound for the time being, I began to hear a new sound. It was a sound I had trouble identifying. First on my left side, then my right, a sort of whispering sound with the cadence of speech, but too indistinct to make out any actual words. It came and went like the sound of tree branches moving with the breeze. At times, it was loud enough and distinct enough to make me turn my head as I wondered who it was that was approaching, but there was never anyone there.

To take my mind off of these tormenting sounds, I read through another article in the newspaper concerning Pridapt. It was about the legislation being considered in Congress regarding our upcoming vaccines. The story focused on the substantial cost savings they would afford. In addition to the "automatic" vaccination of teachers and students in public schools, insurance companies would be mandated to cover the vaccines without a copay. One of my coworkers had joked that with all these mandates, there would be an instant guaranteed market with no need for advertising.

"The boss won't need your slogans anymore, Noah. There goes your marketing career."

Though it was a joke, I did feel a momentary stab of panic. Is that all I was? Would I still be considered for the scholarship to support my education? Would Mr. Stone want me to come back as a researcher, or was I really just the slogan guy, a soon-to-be obsolete slogan guy?

I also cringed whenever I read about mandates. Would people know what's in the vaccine? Would they know about the primordium? Would there be more patients like Carter? If there were to be more complications, they would not occur in people on the verge of death with nothing to lose—they would occur in perfectly healthy people with everything to lose.

My mother was right. I needed to keep my mouth shut about these things. Still, there was a small voice inside me that maintained the alarm. In an instant, it was swept away by a crescendo of ringing and a new wave of whispering. I threw the paper down and searched the rising tree trunks around me for the solace I was accustomed to receive from them.

"Found you!"

The voice rang through the trees and wrenched me back to reality. It was Zoe.

"I've been looking for you for days!" she exclaimed. "Two days ago I came by, and they said you went off somewhere with a doctor. Today I come, and they say you went out to lunch, but I thought maybe you just came to the woods, and here you are!"

I kept looking at her, wondering if she really was Zoe or if this was another hallucination. I briefly considered the idea of pinching her but couldn't imagine anything good coming from that.

I reveled in the fact that *she* had been looking for *me*. I felt the need to clarify where things were with the diabetes trial since I was pretty sure that was why she had come.

"About the diabetes trial..." I began.

"That's what I wanted to tell you!" she beamed. "I told my mother about it right away, a few days ago when you told me. She was so excited; I couldn't believe it. She's never been this positive with me, not as long as I can remember anyway. She said she was 'proud of me,' and 'my new boyfriend sounded wonderful,' and she went on and on!"

Did she say, "boyfriend"? The word kept repeating in my mind, over and over. The idea of a hallucination seemed likely. I would hate to fall for that again.

"Noah?" Zoe prodded. "Hello?"

I had been staring at her without listening, considering the audacious notion that Zoe Halpern should be standing there before me, calling me her boyfriend.

"Yeah," I said, returning to the conversation. "It's great isn't it? So much good coming from this, it's amazing."

"I feel like I can get past all this stuff with my dad. I just want it out of my head, once and for all, you know? Well, I guess you wouldn't know."

"My dad left me, too," I boasted in the interest of fostering our camaraderie.

"Yeah," Zoe admitted, "but, at least he ditched you before you were born. He never knew you. If he had, he would have liked you and stuck around because you're a cool kid. At least you can tell yourself that. It's a possibility. My dad knew me and walked by me every day like I was invisible. All he cared about was his horn. He'd run into the house to pick it up for some gig. God forbid it wasn't exactly where he'd left it, like anyone would care to touch his precious trumpet."

Zoe had originally been speaking to me but was now ranting to the space beside me.

"Why don't we go see if we can get those forms for your Mom?" I suggested. The change of topic seemed to bring Zoe back to the pleasant mood she'd arrived in.

"Sure." She smiled. "Let's do it."

We left the woods and returned to the Pridapt lobby. My mother must have seen us coming up the drive, because she was there in the lobby to meet us.

"Where are you two going?"

"Don't worry, not the East Wing," I assured her. "I was thinking Zoe might be able to get the paperwork for the diabetes trial... for her mom."

"Sure," my mother replied with a grin. "Zoe, why don't you come with me, and I'll get you those forms?"

I stood waiting for them to return, thinking of how suddenly things seemed so much better. There were no scratching sounds, no whispers. As I thought of it, I could still make out the background ringing in my ears, but it was hardly noticeable. *What a difference a positive mood can make.*

My mother returned with Zoe nearly skipping along beside her.

"Thank you so much, Mrs.—Noah."

She left the lobby and trotted out to her car, her arms straight up in the air, her head rocking side to side as though she were singing and dancing.

"Nice girl," my mother quipped. "Doesn't even know your last name."

"She knows it," I offered in her defense. "She was just... so excited and all."

"I see." My mother sighed. "Is your work done in the lab?"

"Yeah, pretty much."

"Come on, we could use a break."

My mother led me to her car, and we drove down to the San Francisco waterfront. It struck me that we had not done anything spontaneous like this for a long time. As we were parking, I looked at her face, trying to discern an underlying cause of her sudden carefree attitude. Perhaps even *she* succumbed to stress at times and needed to escape.

"Are you okay?" she asked me, beating me to the punch.

"I'm fine. I was going to ask you the same thing."

"We both needed a break. You have some time now, before you start your applications for college and for the Pridapt scholarship. Let's forget all that for the afternoon, forget the deadlines and everything, okay?"

"Sounds great," I agreed.

We stepped out into an expansive farmers market around the Ferry Building. I breathed in the damp sea air mixed with the smells of fresh produce and fried food. I looked around the sea of people and up at the intricate stone work on the top of the old building, just as I would gaze at the panorama in the woods. There were so many sounds, of children, voices, cars, and buses, that I couldn't even begin to hear ringing or whispers in my head. I took my mother's hand with a broad smile. I remembered having come to this place before, when I was younger, how I would run from stand to stand, tugging at my mother's arm to follow me. I felt the urge to do the same thing again.

"Feel better?" my mother asked.

"I feel great!" I pulled her over to the first stand that caught my eye and then another. We made our way into the Ferry Building and walked by all the shops. Watching the people, moving within the crowds, seeing the little children running up to store windows, I felt a peace like that of my wooded sanctuary. Then, we passed a shop with newspapers displayed out front, and I caught another headline about our "curing cancer before it begins." My mother saw my expression change as the stress began to return, and she suggested we take a walk out on the pier. I readily agreed.

As we stepped outdoors, an image came to mind of me fishing there once as a young boy. Sitting on one of the benches, we looked across the line of fishing poles. There were children, adults, and seasoned pier fishermen, as much at home there by the water as the gulls that stood expectantly along the tops of nearby posts, waiting for scraps from the cleaned catches. On a bench opposite us, there was a man sleeping on his side with newspapers over him. Judging by the state of his clothing, I assumed he was homeless. I watched as people walked past him. Except for young children, who craned their necks to examine what to them was a curious scene of a man sleeping in the middle of the day, no one seemed to notice him. Unseen and unwanted, he was as invisible as the primordium, arrayed in its bark-colored skin beside a tree trunk.

Across the bay, Alcatraz Island jutted up from the water line, its peak crowned with Alcatraz Prison. Having once held the infamous Al Capone and the "Birdman of Alcatraz," it was now a museum and tourist destination. The sight of that old place of incarceration, a literal island in a sea of humanity, brought to mind the patients at Whispering Acres, isolated on their allegorical island, and the homeless man we had just seen, virtually invisible on his bench. *How many of these islands are there?* I wondered—hidden in plain sight. Was the East Wing at Pridapt another Alcatraz Island? Were my woods?

We walked back to the waterfront, passing a collection

of barking sea lions in the water to our right, a welcome distraction from the man on the bench to our left. As we returned to the crowds around the food stands, I once again felt the electricity of humanity, the joy of community, of children, entertainment, and food. We got a couple mugs of chowder and some hot chocolate and sat on another bench looking out over the bay.

As twilight began to fall, we watched the lights come on over the Bay Bridge. They were like the stars coming out. With every minute, they became brighter, their reflection in the water becoming more and more distinct. Neither of us had spoken more than two words during the last half hour, both of us content with the notion that all that needed to be said had been said. *What could be better than this?* The warmth of our chowder and hot chocolate had passed, but neither of us were cold, despite the cool, damp breeze blowing in from the bay. It was a perfect moment, a perfect day. I was happy. I was so happy!

The evening turned from twilight to night, and it was time to go home. As we returned to the car, I kept looking at my mother and smiling.

"What?" she asked.

"Nothing," I said. "I'm just happy."

"I'm glad, and I'm sorry," she added.

"For what?"

"For forgetting to do this more often. We'll do it again soon, okay?"

"You got it," I said as we began the drive home. I kept the window down until we reached the highway, to hold on to the afternoon's experience for as long as possible. Once we merged into the highway traffic, I closed the window, shutting out the sounds of buses, passing cars, and wind, and there it was—the ringing in my ears, as loud as ever. My heart began to race. It was like coming upon a fearsome stranger in your kitchen after a crowd of happy guests leave. You realize that behind the festivity, behind every conversation, every smile, and every laugh, something menacing had been there the whole time, waiting!

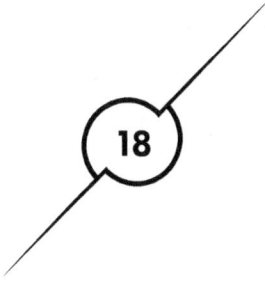

WHISPERS

I woke again to the sound of scratching, so loud this time I was certain I would open my eyes to find a rodent inches from my face, gnawing on my bedpost. Seeing nothing but the dim gray light of the early morning, I sat upright in bed, my hands clasped tightly over my ears, moaning to drown out the sound. Eventually, the scratching faded to ringing, and I was able to get myself dressed.

My mother had gone in to Pridapt before me this morning, probably to catch up on the time she had lost the day before with our outing to the waterfront. Recalling our time there lifted my mood. It was as though that afternoon had gathered everything good and happy in my life, brought it to the surface, and presented it to me, to be drawn upon as needed. I had a great family, a great life, it was summer break, Zoe had referred to me as her boyfriend. My future was the brightest it had ever been.

Falling asleep the night before, I had hoped the tormenting sounds in my head would dissipate and become just a curious memory, but they were back with a vengeance this morning. Clearly, that thing had a hold on me. It was in my head and was not letting go.

I made my way down the hall to the kitchen, turned on the radio for a distraction, and grabbed a box of cereal. Looking at the curtained front window, I began to have a most unnerving sense that there were several people standing outside our door, whispering. We lived in a condominium complex, so it would not be unusual for pedestrians to be passing by, but why would they have been standing there? *Were they talking about me?* I strained to listen more closely but could only make out the vague whispering sound I had been hearing off and on for days.

I thought of crawling on all fours to the window to peek around a corner of the curtain, but worried, *what if they saw me?* I began to panic. I tried to tell myself that I was being unreasonable, that this fear was completely irrational, but I couldn't stop it. The front door was the only way out of our condominium. I considered the windows, regretting that my mother was not there with me. *Why did she have to leave early today?*

I raced back to my room and wrenched my neck to look out my window, but it had no view of the front door. Deciding to face whoever was out there, if, indeed there were people there, I prepared to leave. Back in the kitchen, I had the same sense that people were on the other side of the wall, whispering. With three long strides, I threw open the front door and, with an involuntary gasp, looked down the length of the walk. There was no one there. I scanned the complex to see if anyone had noticed me bolting out the front door like that, and fortunately, no one was out. Down at the road, there were people at a bus stop, but they were too far away to have seen me.

I breathed a sigh of relief and walked to my car in the parking lot. My nerves were still on edge as I made my way onto the highway. I kept my eyes fixed on the road in front of me, afraid to glance at passing cars, worried that I would discover that their drivers were staring at me. After exiting onto the side roads that would take me the rest of the way to Pridapt, I felt calmer.

Whenever I stopped at a light, the whispering sounds resurfaced. I sensed that people were looking at me. When I glanced at them on the streets, it always seemed that they were, indeed, looking at me. They had been watching me the whole time!

They're whispering! I thought. *Whispering about me! What do I do?* The honk of a car horn behind me startled me, and I realized that I had been driving very slowly, at least twenty miles per hour below the speed limit.

I accelerated, but as I tried to read the speedometer, my vision seemed blurred, the steering wheel a sort of disjointed set of rings. As I struggled to regain my bearings, I was jolted upward and backward as my car jumped the curb. I looked up and saw a tree trunk rapidly approaching my windshield, so I stood on the brake.

There was a loud crash and I felt something like sand being thrown onto me. When my eyes opened, I saw a mosaic of the tree trunk through the shattered windshield, little squares of glass sprinkled over me, and felt a sharp pain in my left shoulder.

I heard no whispering, which was odd, because I was certain they would be talking about me now, now that I had driven off the road. I heard the sirens approach, then shortly afterward, my car door opened, and I heard the voices of the paramedics.

"What's your name?"

"Don't try to move. We'll get you out of there."

"Do you remember what happened?"

"Noah," I answered eventually. "Noah Bolton."

"Well, take it easy, Noah. Everything's going to be all right."

I had fallen over onto the passenger side of the car. They fixed a neck brace on me and then slid me onto a flat board. After laying me onto the ground beside my car, they left momentarily. They must have thought I was unconscious because I heard them talking about me as though I wasn't there.

When they returned, they lifted me up and put me into an ambulance which then took me to the emergency room. As we were driving, the ringing in my ears became unbearably loud.

"Can you hear it?" I asked one of the EMTs.

"Hear what?"

"Ringing."

"There's no ringing. Maybe you're hearing our siren."

As they were transferring me into the emergency room, the doctors were getting a report.

"He was alert and oriented at the scene but confused. Talking about ringing."

"I'm not on drugs!" I interjected. The doctors and nurses peered at me. "I'm not on drugs. I heard what you were talking about. You kept asking, 'Are you sure he doesn't have a drug history?'"

The EMTs looked at each other and frowned. "We just asked your name, to make sure you were conscious."

"I heard you," I insisted.

"Something made him drive off the road," one of the EMTs muttered, rolling his eyes at the nurses. "Though it doesn't seem to have hurt his hearing any."

You have no idea! I fumed to myself. *If you saw what did it, you'd run your rig off the road, too!* But before I could defend myself any further, they were gone, and I was descended upon by a team of technicians and nurses.

They did blood tests, X-rays, EKGs, and a CAT scan. Before too long, the alcohol and routine drug screening came back negative, so they began to look for another cause of my accident. The doctor came in and told me they couldn't find anything in my head on the CAT scan, but I could have told them that. Of course, they couldn't see what was in my head; no one could see it but me.

I kept waiting for my mother to arrive since they told me that they had notified her. I knew she was the only one who could help. I looked down at my right arm, which was scratched and bleeding, and like the steering wheel, it suddenly became disjointed and blurry. Whatever had happened in the car, it was happening again! My wrist was numb and tingling, my vision went out of focus. I looked across the room to find someone to call out to and saw my mother standing there talking to one of the doctors. They were whispering. *Come in here! It's happening right now!* I thought. Why were they talking for so long?

My mother finally came into the room and rushed to the side of my stretcher.

"Noah, are you okay?" she asked. "What happened?"

"It's the hypnosis!" I whispered. "I can't tell them that, but it's still affecting me. It's making me hear things and see things. I don't know how to stop it! Can't you make it stop? Make *her* stop!"

"Who is? What are you talking about?"

"Who do you think? The primordium!" I hissed.

"She was nowhere near you," my mother protested.

I looked behind my mother and noticed that the aids and nurses were looking at me and whispering. They were talking about me; I was sure of it. *It must have gotten to them, too!* I looked at my mother and motioned my head toward them. "Look at them! That thing is using them to get to me again," I whispered.

"Noah, do you hear yourself? You're not making sense."

"Just look at them!"

A man in a white coat came up to us and explained that the emergency room doctor had asked him to come speak with me. He was a psychiatry resident. He asked a battery of questions, most of which were simple, like the date, my name, where we were, and who the president was.

"Do you ever hear voices?" he asked, after all the mundane questions.

I had to think about that one, because while I had been hearing a whispering sound for days, I could never make out any words, so how could I be sure those were voices?

"Well, I hear whispers."

My mother looked at me and appeared startled.

"Whispers?" the resident repeated.

"I can't make out what they're saying, but I know they're talking about me."

"What are they saying about you?"

"I told you, I can't make it out."

"Are they derogatory? Do they say that you're bad, that you're no good?"

"I just told you…"

"When do the voices come?"

"I don't know that they are voices; it's a whispering sound."

"But you know they're whispering about you."

"Well, I know *they* are," I said, pointing to the nurses standing against the wall, looking at me. "I can hear them."

The resident looked behind him at the nurses, then excused himself, saying he would be back shortly with a colleague.

"What can I tell him?" I asked my mother. "I can't tell him what it really is."

"What is it, really?" my mother asked me.

Stunned, I stared at her for a few moments. "It's *her*, obviously!"

"I told you," my mother spoke quietly, turning her back to the ER personnel, "Eve could only affect you directly by bringing on a slight hypnotic state. She can't make you drive off the road or hear voices."

"How do you know?" I challenged her. "You've never felt it. I have. You don't know what it's like to have that *thing* in your head!" I was done calling it *her*. I had expected my mother to jump in on my side, but, once again, she took the primordium's side. *They're all against me!* I thought.

The psychiatry resident returned with a more senior-appearing doctor and asked some additional questions. They asked me if I had ever seen things that weren't there.

You mean, like Zoe crawling on a rafter? I thought. "I see blurry shapes sometimes," I offered.

"Could be floaters," the junior doctor suggested.

"At seventeen? Not likely."

They continued, moving on to questions directed at my mother. The issue of my father was raised, questions about my childhood: was I social, did I get along well with others, was I a loner? I didn't like the picture they were painting of me. They were making me into something I was not. It wasn't fair. I began to wonder if they were in on it, too.

After the junior and senior psychiatrist stepped out again to confer, they returned and asked my mother to sit down.

"I'm afraid I have some bad news for you," the senior doctor began. "Your son may have schizophrenia. The presentation can be variable, but he has a number of the classic signs: auditory hallucinations, paranoid delusions..."

They're not delusions! I turned to my mother looking for her to defend me, but she just sat there listening. *Say something!*

"Visual hallucinations, while less common, can also occur. This is the age that the illness often manifests itself. Here is the name of a good psychiatrist who specializes in schizophrenia." He handed my mother a business card. "We've made great advances in recent years with newer medications and customized protocols. People with schizophrenia can go on to lead nearly normal lives."

My mother nodded her appreciation and put the business card into her purse, and the two doctors left.

A nurse arrived with a sheet of instructions for me and a sling which she put on my left arm. I was to call if I developed a very bad headache or had persistent nausea and vomiting, and I was to follow up with my pediatrician, an orthopedic surgeon for my strained shoulder, and, oh yes, a psychiatrist for my schizophrenia.

So that was that. I was crazy—end of story.

And my mother said nothing.

In all those years she had never felt any hypnotic effect from the primordium. Was she right about the limits of the thing's hypnotic effects, or was she in denial?

The ringing, the whispers, the nonstop harassment I'd been enduring for days was definitely coming from a monster, but was it the monster in the East Wing, as I had suspected all along, or was it, as the doctors and nurses and now even my own mother believed, the monster in me?

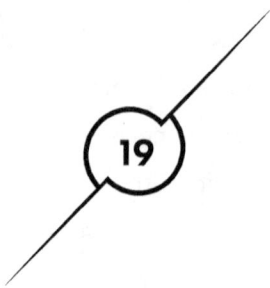

THE MONSTER IN ME

I went to work as usual the next day, though my mother had to take me, since my car was being repaired. My mother thought it best that I continued my regular routine for a sense of normalcy. There was nothing I wanted more right now, so I agreed.

With my left arm in a sling, I was slower at my work, but I still managed to finish before noon. My mother would not be free to drive me home for another hour, so I went outside for a walk. I decided to stay on the pavement and level ground, as opposed to the trail in my woods, having one less limb with which to steady myself.

With no immediate goal in mind, I soon found myself heading around the back side of the East Wing. The walkway on the side of the building led me to a loading dock which abutted the high fence surrounding the wooded exterior of the primordium's habitat. Surveying the line of trees along the fence, I wondered if it was hiding there behind the branches, watching me.

There was a tractor trailer backed up to one of the loading docks beside the fence, and it struck me how easy it would be to climb to the top of the trailer and get over the fence. I didn't suppose there were many people who would want to do that. I certainly had no inclination to do so. However, looking at the fenced-in wooded habitat, I felt envious of the primordium. There, in that controlled environment, it was safe: safe from accidents, cars, doctors, and emergency rooms. But then, was it really easier to be a monster hidden in a habitat, rather than one living in the real world? Didn't it amount to the same thing? I began to feel a bond of sorts between us—the monster and me.

I strode back to the lobby and took a seat by the front desk. The security guard informed me that Zoe had been by the day before, looking for me.

"If she comes by again," I advised, "just tell her I'm out."

How could I see her now? I felt like the foundation of reality had been washed away from beneath my feet. I was floating, weightless, completely disoriented. Everything I had ever known had come to me through my senses, and now I could no longer trust my senses. Information was coming to me through the bizarre filter of that creature's hypnosis, or worse, through the filter of schizophrenia. How could I be sure of anything?

"Okay, Noah," my mother called out cheerfully as she entered the lobby. "I can take you home now."

We barely spoke during the drive home, my mind racing with so many thoughts that I could not remember whether or not I had heard any ringing. She had to get right back to Pridapt, so she just dropped me off at home and left.

Inside, I sat at the table covered with my applications, both for the Pridapt scholarship and a number of colleges. Just a few days earlier, I had been so excited about diving into them, but now I wondered, *Why bother?* If the whispers were there, I didn't notice them. I was too preoccupied with the ramifications of schizophrenia. "The medications have made great strides," the doctors had said. "You can live a normal life, maybe even have your own apartment someday and buy your own groceries!"

I didn't want to just be normal, to achieve the tremendous accomplishment of living on my own. I wanted to be a researcher. I wanted to contribute, to be somebody special. Before this day, I had never doubted my ability to achieve these goals, but now they seemed out of reach. Longing to experience my prior certainty and optimism again, I pulled out a box of mementos and papers from my mother's closet.

At the top was a photograph of my mother and me in front of Pridapt. I looked to be about eight years old. There were several other photographs from about that time, some when I was a bit younger. Then, there was one with my mother twirling me around in her arms. She was smiling the biggest and broadest smile I had ever seen on her. It was so rare that she smiled like that anymore.

Now that I thought of it, she was quite serious most of the time, especially the past few years. There had been times when she would look at me with such a worried look, I'd thought something bad had happened. Whenever I'd ask her about it, she always said it was nothing and changed the subject. Had she known? I wondered. Did she suspect there was something wrong with me?

Beneath the photographs, there was a medical form, some sort of prerequisite physical exam for me to enter high school. I pulled it out, along with other papers clipped to it. There were a few segments that had been whited out, with nothing written over them. I set about uncovering what had been deliberately obscured.

Next to the "general" part of the physical exam, there was a blotch of white, which I managed to take off in segments with a razor blade. The exposed script read, "blunt affect." I had always been a quiet kid, but I took offense at the description, "blunt." I supposed this was a medical term.

I skipped down to the bottom of the form where there was a line labeled: "Abnormal Findings." The box marked yes had a spot of white-out within it, which I assumed covered a check mark. Beneath this was a line for recommendations. This area was also whited out. I took pains to scrape off the white camouflage, occasionally tearing the paper slightly. Once the white was cleared, I could read in a scrawling script, "Recommend additional evaluation with Psych, see attached."

I quickly flipped the page to find another official-looking sheet with a list of check boxes. The list of questions all seemed to pertain to psychological issues, so I assumed this sheet was the referenced "attached form." To my relief, all the pertinent boxes were checked off in the negative, boxes next to: "Does the student demonstrate any suicidal ideation?" "Any risk of harm to others?" and so on. I scrolled to the bottom of the page, and was astonished to find that it recommended a "specialized institution."

Another medical form under these two was one for employment at Pridapt. This form was not altered and reported everything about me as normal, which was a relief, until I noticed that the signature at the bottom of the form was David Bernstein, MD!

I knew that Dave was a medical doctor, but I was certain

that he did not do employee physicals. Even if he did, he was too close a friend to be an objective evaluator. Clearly, my mother had used him to sign off on this form. *She did know! She knew all along that I had schizophrenia!*

Hearing my mother come through the front door, I hurriedly pushed the papers back into the box and stood up quickly, a bit too quickly. I felt a warm rush, and the floor began to sway under my feet. The whispering and the ringing rose in my ears as the room spun. I felt a sharp blow to my forehead and hit the floor with a thud.

As I oriented myself again, I saw my mother leaning over me, pressing on my forehead.

"What happened, Noah?" she asked.

"I guess I got dizzy."

She did a quick check for other injuries, then went to get her first aid kit. After washing off the area and dressing my superficial forehead wound, she asked me again what had happened.

"Why did you change those medical forms?" I asked her. "You knew! You knew all along! Why didn't you tell me?"

"What are you talking about, Noah?"

"You knew I had schizophrenia. Why lead me along, letting me think I could ever amount to anything?"

My mother scanned the room and spotting the open box of mementos, understood what I had seen.

"Because you will," my mother cooed. "You can and will amount to anything you choose to. You can do anything, Noah."

"Not according to those forms. That doctor also thought I had schizophrenia."

"That medical evaluation didn't say you had schizophrenia."

"Then why change it?"

"You're gifted, Noah. You've always been gifted. You're very intelligent and perceptive. Yes, I hid things on those forms, but not because they said you were sick. I hid them because they said you were exceptional, that you should go to a special school, but I thought you'd do better here with me rather than at some boarding school. You weren't ever bored or stifled, were you, Noah?" she asked, sounding almost desperate. "I thought I could make up for whatever you missed by not going to that school, by getting you involved at Pridapt. And you did so very well, only thirteen and you were grasping the concepts as well as our seasoned technicians. They were all so impressed. Those forms didn't say you were sick."

"Then why have Dave sign my medical form for Pridapt?"

"That was just a technicality. Dave was doing me a favor." She pulled a bottle out of her purse. "By the way, I filled the prescription that the emergency room doctor had written for you. You have been under a lot of stress lately. These may help."

"So, do you think I could have schizophrenia?"

"Yesterday, yes, I started to wonder if maybe you did, since so many patients with schizophrenia are exceptionally gifted like you are, but now I don't think so, Noah." I felt a rush of relief that must have been visible to my mother. She sighed, gently rubbing the dressing on my forehead. "Tell me, Noah, what do you hear, exactly?"

"Just whispers."

"You can't make anything out?"

"No, that's what's so maddening."

"And what do you see exactly?"

"Blurry things."

"Can you tell what they are?"

"No! They're not real things; they're just shapes!"

"And it all began after you looked at Eve the other night?"

"Yes, I told you. All except for the shapes," I confessed, "I'd been seeing those before, but I never made much of them."

"Noah," my mother said, with the trace of a smile, "I'm now quite certain that you don't have schizophrenia or any mental disorder."

So it is all from the primordium! I thought.

"I can explain things for you better in the East Wing. Why don't you come with me there?"

"Now?"

"We can get something to eat on the way. It will be quieter now that everyone else has gone."

The thought of us being alone there in the East Wing was disconcerting, but I had the sense that whatever my mother had to share with me, it was significant, so I agreed to go along with her.

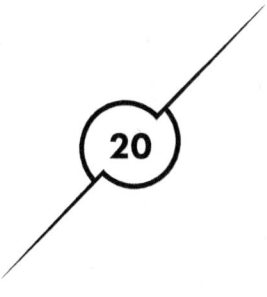

THE TRUTH

The night security guard was just starting his shift when we arrived at Pridapt. It was very quiet after hours, and as we made our way to the East Wing doors, I remembered my mother's warning about how we could be seen and heard by the primordium even from the hallway. This time, I didn't really care. My mother was going to share something with me that would help me break free of its control.

Entering the front room, we sat down by a file cabinet from which my mother pulled out a folder of papers. I glanced briefly at the window into the next room but did not allow my gaze to linger there, for fear of catching the primordium's eyes again. I tried to keep a check on my mouth, too.

"Do you remember this?" my mother asked, showing

me a photograph of the two of us standing in the lab by the electrophoresis machine. I had just run my first set of specimens. I actually did remember that day, quite vividly. It was an especially exciting one for me as it was the first time that the other lab workers showed respect for me as a coworker instead of just "Dr. Bolton's kid."

"Oh, this was a special day," she remarked with a sigh. "Your thirteenth birthday!"

"Why is that in there with your work files?" I asked, wondering when she would get on to the reason we were there.

"I have a drawer full of empty frames," she explained. "I meant to get these photos into them but never got around to it. Oh, the farm," she exclaimed, pulling out another photograph. "I bet you remember the farm." She held up the scene for me to revel in. "Do you remember the llamas?"

I don't care about the llamas! I was losing my patience with my mother's inexplicable nostalgia. "Can we get back to why we came?" I asked, with as much gentleness as I could muster.

My mother nodded but continued flipping through photographs as though she didn't really hear what I had said.

"You said I didn't have schizophrenia. That's great! But what is going on? How do I get that thing to stop?"

"Do you remember your first primordium?" she asked

me, this time looking at me instead of a photograph.

"Of course! It was a reptile primordium." How could I forget? While my role in the experiment was minimal, I had been there at every stage: the stimulation of the initial one-celled embryo, the development of the early primordium, the extended dormant stage, then the cocoon and its division into male and female. "I remember running down the hall telling everyone..."

"We have two!" my mother burst out, laughing. "That's what you yelled to everyone. You were so excited."

"I was," I agreed, joining in her laughter. "I stuck my head into every lab all the way down the hall."

"You couldn't have been prouder. I couldn't have been," she added. "I still couldn't be more proud of you than I am."

I looked at my mother's loving eyes and thought of how I longed for that day again. That had been a happy day, and they had been happy times.

"Afterward," my mother continued to remember, "you and I went down to the cafeteria to celebrate."

"And I had a hamburger and a strawberry milkshake," I reminisced.

"Two milkshakes, as I recall," my mother clarified, wrapping her arm around me. "That was a whole lot better than studying a bunch of nonsense at some elite prep school, wouldn't you say?"

"Absolutely," I agreed. Those were some of the best times in my life, and I'd had such a happy life. But that was long before I began hearing whispers. I needed answers now, not memories. "What about the hypnosis, Mom? How do I stop it?"

My mother put down the folder and sighed quietly. "Eve was responsible for starting these things you're experiencing," she admitted.

"I knew it! Then why do you always defend it!" I asked.

"For one thing, she's a living person, not an *it*! But more than that..." She stopped and handed me a sheet of paper she had pulled from the folder. It was a consent form for the donation of an embryo for experimentation. "This was the form for the embryo we received from the in vitro lab, the single-celled embryo I told you about before."

"The cell you developed the primordium from," I recalled, glancing briefly at the page.

"Look at the signature."

My eyes ran down to the bottom of the page where I saw that the signature releasing the embryo for experimentation was "Annette Bolton!"

"It was yours?" I gasped.

"I told you I was married once," she explained. "It was a long time ago. We had tried to have a child with in vitro fertilization but were unsuccessful. There was one embryo left over, a single-celled embryo, no good for implantation. They can only keep them so long, and nine years ago they contacted me, and, well, you know the rest. Rather than destroy the cell, I thought some good could come from it. In place of destruction, there could be life, and more."

"The cures."

My mother nodded. "The cures have surpassed my wildest dreams. But I never expected the adult form to arise so quickly. I told you we didn't know what to expect. You understand, don't you? Noah?"

I had stopped listening. I was so overwhelmed by the concept that it was hers, that thing was her daughter! She was its mother! What a nightmare!

"She's your daughter?" I thought out loud.

My mother looked back at me with a glare, which I understood to mean, "Figure out all the relationships."

That would make her... Talk about an evil stepsister! I thought but did not say. All I could think of now was my mother and how she must have suffered, then and now. How hurtful it must have been to hear me refer to the primordium as "it" and as a "monster." As accurate as those titles may have been, it was my mother whom I had been hurting all along, and her feelings that I now cared most about. I was overcome with empathy for her and agonizing regret for the pain I had caused her.

"I'm so sorry, Mom. I didn't know. Why didn't you just tell me?"

"I didn't tell anyone."

"What do you mean, you didn't tell anyone?" I asked, staring at her. "People here must know. Dave, he must know, doesn't he?"

My mother shook her head quietly.

"But, this form... they had to see."

"I arranged for the donation and took care of the paperwork. Then, I was the only researcher overseeing the work. Once she developed into an adult form, well, I've been keeping things quiet, waiting to mainstream her someday, like I said."

"I won't call her *it*, anymore," I promised. "I'm so sorry."

My mother looked at me with such sadness, I felt the guilt rising in me for my lack of sensitivity. But then, our main reason for going there that evening resurfaced in my mind, with an even greater urgency to settle the matter.

"You have to call it off," I said to her. "Now that I know that you are her mother, then clearly she will listen to you. Tell her to stop what she's doing to me. Just draw the line. Make her stop!"

"She's not doing anything anymore," my mother insisted. "She just started something."

"If she started it, she can stop it," I argued, but it was as though my mother didn't hear me.

I had thought it was good that I didn't have schizophrenia. Now I wasn't so sure. At least there were medications for schizophrenia. My mother's ambivalence about the primordium's influence over me was frightening. Was I a lost cause? Would I just have to learn to live with the ringing, the whispers, and the hallucinations?

My mother brought out another collection of photographs. They were of me again, this time looking to be about six years old, then eight years old, and then thirteen. "How quickly time flies," she mused, looking at me, then the photographs again.

"That's nice, but you're not helping me."

"I've tried," she said in a pitiful, almost whimpering voice. "I've tried so hard. What else could I do? I had to take care of her. You understand, don't you?"

"You said there was something here that could help me," I reminded her, trying to bring her back to the issue at hand. "What is it? How does knowing that Eve is actually your daughter help me? Can I stop her better if I understand her better? Is that it?"

My mother continued to leaf through papers in her folder. Another sheet slid out from her stack and onto the table. It was a letter from a dermatologist.

"I don't remember going to a dermatologist. What was that for?" I asked.

"Oh, you know, adolescence, acne and all that," my mother answered flatly, without looking up from her folder of papers.

She's stalling, I thought, *but why?* The thought that Eve was manipulating her mind as well as my own seemed to be a real possibility. I rapidly scanned the room for her, jumping up to check the lock on the door and craning my neck to look through the window at all four corners in the next room. I saw nothing.

"What are you worried about?" my mother asked, looking at me with a truly forlorn look that I had never seen before. I sat down beside her and asked her the same question.

"What are you worried about, Mom?"

She just looked down at her hands and sat in silence. My eyes ran over the letter from the dermatologist again, stopping at an unusual word. The last line referred to skin "mottling."

"Mottling? What is that?" I asked, but once again, my mother did not seem to hear me. The discolored faces of the patients at Whispering Acres flashed before my eyes.

A realization came over me, like a sudden chill, spreading across my shoulders, through my chest and down into my gut. After another wave of chills, a general sense of nausea set in, and a cold sweat broke out on my forehead.

The ringing in my ears resurfaced with increasing intensity, rising and lowering in pitch, becoming more of a scream than a ringing sound. It took on the resonance of an unnerving, muted cry, which then became a full-throated shriek.

Time seemed to stop, silencing all sound, except that of the horrible shrieking, which, though deafening in its intensity, seemed muffled, as if coming from behind a padded door. It was like the battle cry of some hellish demon about to tear me apart.

It was truth: the truth of who I was, my nature, my life. I had seen the discrepancies, the changing story about my father, my absence from my mother's college pictures, my naturalization papers dated only nine years earlier. I had been hearing things, seeing things. There had been so many signs. Had I simply chosen to ignore them? Was it because everything in my life was coming together for me? My dreams were coming true: college, research, even a girlfriend.

The more apparent the truth became, the more I pushed it away. I had only been with my mother nine years, not seventeen. I was not there during college. The story of my adoption was fake. I was not who I was led to believe I was. I didn't want the truth. *Give me back the lie!*

But truth continued its relentless advance, closing in on me from all sides, as though I were in a vacuum and the walls were falling in on me. I feared it. I looked to my mother for help, but she gave me none. She spoke with a gentle deliberateness as though nonchalantly about to open the padded door and release the shrieking demon into my head.

"Haven't you ever wondered where the other primordium was?" she asked quietly, tears now running from her eyes, those steel-gray eyes, always so cool, always barring the path to truth, concealing the pain and mysteries of the past, now flooded with tears—a torrential release of the secret they had held fast for over nine years, the secret that was me. "You know there are always two: both a female and..."

"No!" I cried. "Stop!"

"You need to know," she said gently.

"No! Don't you dare!" I snapped, trying to stifle the shrieking in my head and the tears welling in my eyes.

"You need to..."

"Don't do this!" I sobbed. "Don't do this to me!"

PART III

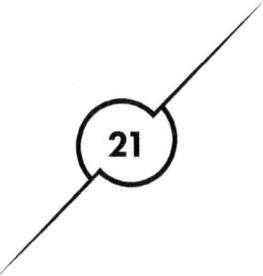

THE CURE FOR STRESS

I spent the next three days in my room, the curtains drawn and the door closed. Despite my mother's pleas for me to come to work with her, I remained in bed, sleeping most of the time. Sleep was the only respite I had from the oppressive realization of who and what I was. Like Eve, I was technically only nine years old. However, also like Eve, I had quickly matured to the equivalent of an eight-year-old in the first month of life. My memories of early childhood were only snippets because that period of my life really was just snippets.

I had come to understand what the ringing and the whispering sounds were. Imagine not being able to filter out the millions of nerve impulses that arrive at your brain on a continual basis. If you were aware of every point of pressure on your skin, every sound, every smell, the position of every part of your body, no matter how insignificant, your mind would be completely overwhelmed. It is only by prioritizing and filtering out some ninety-nine percent of those impulses that we can function. Somehow, that hypnotic experience with Eve had flipped a switch in me, turning on this increased awareness of my senses, including some extraordinary ones I never knew I had.

The ringing was an overflow of background noise that most brains would normally filter out. The whispers were actually conversations of people some fifty feet or more away from me; the shapes, infrared images of people and animals around me.

The reality of it all overwhelmed me—I was the other primordium, the male twin of the monster, the sibling of the thing that had so revolted me I could barely stand to look at it. It—she—was my sister. Over the past three days, my mother had explained it all to me. Eve and I had begun, like all the other primordia, as one. In cocoon form, we then divided into two—male and female—but my mother did not realize what this separation was. When my half developed into what appeared to be a normal baby boy, my mother took me and hid me, thinking the other half was simply a mass of primordial cells, not another baby. Stone came by later that day to see the progress with the research, and saw only Eve's primordial cocoon. Although he was disgusted with the cocoon's appearance, he had my mother begin the experiments anyway. They began with several rounds of radiation to cause cancer with the intention of stimulating an evolutionary adaptation—the cure. That much was a success; the cells that would make the cancer serum were harvested shortly thereafter. But then, the cocoon went on to develop into a baby girl, and the other effects of the radiation became evident: the fibrosis of her eye muscles and the extra vertebrae in her neck.

I had not received any radiation and so was spared the owl eyes, but we both shared the earlier adaptations from the reversion to the primordial form. I could sense infrared though I'd never understood what those oval shapes in the dark were. My skin had the ability to camouflage itself, though the ability had remained dormant until I was an adolescent, and then only in situations when I was especially frightened. That was why my mother was so startled when she came into my room that morning weeks before. She had seen me in a camouflaged state. It was not clear yet whether I had any of Eve's hypnotic ability. My mother tended to think I did not.

As horrible as the prospect of being a schizophrenic had been to me, this was much worse. There were many people with schizophrenia in the world with whom I could commiserate. There was only one other human primordium in the world, and I did not feel capable of commiserating with her. I sat in my room and stared into the darkness.

Within the blackness, I saw an oval shape hovering against my wall. I assessed it fearlessly, with only mild curiosity. I knew now that it was not the primordium, nor my imagination, nor a psychotic delusion. It was simply my hyper-acute perception. Looking at the oval, I concentrated on separating its shape from the other vague shapes I could make out in the dim light. When I closed my eyes, the oval shape remained.

Soon it began to move, sliding along the wall toward my door. The door opened, and my mother stood in the doorway. This time, there was no surprise, no startled rising to the edge of my bed. I had seen her coming. I closed my eyes again and turned my head away from the door. Even with my eyes closed and my head turned, I sensed her presence. I could *see* the oval shape behind me. I strained to see details in the infrared image, which seemed to move slightly.

"Noah?" my mother pleaded. "Won't you please come out?"

"I'm learning to see you the way she does."

"You could learn better from her directly. Why don't you come with me today?"

"You want me to become her apprentice?" I scoffed.

"I'd be happy if you did anything besides sit in this room," my mother rebutted. "Come on. Your car's fixed; we can pick it up on the way."

"Fair enough."

I felt none of the enthusiasm I used to feel about going to work at Pridapt. How would I ever fulfill that dream of earning a PhD and returning to Pridapt as a researcher, when I couldn't see myself as anything but a freak? Then again, I couldn't stay in my room forever, so I went to work that day.

When we arrived at the Pridapt lobby, the security guard had messages for me.

"Mr. Bolton, a Miss Zoe came by two... no, three times for you. She's come just about every day; left her phone number each time too. She's also called here some six or seven times." He handed me the little stack of notes with her phone number on them. "Call her back, will you? We're running out of note paper here."

My mother looked at me with one of those looks that seemed to speak volumes but was completely incomprehensible to me. I had no intention of calling Zoe back that day. I was not up to the task of explaining what I was to her yet. It was enough that I had gone outdoors.

My mother was heading straight for the East Wing

without even giving me a few moments in my lab to acclimate. As we passed Dr. Strauss's office, he called out to us.

"Noah! Annette!" He raced out of his office to intercept us, his white forelock bounding with each stride. "We missed you this week at Whispering Acres, Noah. Are you feeling better?"

After I stared blankly at Dr. Strauss for a few moments, my mother broke the silence.

"I told Dr. Strauss how you've been feeling under the weather," she explained to me, then looking at Dr. Strauss added, "Sometimes these flus can really hang on."

"They sure can," Dr. Strauss agreed, and I nodded, eager to avoid any discussion of the real reason for my seclusion. "Carter has been asking for you," he mentioned to me. "You'll join us next week?"

"Sure," I replied, now realizing that I had much more in common with the patients at Whispering Acres than I had previously imagined.

"Annette," Dr. Strauss said in a hushed voice, "has Dave spoken with you yet?"

Dave! For the past three days I had all but forgotten about my mentor and father figure. He never even knew about Eve. *What would he think if he discovered the truth about me?*

"Spoken to me about what?" my mother asked.

Dr. Strauss glanced awkwardly at me, then back at my mother.

"It's okay; he can hear anything you have to say," my mother clarified. What could be worse than what I had already heard?

"The vaccine alternatives are not going to be pursued."

"What do you mean? I just sent that data over yesterday!" my mother protested.

"They're burying your data," Dr. Strauss whispered, then moved closer to my mother and added, "Look for it in the system. You'll see. It's gone."

For a brief moment, a worried look flashed across my mother's face, then it passed. "Let me check," she said with renewed confidence. "I'm sure it's just been put into some other folder."

"There's more," Dr. Strauss breathed, and with the motionless face of a ventriloquist, continued, "Stone has said we need more experiments, something to do with stress and aging. The experiments would be based on a human adult. Now, I'm the chairman of the ethics committee, and I haven't seen anything about proposed stress or aging experiments on human subjects. I asked about it as soon as I heard, but I'm not getting any answers."

My mother seemed to be staring through him. "What type of experiments, did you say?" she asked.

"Stress and aging," he answered. "When you're talking about stressing a human subject, that must be run by an ethics committee. I'm not at all comfortable with their track record on safeguarding human subjects, as you know, Annette."

My mother still had a distant look in her eye as she thanked him for the information.

"I'm meeting with Stone later today," Dr. Strauss continued. "If I don't get some answers, I may have to go to the press."

Surprisingly, my mother said nothing in reply. I would have expected her to admonish him for his alarmist thinking. Instead, she simply nodded and said she would also have to talk to Mr. Stone.

"Look for your data, Annette," he added, barely above a whisper. "I'm telling you, it's gone."

As we approached the East Wing doors, I asked my mother about Dr. Strauss's concerns.

"What data was he talking about?"

"The data from our work on the vaccine alternatives," she explained. "We found a way to make the vaccines effective without inserting genes. It's worked on mice, so it looks very promising for humans. It will take some time to get through the trials again, but at least the protocol will be ready in time."

"In time for what?"

"The next deadline of course: this year's cure."

"These alternatives, they don't insert the primordium's... Eve's genes?"

"Correct."

"Well, that's good, right? Why did Dr. Strauss think it was being buried?"

"I hope he's wrong about that. I told you, he always anticipates the worst-case scenario. One could imagine the data being buried to protect profits since the compounds used for the vaccine alternative are not patentable. But that would be totally unethical. I can't imagine that happening."

"Profits? Wouldn't we still make money off the alternative?"

"So would everyone else. Without a patent, other labs could easily figure out our formula and compete with us."

Remembering how stunned my mother looked when Dr. Strauss mentioned a treatment for stress, I asked, "What was that about stress experiments?"

"We have no serum to treat stress," she replied. "Our initial experiments led to a cancer serum and a diabetes serum. That's it. I'm concerned that he may be thinking of stimulating more adaptations."

"Stimulating? You mean, in the... in Eve?" I asked. My mother nodded. "What will they do to her? Doesn't there have to be a review, like Dr. Strauss said? Doesn't some committee have to okay research on people?"

"Technically, she's not a person. She's an *it* as far as Mr. Stone is concerned."

I felt a flash of indignant anger rising in me. *How dare he?* Even though I had held the same view of her just days earlier, I would never have considered experimenting on her. At least, I hoped I would not have. "He has no right," I said, looking for further affirmation from my mother.

"We don't know what the plans are yet," she said, "but..." She stared across the hallway.

"Are we going in?" I asked. She swiped her card, and we passed through the outer room and sat at the table in front of Eve's habitat. I searched for her with an entirely new perspective. We were twins. The word kept repeating in my mind.

I remembered my first views of Eve as she scurried along the ceiling beam like a squirrel on a telephone wire. If my mother hadn't hidden me, I would have had the same deformities, the same monstrous appearance. As I slowly scanned the habitat, she appeared, sitting in a chair along the side wall. I looked at her again but this time felt no revulsion and saw no deformity. After days of wallowing in self-pity, I now only felt pity for her. *That would have been me,* I thought. I could see myself there, in the monster. For the first time, I saw the depth of her pain, her struggle, her burden.

She looked at me differently, too, without the hypnotic stare. I glanced back and forth between my mother and Eve.

"You can't let him," I blurted out. My mother turned to me with a genuine look of surprise. "You can't let him do it! You have to stop him."

My mother smiled for the first time in days. "*We'll* have to stop him," she said, putting her arm around me and pulling me in for a hug.

COLLATERAL DAMAGE

M y mind was racing. *What are we going to do? How do we protect her? What do we say? How would we stop him? What if Mr. Stone's coming in here right now?*

I glanced at my mother who was busy typing on a computer keyboard and scrolling through files.

She's not ready. We're sitting ducks in here, I thought. He could open that door at any second and we would be caught completely unprepared. He could be marching up to the door at that moment, his enormous hand about to swipe his card. My nerves were on edge anticipating that swiping sound, when I realized that there was no one outside the door. In fact, there was no one anywhere near the East Wing doors. I could see through walls!

Fear and panic released their hold on me. My fluttering pulse rate slowed, and I stood guard with my back to the door, facing my mother. It was like I had eyes in the back of my head! Things were going to be okay. We could get the upper hand in all this. Maybe there was a silver lining in my condition after all.

Wait! What if it's already begun? I thought, my heart pounding once again. *What if there's something in Eve's food and water? What if it's too late?*

"Where's her food?" I blurted out as I nervously paced the length of the outer room.

My mother did not reply.

"What about the food?" I asked again. "They could be putting something in there to stress her." *Was she even listening?*

"I bring in all her supplies," my mother replied despondently. She had stopped scrolling through files. "It's gone," she muttered. Swiveling her chair around toward me, she repeated, "It's gone!"

"The vaccine alternative?"

"The whole folder is gone and the data with it!" she groaned. Bolting out of her chair, she pulled a small drive out of the side of the computer and handed it to me. "Keep this safe. I have a copy too. I'm going to talk to Mr. Stone about this right now!"

"What's on this drive?"

"My notes, an explanation of the research data that's missing, and as many details of the work as I could remember."

"What will you do if they've deleted the data?"

"I'll give Mr. Stone a chance to show me where the data is, and clarify what he means by, 'additional experiments.' If what Dr. Strauss said turns out to be true," she paused, looking back toward the habitat, "then we do whatever it takes to make things right."

I liked the sound of that, and my mother's newfound rebelliousness. "I'll go with you," I suggested.

"Come on," she agreed, "but you stay out in the hall. It won't take me long to get to the bottom of this."

I was a little disappointed at missing this bold confrontation, but then realized that I would be able to hear and see the whole thing through the walls.

As we drew near to Mr. Stone's office, I tried to focus on my infrared perception of the room. There was a person sitting at a desk by the door, then two more people standing farther away from them. I assumed that was Mr. Stone's inner office. My mother entered the front room and greeted Mr. Stone's secretary.

"I need to see Mr. Stone," I heard her announce, just as the glass door swung shut. I turned my attention away from the level of sound that would normally occupy my mind and centered instead on the background noise. The more I concentrated on it, the clearer it became. Buzzing became ringing, which became whispering, which then settled into distinct words.

"I told her you're not in," I heard the secretary say. Below this was another layer of sound, farther away and with lower frequency. It was Mr. Stone's voice. He was in his office, speaking to the secretary on the phone.

"Tell her she may speak to my assistant. He'll be out momentarily."

I watched the two shapes in the back room separate and one come out to the front room by the secretary and my mother.

"Yes, Dr. Bolton?" I heard the assistant ask.

"I need to see the data I had transmitted to the secure server," my mother explained, "but when I looked for it, it had been moved. Where can I find it?"

"I'm afraid that is something only Mr. Stone can discuss with you, and he's not here," he said.

"I'll wait. When are you expecting him?"

"He won't be in today."

"What time tomorrow can he meet with me?"

"I couldn't say."

"I'm not leaving until you give me an appointment with

Mr. Stone," my mother insisted.

After a short silence, the assistant looked at the secretary's desk, then he said, "Why, certainly, Dr. Bolton, we can arrange something. Sue, give Dr. Bolton an appointment for tomorrow afternoon at two o'clock." My mother thanked them, then met me in the hall.

"It was Mr. Stone's assistant," my mother grumbled. "He was stalling."

"Totally," I agreed. "Stone was in there."

"Where?"

"In his office. I saw him. He sent the other guy out. I heard them talking to the secretary. He told her exactly what to say."

"You saw him? You mean with infrared? And you heard?"

"Yes. I'm getting good at it."

She grinned and put a hand on my shoulder. "You're a quick study."

"What are you going to do?" I asked her.

"I don't know. I'd like to talk to Dr. Strauss again. He should be in the cafeteria right now. He always takes his lunch at eleven forty-five. He's very punctual that way."

As the dining area came into view, I stopped momentarily, looking up and down the hall to make sure we were alone.

"So why can't you just publish it yourself?" I asked.

"I only have my notes, not the raw data, but I'm thinking that would be better than nothing. If Mr. Stone refuses to publish it, maybe my threat to release what I do have would convince him otherwise."

"Sounds like a plan," I whispered as we entered the cafeteria. There was an odd silence in the normally hectic dining area, with a circle of people standing around something and pointing. Even the display chefs were staring across their counters at the commotion.

"What's going on?" I asked a woman who cast a worried glance at the crowd.

"He choked on something. It's terrible." She sobbed, wiping tears from her eyes. "He was waving for help. I tried, but I didn't know what to do. They're doing CPR now. It's terrible."

We rushed to the edge of the crowd and pushed through the circle of gaping employees. Two men were kneeling on the floor trying to resuscitate the victim.

"Has anyone called 911?" one of the men asked as he straightened up, exposing the man lying prone beneath him. It was Dr. Strauss!

"They're on their way," an answer came from behind us. I instinctively dove in alongside the men, staring in disbelief at Dr. Strauss's ashen face, his white mane lying motionless across his forehead, his eyes open and opaque.

I was desperate to help, but like the tearful woman we had just seen, I didn't know what to do.

"What happened?" I cried out, looking at the table for any sign of what he might have choked on. There was nothing but a Styrofoam cup of coffee. "How do you choke on coffee?"

"Went down the wrong way," one of the men suggested. "He's in spasm now. We can't get any air into his lungs."

"You have to do something!" I insisted. The crowd parted to allow a team of paramedics through.

As I stood up with the people who had been trying to revive Dr. Strauss, I noticed something. "Do you smell that?" I asked.

"Smell what?"

"In the coffee," I thought out loud, leaning over the table to get closer to Dr. Strauss's cup.

"Flavored coffee?" the man suggested.

He hates flavored coffee! I remembered. *Why would he...* I suddenly recognized the smell. It was nutmeg! I stumbled away from the scene and stood frozen, afraid to speak. My mother, too, was petrified, staring with a look of wide-eyed horror at Dr. Strauss's face. His jaws were clamped shut, his cheek muscles twitching. I could tell that she knew what I knew.

It was the toxin, the one they had developed from the

reptile primordium. It had the distinctive smell of nutmeg and worked by creating an instant sort of tetanus, a tight spasm of all the muscles it came in contact with. Sprayed into the face, it caused a spasm of the jaws and facial muscles. Swallowed, it rendered one unable to talk or breathe.

I pushed my way over to my mother and whispered into her ear, "What's the antidote?"

"There is none," she breathed back, gripping my forearm and leading me swiftly through the crowd and out of the cafeteria.

Out of the corner of my eye I saw two of Stone's security men standing against the wall, calm and still, as if nothing extraordinary were going on. I glanced at them and immediately turned away.

"They're watching us," I gasped.

"Just walk with me." My mother and I walked briskly out the front door to the parking lot. Once outside, she called Dave. "Meet me in the parking lot," was all she said.

While I would have no reason to doubt Dave's loyalty, having always thought of him as a father figure, I was suspicious of just about everyone at that moment. "Are you sure you can trust him?" I asked. Surprisingly, she didn't answer.

"I don't know who we can trust," she said finally, as Dave was coming out of the lobby, "but we have to tell someone. Give that drive to your blogger friend. Have him get the word out. I'm going to speak with someone in San Francisco, at an office for whistleblowers."

"Annette," Dave called out to us, smiling with a fore-head-full of folds. "What's up?"

"Strauss is dead."

"What?" he gasped, his forehead suddenly smooth and still.

"He said he was going to go to the press with some of his concerns," my mother explained.

"He was always saying that."

"Well, someone took his threat seriously this time. He was poisoned." She described the scene in the cafeteria, the unlikely scenario of Dr. Strauss choking to death on coffee, the uninterested security guards, the muscle spasms, and the telltale smell of nutmeg.

"Nutmeg? The reptile toxin?" Dave asked. "But, that's locked up somewhere. No one except the administration has access. You're saying the company murdered him!"

"Of course she is," I shot out.

"That's some accusation," Dave countered. "Are you absolutely certain? I mean, can you prove it?"

"You know we can't prove it," my mother retorted. "There's no test for this toxin. It's unknown to anyone else in the world."

Dave considered this point, glanced back and forth from my mother to me, then said, "Okay, what do you want me to do?"

"Nothing," my mother replied. "Just copy any files you have and keep them safe. I wanted to make sure you knew what had happened, just in case."

"In case what?"

My mother looked at me and took my arm. "I'll be back later. I still have some unfinished work to do."

We walked briskly to the parking lot, then my mother left to go downtown. I contacted Isaac and asked him to meet me at a highway rest stop we were both familiar with. Always on the hunt for scandalous news, Isaac was happy to comply.

I arrived first, leaving my newly repaired car at the end of the parking area, and scanned a wooded picnic area for any sign of spying eyes or ears. I sat at a wooden table near the periphery and focused intently on any and all infrared shapes around me. Before long, an oval shape became apparent to me, approaching on the grass. Even before I could make him out with my eyes, I recognized Isaac's gait in the motion of the infrared shape.

I waved and called out to him. After he joined me at the table, I asked, "How did you know to look over here?"

"I found you with my GPS," he explained.

A bolt of fear shot through me as I realized I was not as hidden as I had thought.

"What do you mean?"

"I could find you based on your last call to me. See?" He showed me the function on his phone.

"Can anyone do that?"

"Only friends, but it depends on your settings. Sometimes the default setting is to make everyone a friend."

I quickly pulled out my phone and fumbled with the settings.

"Here, let me look at it," Isaac offered. "It looks like your location settings are turned on for everything and everyone. Do you want that?"

"No! Not if it means everyone can find me."

Isaac made the necessary changes on my phone, then handed it back to me. "There you go. Though they say," Isaac leaned in to me, speaking more softly, "that your microphone and camera can be used remotely by someone else, even when your phone is switched off."

"Really?" I stood up and motioned to Isaac to follow me to my car. I tossed my phone onto the floor of the car and asked Isaac to do the same. We then returned to the picnic table. After sitting there for a few moments, Isaac broke the silence.

"So, who's trying to find you?"

The question made me focus on the background images around us, ensuring that there were no new shapes approaching. "I need your help, Isaac."

"Is it an ex-girlfriend?" he jabbed.

"It's about Pridapt." I pulled the small drive out of my pocket. "Things aren't what they seem. There's corruption, a cover-up of important research, and even..." I looked again around the picnic area. "There's a doctor who was threatening to go to the press with this information, Dr. Joseph Strauss." I handed Isaac the drive.

"Dr. Joseph Strauss, okay," Isaac said, jotting down the name.

"He was murdered this morning."

"Murdered?"

"They'll brush it off as a tragic accident, but my mother and I were there. We recognized the toxin used. It was from a primordial reptile. A reptile that either never existed or hasn't existed for millions of years."

"Messing with extinct species! See? This is what we were afraid of!" Isaac exclaimed.

"And that's nothing compared to what's behind the miracle cures. The notes on this drive describe research that found a natural replacement for the cancer vaccines, one that would avoid the use of retroviruses and gene splicing. Now, that research has been buried just to protect the profits from the vaccines. Here, take it," I said, giving him the computer drive. "Get it out there. Don't say where you got it or heard it. Just start a rumor; get people talking. Then maybe they'll start asking the right questions. Can you do that?"

"You better believe it!"

We worked out some code words and phrases we would use when communicating by text or online, and chose that rest stop as our emergency meeting location.

"Be careful," I warned as we stood up to leave. "Don't make yourself a target. Remember, they've already killed one of their own!"

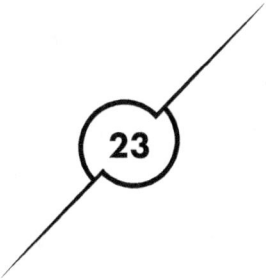

THE TRIPLE CROWN

I returned home and parked a good distance away from our place. Sitting on the curb at one end of our condominium complex, I worked on fine-tuning my infrared perception. As I stared across the lawn in front of me, it soon faded into a blurred sea of green, through which I could make out small ovals of infrared throughout the complex. Keeping myself in that frame of mind, I walked toward our front door. Only when I was certain that there were no infrared shapes inside did I dare to enter.

Once inside, I locked the door, and as I was checking behind the curtains for the third time, I began to feel pretty silly. Just because Isaac had tracked me down didn't mean anyone at Pridapt would be doing the same. They had gone after Dr. Strauss because he threatened to go to the press. Why would they be tracking me? While it didn't hurt to be cautious, there was no need to overreact, either.

Having reached this conclusion and let down my guard, I became aware of an infrared image coming toward the front door. With little time to react, I instinctively ran to hide, discovering that there weren't many good hiding places in our little place. As the front door opened, I slipped into the hall closet. The infrared shape might have been my mother's, though I couldn't be sure until I'd seen her. I peered down the hallway through the vertical slit of light along the edge of the door, the ringing in my ears becoming louder as I strained to hear any conversation. Then, the infrared form turned the corner, and I saw clearly that it was, indeed, my mother.

"It's you," I sighed, nonchalantly opening the closet door. My mother screamed and jumped backward. "Oh sorry," I apologized. "Did I scare you?"

"Of course you did! Why were you in the closet?"

"I thought maybe they were following me."

"Who?"

"Whoever killed Dr. Strauss."

My mother seemed surprised by my answer. "They know where we live, but I doubt that they would ever come here," my mother reassured me. "Although..."

"What?"

"Something strange happened when I was in the city," she explained. "I met with a federal worker who processes whistle-blower cases. At first, she was very interested in what I had to say. I didn't accuse anyone of murder, but I did mention the possibility of stolen data which could impact public health. She wrote everything down and left to get another form for processing. But when she returned, the phone rang, and after speaking with someone on the other end, she was very different. Suddenly, she was not interested in more information about the data I was referring to, just more information about me. They asked where I would be the rest of the day and where I would be tomorrow. I think Mr. Stone must have gotten to someone in the agency."

"It's because you went to Stone's office this morning, demanding to see the data," I suggested. "They suspected you might tell someone about it."

"But why think of a federal office instead of the press, like Dr. Strauss was threatening?"

"Let me see your phone." I took my mother's phone and scrolled through her settings, modifying the privacy settings for the GPS.

"Where did you learn all this?" she asked me.

"Isaac showed me earlier today. He found me just by

tracking my phone location after I had called him. Both our phones are company phones, right?"

"Of course."

"I think they tracked your phone. That's how they knew where you had gone. Mr. Stone must have connections everywhere, so he knew the right person to call to intervene. We need to get out of here and away from our phones."

My mother hesitated. "I thought you just turned that off."

"Isaac says even with the phone turned completely off, it can still be tracked. Leave it."

"I need my phone at work," my mother explained. "Mr. Stone calls me on it all the time."

"Then we'll take our phones to the lab and leave them there."

After grabbing a few things, we prepared to leave.

"What about Eve?" I asked, beginning to panic once more about Mr. Stone going to the East Wing.

"She knows to hide when it's not me entering, and she can get out undetected through the woods," my mother reassured me. "But, we should fill her in on what's going on."

When we returned to Pridapt, we passed through the lobby and by security without incident. Once in the East Wing, I stood guard in the front room, using my infrared senses, while my mother spoke with Eve in the habitat.

"We're good," my mother announced as she joined me in the outer room, "Eve will be extra cautious."

"Excellent! The coast is clear," I assured her, after scanning for any infrared shapes in the halls around us. "Let's leave our phones in here," I suggested.

"Okay, but wait, what if you need to get in?" My mother quickly jotted down something on a piece of paper and pressed it into my hand.

561947—I recognized her code immediately.

"What's this?" I asked awkwardly.

"It's my passcode; you can use it on the door's keypads."

I feigned a nod of thanks. My old guilt about stealing the code resurfaced briefly, but was quickly replaced with relief, now that she had freely shared it with me.

We made our way back to the lobby and were just passing the security desk when I heard my name ring out.

"Noah!"

My mother grabbed my hand, and the two of us rapidly scanned the area.

"Noah! Where have you been?"

Then I recognized the voice—it was Zoe's. Unlike the cheerful cooing I'd been graced with the last time I'd seen her, the day she'd referred to me as her boyfriend, this had the shrill tone of irate censure which was turning the heads of everyone around us.

"She has to do this now?" my mother murmured. "Take her outside. Keep her quiet!"

I hurried to meet Zoe and tried to direct her toward the front door, but she had planted herself firmly before me and was not moving.

"A week?" she began her denunciation. "A whole week you don't return my calls?"

"It's been a crazy week," I hastened to explain, again, trying to move to the door.

"No, I'll tell you what's crazy is you ignoring me. What's up with the diabetes thing? My mother is on me every day."

"Oh, things are kind of on hold right now," I explained.

"On hold?"

"Let's talk outside."

"On hold? You know what? Forget it. Forget everything! I'm done. Goodbye!"

She finished the broadcast of our relationship termination by spinning on her heels and marching out the front door. Seeing nothing but a typical scene of adolescent melodrama, the curious around us, including the security guards, smiled and turned away. I moved swiftly over to my mother, and we exited quietly.

Thinking of Zoe's tirade, I was struck by my lack of emotion. If I felt anything, it was relief. *Now I don't have to tell her.*

With our phones stored in the East Wing, we would need a new way to communicate. We stopped at a discount store and picked up two new phones with prepaid data and minutes. Just off the highway, down the road from Pridapt, we rented a hotel room and settled in for the evening. On the news that night, there were breaking stories about Pridapt. Apparently, Isaac had wasted no time in getting the word out online. A master at capturing the hottest keywords in online newswires, he had managed to tie together the report of an unusual death at Pridapt with a cover-up of medical risks and data tampering. His posts were being picked up everywhere. "Profits Before Patient Safety," was the most common headline, and a commonly reposted story was, "Death by Coffee... or Poison?" Dr. Strauss was referred to by name as the person who leaked the information just prior to his death.

The next morning, we found that the story had continued to snowball, with talks of protests against Pridapt around the country. Isaac had also leaked allegations that a novel animal species had been developed despite the moratorium. Isaac couldn't resist starting this rumor after hearing from us about the reptile venom. He didn't link Dr. Strauss's murder to the new reptile, but instead implied that this novel life form had something to do with the cancer vaccines. He must have felt that such a suggestion would be frightening enough to warrant further investigation, and it appeared that he was right.

Mr. Stone was being interrogated by the attorney general that very morning. While he had not been officially charged, the press was told that he was being questioned regarding allegations of impropriety and the suspicious death of Dr. Strauss. Later that morning, congressmen and senators arrived and joined the investigation, announcing that they had found some new information. We were certain this meant that they had retrieved the buried research regarding the safer vaccine alternative.

These events filled us with confidence, so we decided to go to work as usual that day, though we still left our new phones in our cars. At the security desk, we passed Daniel Smith, the guard who had caught me with Isaac and Zoe in the habitat weeks earlier.

"Morning Daniel," my mother greeted him.

"Morning Dr. Bolton."

"If Mr. Stone comes back, do you suppose..." I began speaking to my mother.

"If?" Daniel's voice boomed from behind us. "If you say, 'if,' you don't know Mr. Stone. It's not 'if,' it's 'when,'" he clarified.

"Right," I agreed with a forced smile. The thought was unnerving. Since Mr. Stone knew my mother had gone to that federal office, what would he do if he came back? *He won't come back,* I thought.

But he did come back, that very day!

After I had spent an hour in my lab, and my mother had checked on Eve, we were back in the lobby feeling light-hearted, when Mr. Stone walked through the front doors. Flanked by his security team, he stood below a lobby television screen which displayed a news clip of the attorney general speaking.

"Turn that up," Mr. Stone called out to Daniel Smith at the front desk who promptly complied, then turned to wink at my mother and me.

"We will find this terrorist," the attorney general was announcing to the reporters. "It is only a matter of time."

Terrorist? I wondered.

We discovered that the new information the attorney general had obtained was not the deleted research, but information that led them to consider Isaac a domestic terrorist. They were now charging Isaac with espionage and cyber-crimes because some of the information he had released, it seemed, could only have been obtained by hacking into Pridapt's computer system. The charges leveled against Isaac, usually reserved for genuine national-level security breaches, were severe. If convicted, he would face life in prison without parole.

"I'll have to tell them," my mother whispered. "I can't let him take the fall for this. I'll have to tell them I leaked the information."

I stared at my mother in disbelief. "No! You can't! Stone will be hot enough about you going to that federal office. If you admit to this, they'll charge you. They'll make you out to be a terrorist!"

"Better me than him. Maybe I can convince them of the truth."

"No, just wait," I insisted. "I can talk to Isaac, tell him to back off, stop posting. No one knows who he really is; he's always kept that a secret."

"No one knows?" my mother jeered. "Someone always knows. As the attorney general said, it's only a matter of time."

"Then we use that time to our advantage. As long as he's at large," I whispered, "we remain quiet." My mother nodded her head slowly.

"As long as he is at large," she affirmed.

"If he's taken," I added, "then, yes, you have to come forward, and so do I."

"What? No!"

"Yes. If the truth is to come out, all of it must come out."

"No, if anything happens to me, you have to take care of Eve..."

"It's all or nothing," I insisted. I knew the prospect of me being taken with her would make her postpone any inclination toward self-sacrifice.

While we were standing off to the side, a small crowd had formed around Mr. Stone at the front of the lobby. After a round of applause, Mr. Stone emerged with his security team beside him. He cast a sideways glance toward us as he walked past.

"Annette," he uttered briefly, not breaking his stride.

He said nothing more to either of us, not that day nor the following two days. We came to work and carried out our normal tasks, but we watched our surroundings constantly. We stayed at the hotel and brought in our own food and drink.

Mr. Stone implemented stricter security measures, requiring all employees and visitors to go through metal detectors and hand over their phones and other electronic devices to be examined. We continued to leave our company phones in the lab, and our new phones in our cars.

Three days passed, and despite the attorney general's best efforts, Isaac remained at large. Mr. Stone referred to him daily as the "terrorist trying to undermine our healthcare system."

In every news story, every opinion piece, every proposition, there was fear—fear of disease, of cancer, of suffering, and of dying, and above all, the fear of this cyberattacker who threatened to close off the only way out, the only answer: the miraculous cures from Pridapt. This online blogger's motivation was portrayed as hatred of the lower class, a desire to limit access to these cures to the rich and powerful. As the ensuing hatred for the unknown blogger rose, so did the country's fear and insecurity, but on the evening news, there was salvation: Mr. Stone, standing in front of the Pridapt sign. He was the way, the truth, the salvation for all. There was no other way.

There was even talk of a bill outlawing homeschooling. For children not to receive the state-of-the-art vaccinations would be tantamount to child abuse, abuse that could slip through the cracks when children were not monitored in the public schools. All opposition to the rapid and universal execution of Pridapt's initiatives was seen by nearly everyone as an act of domestic terrorism.

The media, the police, the politicians, even religious leaders eagerly supported Stone's cause and just as eagerly demonized Isaac. He was characterized as an uncaring, wealthy elite, looking to eliminate the poor by depriving them of the readily accessible cures for life-threatening diseases.

Stone had done it. In a matter of days, he had mastered the spirited horse of bad publicity that had begun to sweep the nation, threatening to destroy him and crush Pridapt, and instead, he had reined it in and redirected its clamorous hooves, hooves that were now ready to trample anyone who might get in his way. The thunder of those hooves could be heard in all sectors of the country. At this point, to take a stand against Mr. Stone would be to stand alone, with no place to hide.

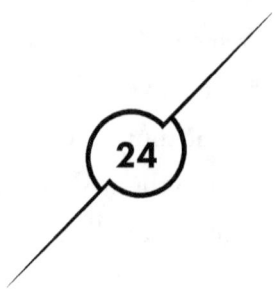

HIDDEN POWER

With all this going on, the East Wing was one of the safest places at Pridapt for my mother and me to talk. Due to the secret nature of the human primordium experiment—Eve's and my beginnings—the central computers had kept no record of it, no audio nor video surveillance of any kind, other than the notes and videos that my mother had made. That could not be said for any other area in the Pridapt complex.

We were sitting in Eve's indoor habitat, a place that only recently had been quite terrifying to me. It was now my safe haven.

"We can't be afraid," my mother explained. "Stone uses fear; it's the only weapon he's got."

"Well, he's awfully good at it. It gives him his power," I noted. "He controls people: the politicians, the media... all he had to do was make a phone call to that office you went to, and you became the suspect, not him."

"He's holding all the cards," my mother lamented.

"Not all of them," I suggested. "He's not the only one who can use fear." I looked at Eve, who was sitting silently across from us.

"I won't have her made a spectacle," my mother snapped at me.

"Nor would I. That's not what I'm thinking."

"What are you thinking?"

"I have an idea, but I need help," I explained, looking back at Eve. Although I had become aware of some hyper-acute senses I had never before appreciated, they were generally undeveloped. Eve was a master at them.

My sense of hearing and infrared perception had become more refined, but my camouflage ability was more like the unnatural skin mottling of the patients at Whispering Acres. It was at best an involuntary reflex.

I walked over and sat beside Eve. While I had come to see her in a totally new light, I had not yet spoken with her. I felt incredibly self-conscious and awkward.

"So," I mumbled, "I guess we're brother and sister. Sorry about before... the things I said."

Eve seemed to show no surprise at our being siblings.

Had she known I was her brother? I felt resentment surfacing. The thought that she had been told while I had not been seemed unfair. As the emotion stirred within me, I looked at her long neck and owl eyes, framed by the walls of her lifelong prison. Of the two of us, I could hardly be considered the slighted one.

"Sorry I made you see that girl," Eve replied to me. The tone with which she had referred to Zoe as *that girl* broadcast her contempt.

"Don't worry about it," I reassured her. "We've got bigger fish to fry now."

Her confused look demonstrated that she did not understand that phrase.

"It's a figure of speech," I explained. "So, we have to be careful with the people here. You know that right? You know you have to hide if they come in here?"

"Oh, I know," Eve answered. "I can also get to the outside woods and hide. I've seen you there. One time you saw me too, when you were with your funny-looking friend."

"Funny-looking? Who? When did you see me?"

"The one with glasses and curly hair."

"Isaac? Wait, the owl? That was you? That *was* you!" I exclaimed, realizing that the owl eyes I had spotted in the woods weeks ago actually were her eyes!

"Wait, just show me what you would do," I asked. I wanted to go through a dry run with her just to be sure she was ready to escape if necessary. We stood up and headed toward the outer habitat.

"Where are you two going?" my mother asked, coming over to join us.

"We're going to fry big fish," Eve announced.

"Just go with it," I whispered in response to my mother's quizzical look. I walked alongside Eve as we made our way down the path.

"Maybe we can help each other," I suggested. "You're obviously very good at this camouflage thing, and I, well, I can help you on the outside."

Eve reacted with great interest when I made this last suggestion, and it dawned on me that my mother had never broached the subject of her being mainstreamed into society. I glanced at my mother, who confirmed my suspicion with a frown.

"You don't want to stay here forever, do you?" I continued, despite my mother's consternation. "Haven't you ever thought about what was outside those woods?"

"I have." Eve nodded. "You'll show me?" she asked, then looked quickly at my mother.

"I will. We both will," I affirmed, glancing at my mother, who smiled in return. Seeing this, Eve also smiled for the first time that I had ever seen. Looking at her, I began to think that her eyes weren't that off-putting once you got used to them. Maybe, with a pair of glasses and longer hair, she *could* blend in. I felt a bond of affection stirring in me, drawing and binding me to her. *My sister*, I thought. It was a connection, a unity, a love I had never known, yet now knew in an instant. What a powerful influence a smile could have.

The three of us went into the outdoor habitat and sat on one of the benches near the center of the woods. "So, where do we begin?" I asked, looking meekly toward Eve, who seemed to be enjoying the situation. When she merely grinned and said nothing, I shifted my gaze to my mother and then out toward the woods with a sigh. "Quiet time, first, I guess." When I looked back to Eve, she was gone! "I know you're good at it," I complained. "Could you please give me some pointers?" I looked throughout the area around us but could see no sign of her.

I let my eyes drift out of focus, and concentrated on the infrared images around me. My mother's was the most obvious, as she was sitting only a few feet away. But, try as I may, I couldn't sense any other images near us. There were very small ovals: workers on the loading dock alongside the Pridapt building, moving back and forth between the dock and the inside of a truck, but nothing else. I closed my eyes to concentrate harder, but to no avail. With a sigh, I confessed, "I can't see you."

I stopped trying and opened my eyes, only to see Eve's owl eyes a foot away from me as she shrieked into my face. She had been hiding behind my mother's infrared image.

I screamed and fell backward off the concrete bench. Reaching for the edge of the bench, I scraped my forearms on the concrete, flailing to find my own arms, the skin of which now matched the background colors and patterns before me.

I was in camouflage! Moving my arms very slowly, I managed to see their blurry shapes and inched them toward a corner of the bench. Grabbing it, I pulled myself upright.

My mother was laughing more heartily than I thought appropriate, but Eve was not. She stared at me with her serious wide-eyed glare, and said, "Remember this. Remember exactly how you feel."

"Annoyed? Terrified?"

"Forget the fear, and forget what you see. What do you *feel*?" She stressed this last verb as if it were a new and unique sense. As I thought about it, I realized that I did feel something different: a sort of tingling sensation racing along my arms and legs and, like the warm surge of a blush, up into my neck and face. It was like the sensation of goosebumps raising the hairs on your skin.

"I do feel it," I agreed.

"Now, relax and let it go away."

Slowly, I could feel it begin to fade, and I started to see the normal skin of my arms again, but then the feeling quickly returned and my arms disappeared. It was like trying to relax while someone was tickling your toes. I could begin, but then it rushed back.

"Think of being warm, like in warm water," Eve suggested.

That did it. The moment I thought of being enveloped by a warm shower, the camouflage was gone and my arms reappeared. *That's an excellent trick*, I thought.

Now, how would I bring it on when I wanted? Apparently being terrified brought it on, but I couldn't recreate that type of fear at will. Eve explained to me that it was like raising your eyebrows. You do it automatically when you're scared or surprised, but you can learn to do it whenever you want, and you can even train yourself to raise one eyebrow apart from the other. So I could train myself to control my camouflage.

I closed my eyes and tried to relive the tingling sensation I had felt on my arms and legs. At first, there was nothing, but then, slowly, I began to sense a hint of that feeling, then suddenly it flashed across my shoulders and arms. Looking down at my hands, I saw nothing but the ground and a blurry pattern of dirt and leaves that moved when I moved.

Eve taught me how to refine the response, to bring it on and end it at will. Like learning to juggle, ride a bike, or tie my shoes, something that had seemed so difficult suddenly became second nature to me, as automatic as walking, or throwing a ball.

"I'm going to need a tan swimsuit like Eve's," I thought out loud.

"I've already picked up two for you," my mother replied. "They're back inside."

Perfect! I thought. My hair was already short enough to not be a problem. As my confidence grew, my fear began to melt away.

Now how do we use fear against Stone?

"What about hypnosis?" I asked. Eve did not seem to understand me.

"She doesn't know that word," my mother explained. "He means, when you look at someone and touch them, in here." She pointed to her head.

Eve shrugged, then turned to me, saying, "You just look at them."

Well, that wasn't much help. I looked steadily at Eve for a few moments, then noted, "I'm looking at you, and it's not working."

"You think too much," she quipped. "You need to look

into them, like you really want to know them. You have to *want* to see them."

As I struggled to understand the subtlety of that instruction, I was startled by the ringing of my mother's Pridapt phone.

"Hello?" she answered. "Right now? Okay, I'll be there." My mother put away her phone and explained that she had been called into Mr. Stone's office. "You two, keep working," she said.

"We will, but right now, I'm going with you," I insisted. Turning to Eve, I said, "Don't worry, I'll look out for our mother."

"He only asked for me, Noah, not you," my mother warned.

"I didn't say I'd be going in to see Stone with you. I'll be listening from out in the hall like before." My mother agreed, so I grabbed my new swimsuits on the way out, tucked them into my pockets, and we headed over to the CEO's office.

As my mother went in, I leaned against the wall, trying not to look too out of place. *What will I say if someone asks what I'm doing?* I wondered. I would say I was waiting for my mother to come out. I had said that so many times before, no one would think anything of it.

I closed my eyes and concentrated on the conversation

that was taking place behind the walls. I could sense my mother's infrared image entering Stone's office. He was not alone. There were three people in his office waiting for her. My mother sat while the others remained standing.

"Annette," he began, "it looks like things are back on track, wouldn't you say?"

"Well," my mother spoke slowly and deliberately, "except for our data. I'm concerned, Mr. Stone, that it may have been stolen."

"By the hacker, no doubt," Mr. Stone replied, raising his mighty hand and index finger, bobbing them methodically toward her. Even as an infrared image, it was impressive.

"Possibly," my mother acknowledged.

"Well who else could it have been? You don't suspect anyone else, do you, Annette?"

My mother did not reply, but I thought I could see her shaking her head.

"That hacker stole our information and has been spreading lies through his blogs. Don't worry about him though—he'll be caught. They say he's Public Enemy Number One right now!" Stone and his men laughed. "It's not him I'm concerned about."

"No?" my mother asked.

"No. It's our own people. I need to know if one of our own helped him. I need to know who is a loyal team player and who is not. In times like these, we can't afford to have any weak links. Don't you agree, Annette?"

"Of course, sir."

"So, I need someone I can trust. I need you."

"Sir?"

"I need you to do something for me. Can you do something for me, Annette?"

"I can try. What is it?"

"I need you to get some files from a computer in one of the West Wing labs."

"Aren't they accessible from..."

"Not these. They are on a lone computer station. I have reason to doubt the loyalty of the individual using that computer."

"Can't you just go in and ask to see them?"

"If I, as the CEO, walked in there, it would alert this person, and they would most certainly log in with an alias, and I would see none of the suspect information. But if you were to enter the room casually, just to say hello, there would be no cause for suspicion. Then, I could arrange for this researcher to be called out, and you could quickly copy the file I need onto this USB drive." He handed my mother a small portable drive. "The file is called 'Alpha Protocol.' Just copy it and bring the drive back to me."

"Would that be legal?" my mother asked.

"Would I ask you to do something illegal? Every computer in this building is Pridapt property, so of course it is legal."

"Who is the researcher?"

"Dr. David Bernstein."

Dave? I thought I must have heard incorrectly. *What could be on his computer?* Mr. Stone went on to direct my mother to do this thing the next day.

"He's setting you up," I whispered to her when she returned to the hallway. "You know that there can't be anything suspicious on Dave's computer. He's either going to fabricate evidence against Dave and say you discovered it, or he'll frame you as a corporate spy for stealing files off Dave's computer. You can't do it!"

"It's a test," my mother explained. "If I don't do it, he'll consider me disloyal."

"And if you do, he'll have something on you, I'm telling you!"

"How could he prove that I was the one who copied the files?"

"You would be recorded on the surveillance cameras."

"Can't they be turned off or something?"

There's a thought. "I'll bet Isaac could find a way."

"I think he's done enough already." My mother sighed.

"Are you kidding? He'd love it!"

I sent Isaac a brief and cryptic text to meet me that afternoon in the woods by Pridapt. We had devised a system of code words to use in texts and even a method for Isaac to communicate to me through his online posts. If he posted a quote from "The Rag Doll," it meant he was in trouble and would be waiting for me at the highway rest stop where we had met before. I texted him that "The Spotted Owl was back on the endangered species list," which meant I needed to speak with him in the Pridapt woods.

While my mother was finishing up in her office, I was in the redwoods, explaining the situation to Isaac and seeing how he was holding up. He seemed to be enjoying the challenge of secretly uploading his posts from hot spots throughout the Bay area. As I had expected, he jumped at the opportunity to help us. He would come to work with me the next day as my guest, disguised as a fellow high school student.

HYPNOSIS

It was with great pain that Isaac parted with his beard, but it would have raised suspicion to see such facial hair on a high school student. When he met us at Pridapt the following day, the security guard, who was accustomed to my high school friend Zoe visiting, gave Isaac a guest pass without question. We went straight to the East Wing for a secure site to work out our plan.

My mother logged in to her computer then gave Isaac the chair to search for a way to interfere with the security cameras in Dave's lab. It was a little unnerving to see how quickly he was able to access the livestreams from the cameras.

"So what is it you have to do in there?" Isaac asked.

"I need to copy a file from that computer," my mother

answered, pointing to a workstation that Dave was sitting at. "I'll go into the lab, then Dave—that's him right there—he'll be called out to speak with Mr. Stone in the hallway. That's when you need to stop this camera, so I can get to the computer and not be seen."

"I can freeze the image right after he gets up. Then you'll have to let me know when to turn it back on."

"I can do that," I interjected, nodding at my mother. She gave me a confused look, then smiled, realizing what I was referring to. I would be able to sense her infrared image from the East Wing and know when she had left the computer station.

My mother left to tell Mr. Stone she was ready. Isaac kept his eyes focused on Dave, waiting to freeze the image as soon as he stood up from the computer station, and I kept my attention on my mother's infrared image. In my mind, I followed her all the way to Mr. Stone's office, then back with him to Dave's lab. As she entered, Stone remained in the hall, waiting for Dave to come out to meet him.

Dave left his station to see Mr. Stone in the hall as requested. "I'm freezing it now," Isaac reported. I kept concentrating on my mother's image which was now at Dave's computer. "You'll tell me when to unfreeze it, right?"

"I'll let you know," I replied. I watched the images of Mr. Stone and Dave together in the hallway for several minutes until my mother left the computer to join them. "Turn it back on," I told Isaac, and with a few clicks on the keyboard, the video stream was live again, showing no one sitting at the computer. "You did it! Fantastic!"

"No problem. You guys need anything else?"

"Nope. I think all we need to do now is get you out of here." Then I breathed a slight gasp.

"What is it?" Isaac asked.

"They're both coming this way!"

"In here? How do you know?"

Stone wants to get the drive from her in here, where there are no surveillance cameras, I thought. "We have to hide!" I ran to the door leading to Eve's habitat and pulled on the handle, but it was locked. The front door was not an option as Mr. Stone and my mother were now in the hallway leading directly to it.

"Find a cabinet or drawer that's open," I whispered to Isaac.

"Why are we whispering? Are they that close?" Isaac asked. They were far enough away that they couldn't hear us, but since I could hear them, I felt it necessary to whisper. "These drawers are unlocked, but they're tiny," Isaac pointed out. "We can't fit into any of them."

"There, keep that one open," I said, pointing to an empty drawer. I pulled off my shirt, pants, shoes, and socks and stuffed them into the drawer, slamming it shut.

"Are we going to swim out of here?" Isaac asked, noting my tan swimsuit.

"Crouch in that corner and don't say a word," I ordered. Mr. Stone was steps away from the door, about to swipe his keycard. I pushed Isaac down into the corner and spread my back and arms over him. The tingling sensation flashed across my whole body as I brought on the camouflage effect of my skin. Isaac caught sight of one of my arms and began to whisper his astonishment. "Quiet!" I hissed, before he could get a word out.

The front door opened and my mother hurried in, a step ahead of Mr. Stone. Scanning the room and not seeing us, she turned calmly back toward Mr. Stone.

"Have you got it?" he asked.

"Yes," my mother replied, pulling the drive out of her pocket. "Did you want to check it?" she asked, moving to plug the drive into her computer.

"That won't be necessary," Mr. Stone explained, putting out his hand to take the drive from her. Slipping it into his jacket pocket, he added, "Don't you think I trust you?"

I had been keeping my back and neck completely flexed, providing as large a stretch of skin as possible for our cover. With my head down like that, I could catch an inverted glimpse of the scene behind me.

"Well, with all that's been going on," my mother said, "you can't be too careful."

"That is true," Stone agreed, "but I do trust you, Annette. I know you're too smart to cross me."

My mother bowed her head slightly and Mr. Stone left the lab, heading back to his office. Turning toward our corner of the room, my mother moved her head from side to side.

"Noah?" she asked. I straightened up from my crouched position, revealing Isaac crumpled beneath me in the fetal position, his eyes glued to me. Thinking of a warm shower, I managed to end the camouflage effect quickly, and Isaac pushed himself up as well, still not taking his eyes off me.

"What are you?" he gasped.

"I'm just a kid, okay?" I snapped. "Look at me. You can't tell anyone, you hear?"

"Sure, but wow!"

My mother just smiled with relief, knowing that we were safe. "That was some quick thinking, Noah," she said to me. She then frowned at Isaac, who was still staring at me. It was unfortunate that he had witnessed my newfound camouflage skills. If I could make him forget... *You just look at them,* I remembered Eve telling me. That was how you touched someone in their mind. Just look at them and *want* to know them.

"Look at me," I repeated to Isaac. He had, of course, been looking at me the whole time, ever since he first saw the skin of my arm change color to match the adjacent wall and floor. But that was just looking at one aspect of me—my arms, legs, and torso—the camouflage effect. I needed him to look into my eyes, so I could reach into his mind.

Finally, he did look directly into my eyes, with a genuine desire to understand. I kept my attention focused on his eyes, too, just as I would do with the infrared images or the distant sounds. Soon, he became more and more relaxed, his eyelids drooping.

"I'll relieve you of the burden," I said to him quietly. He made no response, but at some level, I sensed agreement from him. Through this connection, I proposed a different scenario than the one that had just transpired: Mr. Stone was about to come into this room but changed his mind and went back to his office. We all felt relieved and safe. I left Isaac with those thoughts, got dressed, then returned to him saying, "It's time to go now."

"Is that all you need?" Isaac asked, suddenly fully alert. "I suppose we should be going soon."

"Yes," I agreed. "Let's get you out of here." He seemed to have no memory of my camouflage.

"Did you get the files he wanted?"

"I think so," my mother replied. "Though he didn't even look at them."

"I don't think he cared about them," I suggested. "He

just wanted to get you on camera taking them, in order to have something to use against you. Once he sees that you're not on there, he won't be happy."

"Then we'd better keep him busy enough that he doesn't get the chance to look through that security camera footage," my mother shot back. "About that, Isaac, I have another request for you. I know we've already asked too much from you, so if you're not interested, I'll understand."

"Don't worry about it," Isaac assured her with a laugh. "What have you got?"

My mother described how we wanted to halt the dissemination of Pridapt's vaccines until the safer, more natural version could be developed. Since Mr. Stone was dead set against that, she wanted to contact a researcher from another company to help them get the alternative out quickly.

"If a safer version was available," she explained, "it would stop Pridapt's push to distribute vaccines from the primordial cells. I need to make contact as an alias, though, from a source that cannot be traced."

"That's right up my alley." Isaac grinned. "You get your message ready, and I will take you to a location where you can upload it. Why don't I meet you both at the rest stop at seven o'clock tonight? You know the one," he added, pointing to me.

Our plan arranged, I walked Isaac out the front door while my mother remained in the East Wing, jotting down notes for her intended message to a Pridapt competitor. When I returned, I saw Eve standing on the other side of the glass, watching my mother. I asked for the key so I might join Eve in the next room, and my mother complied without looking up from her paper.

"I saw you; you did it," Eve noted, as soon as the door closed behind me.

"I did what?"

"You looked into his mind."

Realizing that she was referring to my hypnotizing Isaac, I was genuinely grateful. "Yes. Thank you for telling me how to do that."

Eve grinned, then looked back through the window at our mother.

"What does Mr. Stone want?" she asked.

"Nothing good. You just get out to the woods if he, or anyone other than Mom or I comes in here."

"Don't worry," Eve replied with a smile, "I will."

Returning to my mother, who was finishing up her notes, I asked, "Figure out your message to another researcher?"

"I think so—the initial one anyway. I'll need to follow up with more details if they're interested."

"Okay then, let's go," I suggested, then paused. "Maybe Eve should come with us?"

"No," my mother answered flatly, then seeing Eve's

dejected look, repeated in a gentler tone, "No, Eve, not yet. You're safer here until we do this. Afterwards, yes, then you'll come with us."

Eve's mood brightened considerably after this promise. I turned and was nearly at the door when my mother's Pridapt phone rang.

"Hello," my mother answered. "Yes. Yes, I can find him and let him know. Very good sir." She hung up her phone and looked nervously around the room.

"Who was it?"

"It was Mr. Stone. He wants to see you in his office right away."

This was my chance! I could start to use my abilities. *What was it he had said, 'Master the spirited horse?'* Yes, I realized that was what *I* needed to do—to master the spirited horse of fear and turn it against Stone.

"Okay," I answered eagerly, starting out the door.

"You can't go!" my mother protested. "I'll just tell him I couldn't find you."

"Then he'll know something's up for sure. No, I have to go, but tell me something: who does Mr. Stone answer to?"

"Answer to? He answers to the board of directors, the chairman of the board, primarily."

"Give me their names."

"You can't go to them. They may be involved as well.

For all we know, they may have been the ones who killed Dr. Strauss!"

"I won't be going to them," I explained. "I'll be using them against Stone. Trust me. I have an idea." My mother looked through a drawer and pulled out a piece of stationery that listed the names of all the board members. I read through the names and put the sheet into my pocket.

"Be careful, Noah. Don't try to outsmart him. He'll see it coming a mile away."

"I can see him a mile away, or at least a few hundred feet. I can see him now," I boasted, closing my eyes and focusing on Stone's infrared shape. "He's scared, pacing back and forth in his office. Don't forget: I'll be able to hear him from the hallway before going in. I'll have the upper hand."

"Act like you know nothing, nothing at all," my mother warned. I reassured her that I would mind my words, and I made my way to Mr. Stone's office. Having just successfully made Isaac forget all about my camouflage ability, I was confident that I would at least be able to plant a few subliminal suggestions into Mr. Stone's mind while not betraying my suspicions of him. I entered his office without hesitation.

"There he is," Mr. Stone announced as I stepped in. "Have a seat, son." He moved behind his desk and sat down, motioning to the chair opposite him for me to sit in. "So, do you not trust me either?"

"Sir?"

"Like your mother doesn't trust me?"

"Oh, she trusts you."

"Let's not mince words," he fired back at me. "I need to know who is on my team and who is not."

You have to want to see them. You need to look into them; I recalled Eve's advice regarding hypnosis. It was a harder thing to do, to *want* to look into Mr. Stone's mind, as opposed to Isaac's, but I kept my eyes fixed on his and answered his question very slowly. "I'm on your team, and so is my mother." My voice sounded odd, even to me, but Mr. Stone made no comment. I thought about trust, how my mother and I could be trusted, no matter what. I thought of each board member by name and how none of them could be trusted. I thought of algorithms: if this, then that. If he suspected my mother or me, it wasn't us, it was someone else. I thought of words that would trigger thoughts, sights, and smells. I suggested that my mother and I should make a copy of the hidden data. I imagined other possible scenarios and planted my seeds, hoping they would take root.

"Well, kid," Mr. Stone said, suddenly regaining his usual hyper-alert affect, "at least I can trust you and your mom."

It worked! I beamed with inner pride. *So far, so good.*

A NEW DEAL

That evening, we met Isaac at the rest stop as planned. I reassured my mother that my meeting with Mr. Stone had gone very well and that we had a window of opportunity now, during which he would trust us. She was not as certain as I was, but confident enough to go ahead with our plan. Isaac would lead us to a public place with open Wi-Fi, a coffee shop outside San Francisco, and my mother would send her first e-mail to an outside researcher from there. Going forward, we would use a different site for each e-mail, he explained.

Inside the coffee shop, there was a counter with computer stations for customers. Isaac tapped out some quick commands on one of the keyboards, jotting down the information that came up, then cleared the screen and wiped off the keyboard with a cloth, leading us outside to a corner table.

"We'll send your e-mail from my laptop, but it will look like it came from that computer terminal," Isaac whispered.

"Where did you learn all this?" I asked him.

"You pick it up. I've known people who specialize in clandestine work on the Internet. This is nothing. Some of the things they can do…"

"So," my mother interrupted. "Let's get to it."

"Right. So, what do you want to call yourself?" Isaac asked.

"Dr. X," I suggested, as Mom seemed stumped by the question. She nodded her approval, and Isaac tapped on his keys.

"Dr. X it is. What about the address we're sending it to?"

"This is it." My mother handed Isaac the address of the researcher she had decided to send her e-mail to. He worked for BayPharmz, a competitor that also developed new pharmaceuticals.

"Wait, what e-mail will it come from?" I asked.

"Some random address. He won't be able to track it."

"But how will he be able to respond?"

"He won't, not by e-mail. But we can follow up to-morrow night. We'll give a link to a public thread open to comments, say on a software help site. If he posts a comment to Dr. X, we can follow up for a minute or two, then we leave."

"Okay. Let me type in my message." My mother wrote all she could to help this researcher figure out the safer alternative to the cancer vaccines. She also gave a brief explanation, without mentioning any names, as to why she was sharing this information. Time was of the essence, she explained. The alternative needed to be out there soon, or it would be a moot point. At the end of the e-mail, Isaac added a link to a public string of comments where the researcher could respond the next night. We sent the e-mail, then left.

The following evening, we met at a different location, and Isaac accessed the Internet on his laptop through one of the cafe's computer stations. He brought up the comment page on his laptop, and we waited.

"Once we post a comment on that thread, how quickly could someone track the source?" I asked.

"Minutes," Isaac replied. "That's why any conversation here is short and sweet, then we go."

The stress of the situation sent a tingling flash across my forearm. Glancing down, I realized it was more than just goose bumps as my arm took on the colored pattern of the counter top. I consciously resisted the camouflage and my arm returned to its normal state. Fortunately, not even my mother had noticed the momentary change. I would have to remain more focused and calm if I was to prevent that from happening again.

"There he is!" Isaac announced, pointing to a short post that read, "Dr. X, most grateful, was already working on this. One question: what factor is needed for the second passage?"

"That's easy," my mother chimed in, leaning over Isaac to type her response.

I glanced nervously at my watch as we waited for a reply. At just under a minute, it came.

"Perfect. Now we have all we need. Thanks!"

"Well," Isaac said, folding up his laptop. "Let's go."

"Strange," my mother muttered. "Why just that? If he had understood all that we sent, he should have known what factor to use for the second passage," my mother thought out loud.

"Let's talk about it in the car," I suggested, feeling the tingling impulse rising once again. As we headed out, Isaac offered to meet with me in a couple of days in the Pridapt woods, just in case there was anything more we needed him to do. We thanked him and agreed on a time.

I felt those woods were the safest place for a rendezvous, as I had been working on my camouflage skills moving unseen to and from them in my swimsuit. I kept a backpack behind a tree, with an extra pair of sweats and shoes. By staying far enough away from the security cameras and moving slowly whenever I sensed infrared images nearby, I was able to go from the woods to the parking lot and back with ease.

I had confidence in the hypnotic suggestion I had made to Mr. Stone; I really believed that he trusted us, so much so, that I had suggested we go to our own home, but my mother felt we should stay at the hotel, just in case.

All we needed to do now was to lie low and wait for the news that BayPharmz had come out with a safer alternative to Pridapt's vaccines. That would put a stop to Stone's mass-distribution of the current vaccines and undermine the power he had been wielding. It might even lead to an honest investigation into Dr. Strauss's death.

The next day, we noticed that chairs were being set out in the Pridapt lobby. Mr. Stone would be giving another speech that afternoon. Attendance was mandatory for all employees, and as we were gathering there, Mr. Stone motioned toward my mother and me.

"You two, sit up here." He motioned to two seats by the podium, then, leaning in to us, whispered, "Keep your eyes open. See how everyone responds to what I say. It seems we have a rat." He looked at us for longer than was comfortable, and I wondered if my hypnotic suggestion was beginning to wear off.

Once everyone was seated, Mr. Stone began.

"I need to warn you all about some difficulties we are facing. I know you may be wondering how anything could be more difficult than what we have already been through. In some ways, you're right. We are definitely past the worst of it. But there are some loose ends—loose ends that could wind up undoing all the great strides we have made. One of these loose ends is the persistence of nuisance lawsuits."

I breathed a sigh of relief with Stone's first complaint. While most people were fully supporting Stone and Pridapt, there was a small fringe group that had continued to file lawsuits against the company. They began shortly after Isaac's online posts had stirred a national wave of protests. While Isaac's activities were clandestine enough to be branded domestic terrorism, this group's attacks were all aboveboard and completely legal, and as such posed a greater threat. I knew that they annoyed Mr. Stone because I had heard him through the walls, complaining about them as a thorn in his side.

"The second loose end," Mr. Stone continued, "is competition. Competition increases our costs, leads to delays in the release of new vaccines, and could even force us to curtail the development of other treatments."

Had the other company released something to the press already? I wondered. It didn't seem possible so soon. I glanced at my mother, whose look revealed the same thought.

"Fortunately, there is one competitor out there who understands how destructive this competition can be. They understand that we can't afford to be duplicating efforts, wasting time and money, and so, they have decided to join our team. I am pleased to say that as of this afternoon, BayPharmz is now part of Pridapt."

I was afraid to move, afraid to look at my mother or show any emotion at all. "See how everyone responds to what I say," Stone had told us. I nudged my mother and turned to look around the room at the lines of faces. I couldn't tell whether Mr. Stone was looking at us or not, but we couldn't afford to let him see our surprise. There wasn't much emotion in the audience, just an occasional frown and some raised eyebrows. Some researchers might have been worried that consolidation could mean layoffs, but beyond that, the business side of research was of little concern to most employees.

"This merger is a start," Mr. Stone went on to explain, "but it is not enough. There will be others looking to capitalize on our successes, steal the fruit of our hard work. As for this other competition, we have a solution in the works. Ladies and gentlemen, there needs to be a single provider of these miraculous drugs, and that provider needs to be the government."

This time, I turned to my mother without hiding my surprise. I had never expected this from Mr. Stone. How could such an ambitious man want to turn control of his company over to the government? My mother was stunned and silent.

"It's for the good of society." Mr. Stone cheered, his look scanning the rows of seats. "Health for everyone. A new deal." Mr. Stone ended his speech with some brief thanks and stepped down from the podium. "Well, what do you think?" he asked us.

"What will happen?" my mother asked. "Who will run things?"

"Oh, don't worry Annette." Mr. Stone grinned. "I'll still be in charge, along with the board. That's all part of the agreement. I'll make sure you're taken care of, too," he added, bobbing his index finger at my mother and then me. "I take care of my friends. As for the stockholders..." He shrugged. "C'est la vie."

"The government is buying Pridapt?" my mother asked.

"More or less," Mr. Stone explained. "It will be paid for with future contracts. But we'll be given a guaranteed income and benefits package right out of the gate, plus bonus incentives based on production. It's not only domestic, Annette; the international market for this is limitless!"

So this was what had gone on between Mr. Stone and

the senators. It turned out that he had made them a proposal, and they had accepted. Not only would he receive a government position with a generous compensation package, but he would also be protected from annoying lawsuits and competition.

"So," Mr. Stone whispered to us, "did you see any surprised looks when I mentioned BayPharmz?" We both shook our heads. "I saw one," Mr. Stone seethed. "I think I know who the rat is." He looked at us again for a bit longer than I would have liked, then nodded and turned to go to his office.

Feeling utterly defeated, we sat back down in our seats.

"Do you think he meant us?" my mother asked.

"I don't think so," I whispered. "I think my hypnotic suggestion is still working."

"Then he still trusts us?"

"Yes," I affirmed. "And I think we should use that trust to get the word out."

"How? Without the data, who will pay any attention to us?"

"Stone will give us the data," I boasted. "I planted the idea that..."

"Dr. Bolton! Noah!" Daniel, the security guard called out to us. "Mr. Stone wants you in his office right now."

My confidence was shaken somewhat as we complied

with the CEO's bidding. Before reaching the door to his office, I stopped.

"Wait, let me look in there." I scanned the office through the wall. "It's just him. I don't see anyone else in there." When we entered the waiting area, Mr. Stone stepped into his doorway and waved us in.

"Now, Annette," he began.

"You can trust us," I interrupted him, looking at his eyes steadily. I reached behind me and closed the office door.

"Yes, I can," he replied slowly. "We need to move some information off a computer."

"So you need a copy?" I asked, reminding him of my hypnotic suggestion that we copy the hidden data. My mother glanced at me with a curious look.

"Exactly," he replied. "The computer is in a secure storage room. You can move the whole thing onto this drive." He handed my mother a portable drive.

"How? I don't have access," my mother said.

"I'll give you access. I could do it, but it would be inopportune for me to log on to that computer."

"What if we're asked why we're going in there?"

"You could always say you needed something for the East Wing project, which is also a secure area. No one would question that. After you copy the data, leave the portable drive on the table, then use this software to scrub the hard drive clean. He gave us a software disc. This will take some time, so keep the software and the drive in your office for now and take care of it first thing in the morning."

He gave us the passcode for the secure room keypad and thanked us.

"Oh, by the way," he added as we were leaving, "I know this Dave Bernstein is a friend of yours, but there's no room for traitors here."

My mother and I stared blankly at him.

"That's right—he's the rat!"

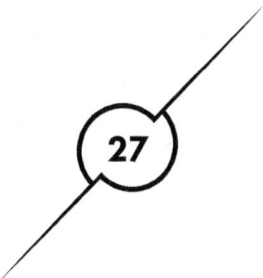

WASTED OPPORTUNITIES

It seemed my hypnotic suggestion had succeeded in deflecting Stone's suspicions away from my mother and me, only to have them land squarely on our dear friend, Dave. Mr. Stone was now convinced that Dave was the "rat" who had given the information to BayPharmz.

"What was that about?" my mother asked. "Is this another setup? And why did you ask if he needed a copy?"

"It's not a setup. I put that in his head a couple of days ago, when he called me in, remember? I told him he could trust us, and I planted suggestions."

"And why does he suspect Dave?"

"Hold on," I said, "Let's see if I can hear him." I left my mother in the corner of the lobby and leaned against the opposite wall which led to Stone's office. It was harder to do from that distance. I had to focus all my concentration on the background sounds to drown out the louder noises around me. After a few moments, it was there, in the dull ringing: individual voices. There was one commanding tone among them all—Stone's. He was saying something about getting evidence against someone. As I shifted my position along the wall, I was wrenched back to my immediate surroundings by the harsh sound of my name being whispered loudly.

"Noah!"

It was Zoe! She was rushing over to me from the security desk, slapping on her visitor's pass sticker. Although she appeared very intense, she did not seem angry like the last time I had seen her.

"What's going on here, Noah?" she whispered more softly. "I saw on the news how there was some scandal, some old guy died, and some blogger's been saying it was murder."

"I told you there was a lot happening," I reminded her.

"Yeah, yeah, okay. That's a pretty good excuse for not calling me, but you know, you could have texted."

Not now, I moaned to myself, but seeing that she really didn't seem angry, my mood softened.

"You know, Zoe," I began, "I don't know what's going to happen with that diabetes trial. I'm sorry, but everything's up in the air right now."

"Hey, that's cool. My Mom was totally freaked when she read what that blogger wrote—about recreated species or whatever. She wants nothing to do with it now anyway."

"Good, I guess." I suddenly thought of a perfect way that Zoe could be of assistance. "Listen Zoe, would you help us?"

Zoe's eyes perked up at the invitation to a potential adventure. Looking around the lobby she suggested, "We'd better go outside. The walls have ears you know."

You have no idea, I thought.

"Just a second, Zoe, wait here," I whispered, then ran back to the East Wing for my company phone. Returning to Zoe in the lobby, I led her through the security line by the front door where they asked to look at our phones.

"So this is new," she commented. "They checked it on the way in, too."

"It's to make sure nothing is being smuggled out." I smiled at the guard, who gave me an apologetic smile in return. Once outside, we walked toward the woods and I began to tell her what had been going on that week. I decided to leave out the bit about me being a primordium for the time being, but did focus on corruption, greed, and extinct reptile venom. I included the last, just to ensure her willingness to get involved. As I expected, it added the thrill that proved to be irresistible.

"Can you come here tomorrow morning, Zoe?"

"Sure! This is exciting! What do I do?"

"You see how everything is checked as we leave the building?" I asked her. "We need to get some files out without them knowing. Here, take my phone. It's a Pridapt phone."

"Cool!"

"Don't use it! Just leave it off for now. Then, at nine-thirty tomorrow morning, come here, turn on the phone, and wait by that front window behind the Pridapt sign. Act like you're waiting for me, looking at the window now and again."

"That's it?"

"We'll send you a file through the company's internal network to my phone. They block regular outside texting and emails. Then, I'll come out at about ten, get the phone back from you, and take it to my car."

Zoe agreed, and as I walked her out toward the parking lot, we passed a small crowd gathering in front of Pridapt. It was Dave speaking to members of the press. I motioned to Zoe, and we both moved closer to hear what was going on.

"If we don't say something soon, we may never be able to," Dave explained. "Competition is a good thing. It is what drives costs down and quality up. A monopoly only leads to higher prices and poorer quality. It's always been that way. We need to keep research companies like ours private, with competition."

Suddenly, two policemen came alongside Dave and, grabbing him by both arms, pulled him away from the reporters and into the Pridapt building. Zoe and I followed into the lobby, stopping at the security station, where the guard informed us that Dave was being taken to one of the "secure" rooms.

"Secure rooms?" I asked.

"Don't ask me what's in there. I don't have access. Only Mr. Stone does, as far as I know."

My mother rushed through security and motioned for us to go back outside with her. After a brief glance toward Zoe, she leaned in to me, and with a hushed voice, explained that Stone's men had Dave arrested after hearing his comments to the press.

"On what charges?" I asked.

"None," my mother replied. "To oppose Pridapt is apparently considered an act of domestic terrorism. He can be held indefinitely without charges."

"Held where? By whom?" I cried. My mother grabbed my arm, holding a finger to her lips.

"Not a word. Dave's being held in-house by local police. Stone has everyone on his side right now. We need to be very careful about what we say and to whom we say it." Directing her steel-blue gaze sternly at Zoe, she added, "That goes for you too!"

Zoe nodded her consent and we went swiftly to our vehicles.

"Nine-thirty tomorrow, Zoe," I mentioned before we parted.

When a statement was later made to the press, it was very critical of Dave. He was referred to as greedy, wanting to keep more money for himself instead of sharing it with the rest of society. It was then that I realized just how powerful Mr. Stone had become. This man, who had never before held any sort of public office, never been elected by the people for anything, now wielded such political power and influence that all he needed to do was point a finger at someone, call them a terrorist, and they were as good as gone.

Back at the hotel, my mother and I worked out our plan.

"So, I assume we'll be making an extra copy of that data before we erase it?" my mother asked.

"Of course."

"But then how do we get it out of there? The secure rooms have metal detectors as well. It's impossible to carry any electronic device out of there without them being found."

"I figured that," I concurred. "That's why I made a plan with Zoe."

"With who?" my mother asked dubiously.

"We'll send her the files."

"Outside service is blocked in the building," my mother countered. "Any outbound e-mail would be stopped."

"We can use our internal network, the intranet," I explained. "I just gave Zoe my Pridapt phone, and she will be standing outside behind the Pridapt sign, where the intranet still reaches. I told her to be there tomorrow morning at nine-thirty. Once you transfer the data to her, I'll go out, get my phone back and bring it to my car."

"That just might work, Noah," my mother said, approvingly. "I hope she can be discreet."

Discreet? That was not a term I would ever have used to describe Zoe, and I nervously considered how any indiscretion on her part might play out. The more I thought about it, the more anxious I became, but I still felt it was our best bet. We discussed what we would do with the data once we had obtained it, deciding that Isaac could distribute it through his blogs. Emotionally exhausted, we had a quick dinner and went to sleep.

The following morning, we were up early, timing our arrival at Pridapt in order to get the data ready for Zoe. I went into the secure room with my mother initially, then returned to the lobby to watch for Zoe. As soon as I saw her starting up the circular drive, I rushed back to my mother.

"She should be there by now," I whispered to my mother, who sent an initial message to my phone as a test.

When she received a text back from Zoe, she began to transfer the files.

"It's going now," my mother breathed, and she connected Mr. Stone's drive to copy the data for him as well. Once the computer indicated that the transfer had finished, I went out to the lobby. I was curious to see how discreet Zoe looked, standing out there waiting all this time.

As I turned the corner, I saw her looking through the large glass window, her hands pressed alongside her face as she scanned the lobby. *That's hardly discreet,* I thought. But then she stepped back and, looking at her reflection, began to fix her hair. *That's more like it.*

I passed through the metal detectors and out the front door.

"Hey, Zoe!" I called out, running over to her.

"Noah, hey."

"Did you get it?" I asked her, standing with my back to the lobby.

"All I got was your mom's text, no file."

"What? She transferred a big file."

"It never came. See?"

She handed me my phone, which I scrolled through, and, while there was the initial message from my mother, there was no subsequent one with the data.

"Noah!" the security guard called out to me from the

doorway. "Mr. Stone needs to see you right away."

I slipped the phone back into Zoe's hand and told her I would see her later, nodding toward the parking lot.

"Right now," the guard stressed.

"Okay, I'm coming."

The guard waited for me at the door and led me through the metal detectors, which alarmed because of his sidearm. We crossed the lobby and went down to Stone's office.

I could see several infrared images in his back room. I tried to listen for any conversations, but all was silent. I realized, as I slowed down at the door, that the security guard had been following along behind me.

Was he making sure I knew the way?

"Go on in," he advised.

There was no secretary in the front office, and the door to Mr. Stone's back room was open. I looked back at the security guard, who nodded toward the open door. Entering the back office, I saw my mother seated with two guards on either side of her and another guard just inside the door. Mr. Stone was sitting behind his desk.

"Where's your phone, kid?" he asked me.

"I... I left it at home," I lied, patting my pockets.

"Really? That's strange because your mother just tried to send a file to a phone over the local network, and I'm betting it was yours. Now, show me your phone!"

"I don't have it. See?" I explained, pulling out my pockets. Mr. Stone did not seem convinced.

"There's something else you don't have." He added, turning his computer screen toward my mother and me, displaying a spreadsheet of data. "Annette, I asked you to copy and erase this data, and instead you tried to send it to someone."

"I thought..." my mother began.

"Don't bother," Mr. Stone interrupted. "There is no explanation I would believe. I trusted you, but apparently, that trust was misplaced." He motioned to the two guards on either side of my mother, and they pulled her out of the chair by her arms and started leading her out of the room.

"Wait!" she pleaded. "Let Noah go. He doesn't know anything."

"The kid?" Mr. Stone asked. "Oh, I can't imagine him not knowing anything. He's sharp, this one is."

His monumental hand and index finger bobbed slowly and ominously in my direction, like an ax about to be raised. All my muscles tightened at the sight of it, cringing in anticipation of the blow.

"You're sharp, aren't you, kid? No, I'll be hanging on to him for a while."

"You can't do that. He's just a boy," my mother argued as they dragged her out into the hall.

"Where are they taking her?" I demanded as Mr. Stone swung his computer screen back to himself.

"She'll be joining your friend, Dr. Bernstein. They're both under arrest."

"For what?"

"Oh, I don't know, how about corporate espionage, theft, domestic terrorism? Take your pick." He got up from behind his desk and began to pace back and forth behind it. "Sit down, kid." I sat in the chair opposite his desk, trying to make steady eye contact with him, but he never looked at me for more than a second. He kept looking up at the ceiling, out the side window, or down at the floor. "Wasted opportunities," he repeated several times, and then he stopped moving. He looked at me, and I hoped I would have an opportunity to make another hypnotic suggestion, but as soon as he caught my eye, he turned away.

"You had tremendous opportunity here, kid, tremendous opportunity. I was looking out for you because you reminded me of myself." He shook his head, glanced at his security guard standing by the door, then began pacing again. "But you didn't recognize or appreciate the opportunity that came your way. Instead, you and your mother picked the wrong team. You picked the losing team. Do you realize that? Just like Strauss, just like Bernstein, just like that online blogger."

He stopped again and faced me. "You've heard about that blogger fellow, I'm sure. Well, he's done for now, too."

Isaac? I thought in horror.

"What blogger?" I asked.

"You know who. Well, he's been found, and we have him for cyberterrorism. He won't be seeing the light of day for a long time."

He moved to a counter and poured himself a cup of coffee.

My mind was racing and my heart pounding. I kept thinking, *What can I do?* I feared for my mother, for Dave, and... Eve! The sensation of camouflage began to flash across my forearm skin, reminding me of the need to be calm. I looked down at the floor, slowed my breathing, then gradually raised my eyes back toward Mr. Stone.

I watched the rising steam from his coffee mug trail behind him as he returned to sit at his desk. Then I remembered one of the seeds I had planted earlier.

"Don't drink that!" I shouted.

He looked at me, perplexed, then grinned at his guard.

"Don't you smell it?" I asked him. "It's nutmeg!"

"What?" he fumed, staring at me for a moment before leaning over his coffee to check for the telltale scent. It was one of the hypnotic suggestions I had made: *When I say, "It's nutmeg," you'll smell nutmeg.*

His face suddenly went blank, and he sat bolt upright, pushing his chair back from the desk. "By God, it is!"

His prodigious hand and finger bobbed at me once more, though this time, not as a slow, menacing gesture, but a rapid, affirming one, like I used to receive following my winning slogans. I had made my way back into Stone's confidence!

Looking at his man standing by the door, then back at me, he gasped, "This kid just saved my life! You just saved my life, kid!"

HIS OWN MEDICINE

M r. Stone was pacing back and forth again, muttering to himself. "How could they? But they must have; they're the only ones..."

My hypnotic suggestion earlier regarding the board members must have taken root. He didn't trust them. He then stopped and pointed a steady, threatening finger at me.

"I'm going to ask you something and you're going to tell me the truth," Stone ordered. "You lie to me and your mother's dead. You understand?"

The affirming hand gesture was gone, the warm sense of being within his confidence, likewise gone. His mammoth hand and index finger stood poised, immobile before me.

I stared at him, eye to eye, but could not even begin to

try a hypnotic effect—I was that frightened. While I had already considered him a murderer, certain that he was involved with Dr. Strauss's death, it wasn't until this moment that I experienced genuine terror in his presence. I nodded readily and began to feel a tingling flash across my forearms. My skin's camouflage effect was coming on again against my efforts to resist it. My arms were covered by my shirtsleeves, but my hands were beginning to blend in with the arms of the chair, so I quickly tucked them under my pants and tried to imagine a warm shower. *Was the camouflage beginning to spread up my neck?* My heart beat so forcefully, it seemed to be rocking me back and forth in the chair.

"How did you know about that smell?" he asked me, his eyes still fixed on mine.

"My mother told me," I answered immediately. "She told me... about the venom from the reptile primordium... how it had a strong smell of nutmeg," I stammered.

"Did she tell you where it's kept?"

"She said it's locked up somewhere."

"When did she go to get it?"

"She didn't. She couldn't. She said it was in a secure area; she didn't even know where."

"Don't lie to me!"

"I swear!" Tears fell spontaneously from my eyes and ran down my cheeks. I was trembling. Unable to calm my breathing, my sobs were like those of a weeping child. I was broken.

Just the day before in this office, I had enjoyed such confidence as I led Mr. Stone on with my hypnotic suggestions. That confidence was now shattered. Before, by listening to him through the walls, I had thought I was in control; but here, face-to-face, it was he who had the upper hand, and he knew it. I was nothing before him.

Whether it was my crying or my shaking, something seemed to have convinced Stone that I was telling the truth.

"There's only one other person who has access," Stone muttered to himself. He looked at me again, but this time without with the fierce accusatory gaze. "No, you couldn't have done it." He kept looking at me but I could tell he was thinking of someone else. I blinked the tears from my eyes to get a clearer look at him, and then, I realized—I had him!

They did it! I thought. *The board! Remember, you can't trust the board. They tried to poison you!* Mr. Stone was silent. He continued to look at me calmly and steadily. *The board did it.* I repeated the thought in my mind to reinforce it in his. Now I wanted to know him more than anything, my fear being cleared away more and more with each breath I took.

"They did it," he whispered. He broke his stare and looked up suddenly at his security guard. "Don't touch anything in here. Leave that coffee cup right where it is. They'll pay for this. They're going to take the fall for everything." He grabbed his jacket and marched toward the door.

"What do you want me to do with the kid?" the guard asked.

Mr. Stone turned back and looked at me with a frown. "Keep him here," he sighed. "But keep him safe."

"What about my mom?" I asked Mr. Stone, trying to capitalize on his momentary clemency.

"I'll deal with her later. I have a board to take care of first," he murmured as he threw on his jacket and rushed down the hall.

I turned in the chair and looked at the guard standing by the door. As I wiped the remaining traces of tears from my cheeks, I regained my composure. *This one will be easy,* I thought, and he would be. He stood there, blank-faced, as though awaiting further instructions.

"Do you mind if I sit over there?" I asked meekly, pointing to a chair directly opposite him.

"Go ahead."

I repositioned myself and set my gaze upon him. "How long will we be here?" I asked.

"Until Mr. Stone says otherwise." The question got him to look at me, which gave me a chance to capture his attention.

You're very tired, I thought. *You need to sit, rest, sleep.* I continued the thoughts of sleep, until the guard's eyes were heavy and he sat in another chair. *It's okay to sleep. Mr. Stone won't mind.* Before long, the guard was asleep.

I slipped behind Stone's desk and found that he was still logged on to his computer, having left in such a rush to confront the board. The file Mr. Stone had intercepted from my mother was still on the screen. I pulled out the drawers of his desk and shuffled through papers until I found a small USB drive. Copying the data files onto that drive, I slipped off my outer clothes in the corner of the office. In my tan swimsuit, with the USB drive in the palm of my hand, I brought on the camouflage effect and stepped out of the office, leaving the guard asleep in his chair.

I stood against the wall, afraid to move. Practicing my camouflage in the East Wing with Eve, or moving from the parking lot to the woods was one thing, but indoors, close to people, where they might notice some irregularity—my hair, my open eyes, or tan swim suit—that was another thing altogether. I started toward the lobby, where I thought the confusion of people coming and going would provide better cover.

As I passed the cafeteria, several employees were leaving to return to their labs. I crouched against the wall and tucked my head like I had done to hide myself and Isaac that day when Mr. Stone had come into the East Wing. The employees continued on past me, until one stopped, saying she wanted to get a drink at the water fountain, which was only a few feet from me. She turned and trotted in my direction. I slid my feet in closer to the wall and a few more inches away from the fountain. If her leg bumped into me, she would stop and look straight at me. My thoughts were racing. *What would I do? Would I make a run for it?* I couldn't just sit there. They would all be poking at me and calling out to everyone. Then she passed me, and I felt the edge of her lab coat brush against my back. I feared she would be even closer as she ran back to her colleagues, so while she drank and her friends were talking among themselves, I took two full steps to the side and crouched back down flat against the wall. I heard the water stop running, and as I had suspected, the clip of shoes was closer on her return trip. I once again felt the brush of a lab coat across my back and I realized that had I not moved, she would have walked right into me!

I waited until there was no one else near me, then crept along the wall to the lobby. Staying along the side walls, I made my way through the foyer, to within five feet of the metal detector. Since the wall on the inside of the detector was the same color as that on the outer side, if I sprinted from one end to the other, I could go through unnoticed, even though the USB drive in my palm would set off the alarm. I knelt against the wall so that my back would blend in. When no one was looking in my direction, I spun through the metal detector and slid flat against the wall on the other side. The guard behind the desk jumped up, but by the time he looked in my direction, there was nothing to see. He walked over to check the machinery, and I slid further away along the wall. Another guard from the hallway joined him.

"Did anyone go through?"

"There was no one near it."

The front desk guard passed through the detector, setting off the alarm again, and checked outside the front doors. Returning inside, he shrugged his shoulders. "Malfunction, I guess." He passed directly in front of me, and I slipped out through the open door as it was closing.

Outside, I kept an eye on the security cameras, moving very slowly until I was beyond their range. Along the far edge of the parking area, I ran out to the woods, pulled my hidden backpack from the brush, and dug out my sweatpants and shirt. As I was coming out of the bushes, I ran into Zoe.

"Noah!" she called out. "What's going on? Why are you dressed like that?"

"Zoe!" I was so happy to see a friendly face! "We were caught!" I explained. Pressing the drive into her hand I gazed at her for a moment.

"What do you want me to do?" she asked.

"Copy the files on this drive and keep them safe. Put them somewhere no one would look."

"Where are you going?" she asked.

"I need to get my mother out; they're holding her in there."

"Holding her? What do you mean?"

"I'll tell you later." I took my phone back from Zoe and, running to the parking lot, left it and my sweats in my car. In camouflage, I ran around the building to Eve's outdoor habitat. Fortunately, there was a tractor-trailer backed up to the loading dock, so I could easily climb up and over the fence, clear of the security cameras. I noted Eve's infrared image inside the habitat, so I entered through the back door and filled her in on what had been going on.

"I need your help," I pleaded. "We need to save our mother."

While I wasn't sure which room they were holding her in, I had a pretty good idea. In addition to the secure area where we had gone to erase data, there were two others, just down the hall.

Eve seemed eager to help as I went over a rough sketch of my plan. We had to move quickly, as I did not know how long they would be keeping our mother on site. We both brought on our camouflage and left the East Wing. Moving through the building, Eve paused briefly to orient herself. I realized that for the first time, she was seeing these halls with her own eyes. Before this, she had only seen infrared images moving through them.

Once in the hallway leading to the secure room, we noticed a policeman stationed outside one of the doors, behind which there were multiple infrared images. Eve grabbed my arm and whispered, "She's in there." Eve had been using her infrared senses for much longer than I had, so she could recognize my mother's image readily.

"Which one?" I asked, closing my eyes to better concentrate on the images.

"The middle one, of the three sitting down."

I could see them now, three seated, and two standing. *The two standing must be guards,* I thought. Eve moved to a corner at the end of the hall and pushed herself up the walls to the ceiling. I crept closer to the officer. Once in position, Eve let out a series of the growling sounds she had made that first time Zoe and I were in the East Wing. This immediately drew the officer's attention, and he stepped out into the hallway for a better view. I rushed to position myself just behind him and cleared my camouflage effect.

"Help me," I whimpered, in as pitiful and childlike a voice as I could muster. He spun around and stared at me in confusion, occasionally glancing over his shoulder toward the growls that echoed off the walls. He must have thought that there was a wild animal in the building. Seeing me standing before him with no apparent injuries, he was speechless. It was just the duration and intensity of contact that I needed. Holding his attention, I made my hypnotic suggestions: *You will do what I say, but you won't remember seeing or hearing me. When you hear, "Primordium," you will sleep for an hour and remember nothing. There is a child who needs help out here. You should ask one of the officers in there to come out and help you. Ask the more senior officer to come out.*

The officer complied, calling out the sheriff to assist him. I stayed behind the door as he exited, and Eve let out some more growls even more unearthly than the previous ones. The sheriff unsnapped his sidearm.

"Help me," I moaned. Once again, the sheriff spun around and as I captured his wide-eyed stare, I planted the same seeds and suggested that he return to the room and send out his less senior officer to assist in the hallway. When the third officer appeared, we repeated the same routine, then I said we should all go in.

"Primordium!" I announced as I entered, following the two officers. Then all three officers slumped onto the floor and closed their eyes.

"Noah!" my mother gasped, jumping up from her seat. Dave stood up beside her, his smooth forehead immediately crunching up into a stack of little folds as he beamed a great smile. Isaac also sprang to his feet, and his eyes brightened behind his disheveled curly hair hanging down onto his face.

"Let's go!" I whispered. "Eve's in the hall."

"How did you do that?" Isaac asked, staring at the guards and then at me standing there in my swimsuit.

"Never mind." I took my mother aside and explained my plan for getting them over to the East Wing without the Pridapt security guards seeing them. "We'll need a few minutes' head start so that Eve and I can distract them, letting you walk by unseen. Give me something metal." She grabbed a round paperweight off of the desk and put it in my hand.

"A few minutes, and we'll be right behind you," she said, beaming.

I returned to Eve, and we set up our diversion. Their pathway to the East Wing would only take them past two security guards: one behind the front desk and another in the hallway behind the lobby. We slipped around those two in our camouflage, and I crawled up to the metal detector. I could sense my mother, Dave, and Isaac coming down the hall already, so I rolled the metal paperweight along the floor through the detector. The rolling sound turned the heads of a few employees nearby, but the alarm did not go off! It had rolled below the detecting panels. At any moment, my mother would step into the guard's view. Before I could think of what to do next, I heard Eve's moaning mountain lion-like growl coming from the ceiling above me. With everyone's eyes turned upward, I ran through the detector, picked up the metal paperweight, and ran back through, setting off the alarm. The combination of growls and alarm brought both security guards running to the front of the lobby. Eve and I then slipped back to the hallway and followed my mother, Dave, and Isaac into the East Wing.

RETRIBUTION

Once the others had all gone through the East Wing door, Eve and I came out of camouflage and joined them. Isaac stared at Eve as she entered.

"Isaac, Dr. Dave," I began, looking at the two people present who had never before laid eyes on Eve, "this is my sister." As one might expect, they were both dumbfounded, looking at me, then my mother. "We can fill in the blanks later," I suggested, "but right now, we have a lot to do before those officers wake up and realize we're all gone."

"How did you get away from Mr. Stone?" my mother asked.

"He stormed off after the board members for trying to

kill him. Then I hypnotized the security guard and left," I explained.

"The board members tried to kill him?" Dave asked, his forehead again as smooth as marble.

"I made him think he smelled nutmeg in his coffee," I said with a grin.

My mother smiled broadly at me, as Dave frowned, asking, "Nutmeg?"

"The reptile venom," my mother clarified.

"Yes, and he immediately recognized it as poison," I added. "He pushed back, scared to death once he thought he smelled it."

"The Chairman of the Board is the only other person besides Stone who has access to that venom," my mother pointed out.

"So should we be warning the board?" Dave asked.

"I don't think he'll confront them directly," I said. "Since he thought he was double-crossed, he said he was going to make them take the fall for killing Dr. Strauss. I'd say he's going to the police."

"Well, why don't we just *see* where he's gone?" Isaac asked. "You must have his cell phone number, don't you, Dr. Bolton?"

"Of course," she replied, jotting down the number on

a piece of paper. Isaac took the phone number and, after typing in a few lines of code on the computer, brought up a GPS map locating Stone's current whereabouts.

"You're right, Noah," Isaac declared. "He's at a police station in the city. So, what do we do?"

I knew that Mr. Stone was able to access his security cameras from his phone, so if he were to check them, he would see that we were gone. I explained this to Isaac, who got to work on blocking Stone from accessing the cameras. I also had him freeze the camera views of the fences around the exterior habitat so we could escape there unnoticed.

"Can you access the previously recorded footage from these cameras?" I asked him as he scrolled down a gallery of security camera views.

"Sure, which ones do you want to see?"

"There, that one!" I stopped Isaac's hand when he came to the room where he, my mother, and Dave had been held. "Look at the other rooms in that hallway," I suggested. We scanned the recorded footage until we saw one of the other doors open. "Freeze that!" Visible in the open door, was a glass tank with a brightly colored creature in it. "Is that the reptile, Mom?"

"Yes," she confirmed after looking at the image. "That's it."

"Can we access this camera footage from outside the

building?" I asked Isaac.

"Sure. You just go to this site," he said, writing down a long web address on a sheet of paper. "I'm blocking that address from Stone's phone so he can't check the security cameras remotely, but you can still log in to it. Just use the passcode you use to unlock this computer, and you can view it from anywhere."

561947, I thought as I slipped Isaac's sheet of paper into my shirt pocket. Isaac logged off the computer, and we all went into Eve's outer habitat.

"So, this is where you disappear to all the time, Annette," Dave commented with a smirk, then with a more serious tone added, "If we go to the police, what makes you think they'll believe us? Most of them are in Stone's pocket, aren't they?"

"They are, but I can give them the molecular formula for the venom. They'll need that to follow up on Stone's accusations," my mother argued, "and when they do, they'll find a discrepancy in his story because there will be traces of the venom in Dr. Strauss's body but none in Stone's coffee."

"Get me a few minutes with the guy at the front desk," I said, "and I'll get us in to see a detective." I didn't want to brag, but I was starting to feel pretty adept at hypnosis.

As I led the group to the back corner of the habitat where the fallen tree lay across the fence, Isaac trotted up to my side and asked, "So why are you and your sister in swimsuits?

Are we going to have to go underwater somewhere?"

"No, it just helps us blend into the background," I replied, hoping to avoid the need for any more memory erasing. With some assistance from Eve, everyone was able to climb up the tree trunk and over the fence. From there, we hiked to my lunchtime area of the woods. To our surprise, we found Zoe waiting there.

"Noah, where have you been? Have you been swimming?" Zoe quipped.

"Did you copy the drive?" I asked her.

"Well, no, I haven't left yet. I thought you guys might need me."

Nice that she stuck around, I thought, but we needed to get that information away from here. "Isaac, we have information on a USB drive that we need to get out to the public. Zoe, give Isaac the drive."

"I'll go with him," Zoe suggested. "It'll be less suspicious. They're all looking for a 'crazy lone blogger.' If anyone sees the two of us together, they won't think anything of it."

Isaac agreed, and the two left to upload the research data. I ran to my car under the cover of camouflage and slipped on my sweats. I then drove down to the park entrance, picked up my mother, Dave, and Eve, and we headed into the city.

It was midday when we arrived, and there was a lot of activity in the streets, though the police station itself was quiet. I parked the car just outside and asked Eve to keep an eye and ear out for us. "If I call your name, it means we need your help," I told Eve, noting a warmth in her face that made me smile. I asked my mother and Dave to give me a minute or two before coming in behind me.

I walked up to the front desk and was greeted by an officer. "Can I help you?"

"Yes," I said slowly. "I need to talk to someone." The officer looked very closely at me.

"Are you okay, son?"

"No... I need to talk to... a detective," I whispered as I kept my eyes fixed on his. When he didn't respond, I added some more suggestions. "All of us need to see him alone. Don't tell anyone else."

The officer went into a back room, and Dave and my mother entered from outside. The officer then returned with a detective, who offered to help us. Dave explained our situation and our suspicions.

"You're looking to grab a pretty big tiger by the tail," the detective remarked. "Mr. Stone is down the hall right now, giving sworn testimony against his board, saying they tried to kill him today and that they killed another doctor last week. You're saying he did it? Did he fake poisoning himself?"

"That part's a bit complicated," Dave muttered.

"In any case," my mother added, "you'll need the molecular formula for the poison if you are to test for it, correct? I can give that to you."

"And who are you?"

"Dr. Annette Bolton, from Pridapt."

"Okay, come with me, and I'll write up a report." Following him around a corner, we walked directly into Mr. Stone and two other detectives.

"What?" Mr. Stone cried, stopping in his tracks and staring at us. "Arrest them!" he commanded. "The board must have gotten them out somehow," he thought out loud.

"Out from where?" one of the detectives asked.

"Never mind! They're in on it with the board. Arrest them! If the board could get them out, it means they've had plenty of time to do away with the evidence while we've been wasting time here! I told you that you needed to work quickly!"

"We've dispatched a unit..."

"Well, dispatch more!" Mr. Stone growled. "And hold them all as terror and murder suspects." The detectives with Mr. Stone quickly grabbed my mother and Dave and were motioning to the third detective to take hold of me, when Mr. Stone interrupted. "Wait, not the kid. Leave him with me."

"No!" my mother cried out. "He's my son! You have no

right! We have a statement to make. I have information..."

"Move!" Mr. Stone boomed, and they disappeared down another hallway. Putting a hand on my shoulder, our CEO, who now commanded much more than just a pharmaceutical company, looked down at me and grinned. "Must have had a pang of conscience, eh, kid?" I looked up at him, genuinely confused. "When you tipped me off about the poison," he explained. "You must have decided to choose the winning team."

He led me into a room filled with people, who I learned were lawyers, police officers, and a court stenographer. There were cameras and audio equipment stationed around a small table and chair.

"Nobody leaves yet," he called out, then said quietly to me, "Now that you're on the right side," he continued, "you're going to tell everyone that it was the chairman of the board who was behind all this. Maybe, just maybe, we'll be able to convince them that your mother and Dr. Bernstein were just pawns, used by the board, and it might go better for them."

Mr. Stone sat me down in the chair in front of the cameras and microphones and spoke to the police officers and lawyers.

"Do you wish to have counsel?" one of the officers asked me.

"He doesn't need counsel," Stone fired back. "Just get going!"

"For the record, state your full name," the officer continued.

I tried to make eye contact with the man asking the questions, but he just glanced up occasionally from his paper. "State your full name," he repeated.

"Eve!" I shouted.

"What? Your full name."

"Eve, Eve, Eve!" I screamed all the louder.

"Listen kid," Stone spat as he grabbed me by the shoulder. "Don't be stupid! This is your only chance. Besides, this is a soundproof room. Whoever Eve is, she can't hear you, so answer the question!"

"Mr. Stone, sit down!" the senior officer barked out, pulling him away from me. "Now, son," he whispered calmly to me. "Don't be frightened. We just want to ask you some questions. That's all."

Tears had begun to well in my eyes again as I felt my previous terror of Mr. Stone returning. Looking up, I caught the eyes of the kind officer. He was studying me with a full, steady gaze, showing genuine concern. I stared back long and hard into his eyes, my thoughts racing as I struggled to make hypnotic suggestions. He extended his hand to me and I grasped it, slipping the paper with the security camera web address on it into his palm. I planted my mother's pass-code into his mind, and an understanding of the significance of that security footage. He quietly closed his hand and returned to his position in the room.

"Once again," the first officer repeated, "your full name?"

"Noah Bolton, sir."

"Where do you work?"

"Pridapt Incorporated."

"For how long?"

"Four years."

"What do you know about a reptile poison developed at Pridapt?"

"I know it exists. I know it smells like nutmeg, and I know it's kept in a secure room that only Mr. Stone and the chairman of the board can open."

"Have you seen it?"

"No, except... maybe once because I smelled it..."

I was interrupted by a piercing sound that rose from the corner of the room, bouncing off the walls. It was the sound a distressed mountain lion might make, a sound I was now very familiar with, but one the lawyers, officers, and Mr. Stone were not.

"What the hell was that?" one of them cried out.

Guns were drawn, and the officers were scanning all

corners of the room. Eve had indeed heard my call and had already answered me, slipping into the room while all eyes were focused on me. Once again, she released her growl, this time from the opposite corner of the room. With the fearful sound keeping everyone's attention on the ceiling, I slid from my chair and out the door. Once outside of the room, I took off my outer sweats and, bringing on the camouflage effect, crouched down against the wall next to the door.

"Where's the kid?" I heard Stone shout. "Get him!"

"You stay put," an officer said to Mr. Stone. "We'll find him."

The door flew open, and police officers ran out, closely followed by Mr. Stone, scattering down the hall and through the police station looking for me. The lawyers and stenographer followed suit, fleeing the unseen beast. As the door closed, I saw my sister's eyes opening against the wall near me.

"Thank you," I whispered.

While Mr. Stone and the officers searched frantically through the precinct building for me, Eve and I found where they were holding our mother and Dave. Eve repeated her mountain lion performance, and I crept along the wall in camouflage to my mother, grasping her arm to lead her and Dave out the door while all eyes were once again fixed on the terrifying sound coming from the ceiling in the corner of the room.

We made a few chairs fall over and staplers fly off desks to distract the remaining officers between us and the exit, allowing my mother and Dave to walk unhindered out the front door. Eve and I followed right behind them, hopped into my car, and the four of us disappeared into the mid-day traffic.

I would later learn that at the same time, the detective who had spoken so kindly to me was remembering my thoughts—the explanations I had rushed to share through my hypnotic suggestions. Having found the web page writ-ten on that sheet of paper, and logged in with my mother's passcode, he was scanning the security camera footage. As we were merging onto the highway, making our escape, and Mr. Stone was barking out orders for our immediate capture, that kind detective was looking at the secure room that had held the venom. He saw the only person who had ever accessed that room, the only person with the means, motive, and opportunity to use that venom, the only per-son, in fact, who could have killed Dr. Strauss: the CEO, Mr. Stone.

NEW LIFE

B y informing the police of the reptile venom, suggesting that Dr. Strauss had been murdered rather than dying from natural causes as the medical examiner had concluded, Stone had, as they say, dug his own grave. He was the only one who had ever accessed the stored venom. The chairman of the board, as well as the rest of the board members, all had very good alibis for the day Dr. Strauss was murdered. The only relevant person without an alibi was Mr. Stone. All these facts became readily apparent to the police, leading to Mr. Stone's arrest.

It was requested that we return to the police station to make our statements. When we did, we kept Eve stationed outside just in case, but it turned out that honesty and integrity had been restored, and it was not a trap. While we were there, we watched Stone in the testimony room, this time from the other side of mirrored glass. It was oddly reminiscent of our primordium observation room, only instead of a primordium gulping water in the room, it was Stone bolting up from his chair in anger and repeatedly being shoved back down again. I was relieved to see him disarmed but also a little sad. He had inspired me initially, and I was disappointed to see the source of my inspiration come to such an end.

Over the ensuing weeks, the story unfolded in its entirety. Zoe and Isaac had been very successful at getting the data out to the public. The truth was going viral, and within days, Isaac was vindicated, taken off the terrorist watch list, and all charges against him were dropped. Likewise, all charges against Dave were dismissed, and he was selected by the board to be the new CEO of Pridapt.

Dr. Strauss's body was exhumed, and chemical remains of the venom were found in his fingernails, sealing the case against Mr. Stone. The government placed a moratorium on the vaccine programs, allowing time to study the safer version, which Dave received a federal grant to develop. He gave press conferences daily, speaking at length about his guarantee of transparency. There was even talk of him running for public office. Imagine that, the guy who needed my help to write his first public address—the passenger pigeon speech at Pridapt—could end up being governor someday.

As all this was going on, I went to see someone I had been meaning to see for some time: Carter at Whispering Acres. He had been crushed by Dr. Strauss's death, and even before there had been anything in the press about murder, Carter had always had his suspicions. I filled him in on all the details, which occasionally made his temper flare and his skin flash odd colors, which reminded me of the main reason I had wanted to see him. I had gained some expertise in controlling my own skin color changes and I wanted to share that with him, as well as a proposal.

It was inevitable that details would come out about Eve and me. In order to protect us and my mother, the three of us were placed in the witness protection program. I had asked that Carter be offered that protection as well. His fellows at Whispering Acres were content to stay where they were, but I knew that Carter longed for a new beginning. He readily agreed to come along with us.

My mother held a patent on the venom's mechanism for transport through the skin, something that would be applicable to hundreds of transdermal medications. We would use the funds from that patent to set up our own research lab in a small, obscure town in the Midwest. Carter, who had a background in information technology, would manage our computer network. As for my full-ride scholarship, as the saying goes, "There's no such thing as a free lunch." You always end up paying for it in the end, one way for another. I would make the money I needed at our new lab.

It was my last day at Pridapt, and Dave was giving another press conference outside. As I sat in the Pridapt lobby with Zoe, the morning sun flickering through the trees outside, a notion that I had been struggling with came to mind—that there was not a great deal of difference between Mr. Stone and me. We both knew of the ethical concerns raised by Dr. Strauss, and we were both willing to overlook them for personal gain—he, for power and money, I, for a scholarship and friendship with Zoe. In addition to being a genetic monster, was I also a moral monster?

We were all imperfect, my mother had explained to me. Our circumstances, hardships, and past mistakes, like our genetic makeup, all had consequences, but those things did not define us. It was what we chose to do in the face of those consequences that determined who and what we really were. It was what we did next that mattered most.

I began to see myself within a great primordial plan, in place since the start of time. Whatever trail of adversity had led me to my particular situation, I was there for a reason. No, I was not a monster, of any sort. Drawn from the brink of primordial humanity, I could see what others could not, and appreciate what they had overlooked. While I still wanted to fit in and be one of the crowd, I understood how important it was to know one's unique place in life.

I realized that even when it seems like no one wants you, you are still wanted, and even if everyone seems to think you're worthless, you are still priceless: you have a necessary role to play.

Turning back to Zoe, I remarked, "You know, Zoe, you don't need to have a circle of fans wanting you all the time. That's not what matters."

Zoe smirked. "Really? Well, things that aren't wanted aren't worth much. Think about it: if nobody wanted gold, it would be worthless. They'd just leave it in the ground and not bother to dig it up."

"You're not gold," I corrected her. "You are Zoe Halpern, a one-of-a-kind, never-to-be-repeated *you*, and that makes you priceless."

She pondered that for a few moments, and with her usual swagger replied, "Priceless—I like the sound of that." She winked, then with a more serious tone added, "I don't want you to go."

"You want me to stay?" I asked, clarifying it with my-self more than her. "Thank you for that." We looked at each other long enough that I could have made a hypnotic suggestion, but it wasn't necessary. We were arriving at an understanding. "Thanks for being a friend, Zoe, but there are things you don't know about me."

"So what?" she replied.

"We need time," I explained.

"When will I see you again? How will I find you?" There was a look of desperation in her eyes that I had never seen before. I fought off the temptation to exploit it.

"Don't worry," I reassured her. "I'll find you."

I made my way out to the woods, looking back a couple of times, each time seeing Zoe at the window watching me. Leaning back against a tree trunk, I looked up at the blue sky, the draping branches, and the columns of light and shadow. Turning toward Dave as he spoke to the press, a sadness tugged at me as I realized I would not see him again for a long time. I pushed off the tree and trotted down to the opening of the trail, where I found my mother waiting with Eve and Carter. Joining them in the car, we started on our journey eastward.

There had been some talk online about me being a superhero. As cool as that may have been for me to read, it was of course, nonsense. I was just a person. But I shouldn't say, 'just,' because being a person is awesome.

It seemed to me that life was like this big relay race in which each person takes a turn carrying the baton. Some might carry it farther and faster than others, and many might prefer simply to watch from the stands and avoid the risk of falling down, getting hurt, or losing. But whether we liked it or not, we were all in the race, and sooner or later, in one way or another, perhaps when we least expected it, the baton would be slipped into our hand. It was then that we had a choice to make: to take it and do the right thing, or drop it and wonder forever, what if?

Dr. Strauss had told me once that a single person in the right place at the right time could change the world. Had one of us accomplished that? Had it been my mother, who had hidden me before I could be experimented upon? Was it Dr. Strauss, whose words opened my eyes to my own rationalizations? Was it Eve, who had helped us to escape, or was it Carter, whose sorrowful story had touched my heart, changing my outlook and eventual actions? It may be true that one person can change the world, but if so, it is through the chain reaction they're a part of—the passing of the baton from hand to hand, including at times, some of the most unexpected, unnoticed, unwanted, and seemingly inconsequential persons on earth. As we drove into the morning sun that pierced the fog and sparkled through the trees, I embraced the new day and our new life and looked forward with great anticipation to the commencement of our next chain reaction.

ABOUT THE AUTHOR

Surgeon, author, and homeschooling dad, Dr. Mario Loomis, has operated in third world missions, done brain and stem cell research, and cared for thousands of patients over the years. He is now writing science fiction novels to both entertain and intrigue the mind. If you've had trouble finding "clean reads" that were thrilling enough to hold your attention or your teenager's, try reading another one of Dr. Loomis's debut novels, *Essence, Assault on the Mind*.

ESSENCE

ASSAULT ON THE MIND

MORE BOOKS BY MARIO LOOMIS

ESSENCE: ASSAULT ON THE MIND

With over a million downloads, eTelepathy is the most popular app of the year. Using technology designed to help quadriplegics communicate, it creates a wireless interface between a person's brain and their smartphone. But once downloaded, it also allows for ongoing subliminal influences from the app's creator, even when not in use. Racing to halt the onset of widespread thought control, FBI agent John Rocco finds that bringing in this perpetrator will be more challenging than he could imagine. From string theory physics and hidden dimensions to premonitions and near-death experiences, he will need to understand the transcendent nature of the mind in order to stop the imminent corruption of free thought in millions.

Learn more at
WWW.MARIOLOOMIS.COM